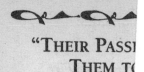 

"THEIR PASS[...]
THEM T[...]

The messenger loosened the bundle from his saddle and threw it. It landed with a sickening thud. As it rolled toward Alaric's horse, its covering fell away, and staring up was the severed head and sightless eyes of the man Alaric had sent to Rome.

The Visigoth gave a cry that was half anger, half anguish. He dug his heels into his horse's flanks. As the animal shot forward, he drew his ax and began to swing. He was on the Roman before the man knew what was coming. The Roman barely had time to raise an arm, no time at all to draw his sword, before Alaric's ax bit deep into his flesh. His blood shot a crimson geyser that sprayed the Visigoth's face like fierce war paint.

Alaric paid no heed. He hacked again and again. Behind Darius, a slow rumble grew as the men saw their leader attacking. The sound mounted. It became a shrill cry as, to a man, the army surged forward to besiege the city.

ALSO IN THIS SERIES:

Available from
WARNER ASPECT

HIGHLANDER™

SHADOW OF OBSESSION

A
NOVEL
BY
**REBECCA
NEASON**

ASPECT®

WARNER BOOKS

A Time Warner Company

WARNER BOOKS EDITION

Copyright © 1998 by Warner Books, Inc.
All rights reserved.

"Highlander" is a protected trademark of Gaumont Television. © 1994 by Gaumont Television and © Davis Panzer Productions, Inc. 1985.

Aspect is a registered trademark of Warner Books, Inc.

Warner Books, Inc.
1271 Avenue of the Americas
New York, NY 10020

Visit our Web site at
http://warnerbooks.com

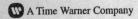 A Time Warner Company

Printed in the United States of America

First Printing: June, 1998

10 9 8 7 6 5 4 3 2 1

Thou, whose exterior semblance doth belie
By soul's immensity . . .
On whom those truths do rest
Which we are toiling all our lives to find,
In darkness lost, the darkness of the grave;
Thou, over whom thy Immortality
Broods like the Day; a master or a slave
A presence which is not to be put by.

—William Wordsworth, "Intimations of Immortality"

Chapter One

Present day, Sudan, Africa

Four hundred years after his birth, Duncan MacLeod was still the chieftain's son; four hundred years and he was still bound by honor and duty to answer a call for help—if the cause be worthy.

And this cause certainly was.

The hot desert winds of Sudan felt like gritty fingers scratching across MacLeod's face as he motioned his companions into the shadows. It was not much farther to their destination, but if distance was measured in safety, they still had miles to go.

The country of Sudan was the quintessential Africa, at least to the movie-fed Western mind. The largest country in Africa, it had wide vegetation belts, alluvial plains and areas of high mountains bordering vast arid expanses. All the wildlife that came quickly to mind when the "dark continent" was mentioned—lion, cheetah, rhino, elephant, gazelle—could be found within Sudan's borders. And it was hot. There were few places in Sudan that could not reach one hundred degrees at any time of the year.

But what might once have been a beautiful country, ancient in its glory and its wildness, was now a land that had been torn apart by famine and civil wars—and lately by something much, much worse.

Jihad.

Duncan MacLeod had long ago recognized the word—often translated as "holy war"—for what it was: *Obsession.* Under the blanket of *jihad*, countless atrocities were sanctioned for religious, cultural, or racial purities. And it was not a thing of centuries past, or even decades. It was happening now. Here.

In 1956, British rule had ended in Sudan, and for the next twenty-five years various factions vied for power. Then, in 1982, a somewhat stable government had been established, but those who now ran the country owed their allegiance farther north—to the heart of Islam. Fundamental Muslims, they had slowly repealed all laws and statutes of religious tolerance, dividing the country into a Muslim north whose Islamic influences had filtered down through Egypt, and the "black south," where Christian missionaries and followers of the ancient African religions had been able to live in relative safety.

Until recently. Now, under unspoken governmental support, Muslim raiders were pushing their presence farther and farther south and all semblance of safety was disappearing. Atrocities were mounting daily. Non-Muslim men were put to death, whether lay people, missionaries, or clergy. The lucky ones were killed outright; some were shot or beheaded, others were crucified as their captors jeered retort to their professed faith. The unlucky ones were imprisoned, starved and tortured first.

For the women and children, concubinage and slavery to Muslim masters awaited. In the past decade, over three hundred thousand followers of the Christian faith had been killed and the slave trade, which had been quietly internal, was now more boldly setting up external routes to other Muslim-dominated countries.

Many relief organizations, some of them religious, others of non-affiliated origins like Amnesty International and the United Nations, were doing all they could. But it was not enough, and the *jihad* continued.

One such organization was led by Victor Paulus. He had come to the country bringing food and medical supplies; he had stayed to help establish a series of "safe houses," a network reminiscent of the Underground Railroad of America's Civil War era, to try and get those in danger out of the country.

Duncan MacLeod had long been an anonymous supporter of Paulus's organization and as such he received regular reports on the foundation's efforts around the world. He followed the work of Darius's protégé with admiration. When news reached MacLeod of Paulus's work in Sudan and the reason for it, MacLeod felt compelled to help.

Now, slowly, he ventured from the shadows in which he and his companions were hiding, inching forward until he could see around the corner of the low, sand-brick building. The street was empty—for now. But that did not fill MacLeod with a sense of security. Gone were the days when raids were accomplished from horseback, with swords and war cries as weapons. Today, it was Ouzies and automobiles, and the enemy could strike from a great distance and without warning.

MacLeod, the Immortal, was safe from permanent damage, and it was not for himself he worried. His companions were five nuns who had run an orphanage in a small village twelve miles north and the eight children who were currently in their care.

So far, thanks largely to the skills MacLeod had acquired in the last four centuries, they were unharmed. But they still had to make it to the other end of the village, where Victor Paulus—and escape—were waiting.

MacLeod had been here for almost two months; Paulus, he knew, had been here for nearly six. MacLeod admired the mortal's stamina and his dedication. Now their funding and supplies were almost gone. MacLeod would be traveling with this group of refugees, taking them to the relative safety of Zaire, where they would either continue their mission work or go on to less dangerous fields in accordance with the decision of their order. MacLeod himself would be returning to the States. He planned to spend the next weeks using his many contacts to raise money and get whatever help he could for the rescue efforts here.

Victor Paulus would be following a few days after MacLeod with much the same purpose—and MacLeod knew Paulus would be successful on a much larger scale. The work here in Sudan would continue in his absence, and Victor's presence in the States would make certain the media attention would get the news out. There were already a series of meetings with the representatives of several world relief organizations and a public rally, the first of many, was scheduled to take place in Seacouver a week from today.

The road in front of MacLeod remained quiet. *Almost too quiet,* he thought, listening to his instincts, the internal warning system that had been well-honed by centuries of use. This village, too small to be even a name on a map, had once been a point of safety in the long trek south. But that had changed. Before he left Sudan, MacLeod would make certain that Victor Paulus and his people moved their headquarters farther south, though they would begrudge every inch they had to yield to raiders, oppressors, and terrorists.

Still it would do no one any good if Paulus or the members of his small rescue team were captured. For MacLeod, it was easier to pass unnoticed. Over the last two months his skin had darkened with exposure to the sun, and his familiarity with Middle Eastern languages and customs, including those of Islam, helped him move more freely about the countryside.

He would use that advantage now, he decided. Taking a deep breath, MacLeod stepped boldly out from the shadows. He walked down the road, forcing his muscles to stay relaxed, while his eyes darted left and right. The village remained quiet; not even a dog barked.

I don't like this, he thought. *I don't like this at all.* If the people of the village had gone into hiding like this, they must know something that MacLeod had not heard.

He casually turned the corner of another building that was little more than a hut made out of the same sand-brick used in constructing all the buildings in this part of the country. Once around the corner, he quickly slipped again into the shadows and turned back toward where his charges were hiding.

The shadows were deep with the bright sun and he kept to them, trying to ignore the breathless heat of the afternoon that wanted to sap his muscles of their strength and turn his mind to fog. On another day, he might have looked for a place where the refugees could wait until evening dropped a veil of darkness over their movements. But MacLeod's instincts whispered again and he knew they must move on.

Sister Mary Patrick inched forward to whisper in his ear. "How much longer must we travel, Mr. MacLeod?" she asked. Even her whisper was husky with her heat-dried throat. "The children are very tired."

"I know," MacLeod agreed. His gaze swept back across the little group, their sad, frightened eyes making small patches of brightness in the shadows, the soft darkness hiding the worst of their weariness. "It's not much farther."

He wished he could tell them that their travels were over and that as soon as they reached the safe house they would be able to rest for a few days before moving on. But he had a feeling that "safe house" had become a misnomer.

Still, they had to get moving, and they had to move now. "Keep the children together and stay close," he whispered, once more turning his attention to the street.

MacLeod counted to ten as he carefully watched the scene before him. Then he gave a small signal. Herding the children like errant chicks, the nuns broke from their hiding place and dashed across the road. MacLeod followed them, hoping to keep his body between them and any possible danger.

They made it across the road and into the shadows again, then began working their way around the low houses to the next road they must cross. They repeated the process three more times before MacLeod heard it—the sound of an automobile. It was still distant, but in the afternoon stillness its noise was as unmistakable as an elephant's trumpet.

And they were still several minutes away from the house where Victor Paulus awaited them. The time for stealth was past.

"Keep as close to the buildings as possible," MacLeod told the nuns, "but run. Now."

They moved out. MacLeod went with them, sometimes running ahead and checking the route, sometimes letting them pass him while he made certain they were not yet being followed. All the while, he was listening to the growing rumble of automobiles in the distance.

Finally, the safe house was only a few yards away. Duncan darted ahead to open the door and get his charges inside, but Victor Paulus was already waiting. Before Duncan could reach the door, it flew open and Victor stood ready to usher the women and children inside.

"They're coming," MacLeod said as he stepped past the

other man and into the dim room. He left Victor to the work behind him, as he quickly crossed to the table in the center of the floor and began to pull it aside. Other hands joined his and he glanced up with a smile of acknowledgment to the two other workers in the cause.

One was a young man named Azziz, a native Sudanese and a recent convert from Islam whose knowledge and guidance had been invaluable in their efforts. The other was Cynthia VanDervane, Victor Paulus's fiancee. With her long blond hair, blue eyes, and fair skin, she would be a prime target for the raiders sweeping through the village, a prize on the market of slavery and concubinage.

She would have to hide with the others; MacLeod hoped he could convince Victor Paulus to hide himself as well.

This house had been chosen largely because of its wooden floor, which was moderately uncommon in this part of the world, a sign of the previous owner's affluence. In that floor, a trap door had been cut and below, a room dug into the ground. It was not a basement by any means, but it was a hole large enough to contain several people. Its presence had already saved lives; MacLeod hoped it would do so again today.

The table was moved and the rug beneath pulled up as the nuns and the children scurried through the door. MacLeod began waving them down. Sister Mary Patrick went first as Cynthia and Azziz began to grab the children and lower them down. They worked with silent, well-practiced precision. The only sounds were the scuffling of feet, the grumble of automobiles in the distance, and the assurances the nuns were whispering to the children.

Sister Mary Patrick, Sister Raphael, Sister Elizabeth, Sister Teresa—MacLeod looked up. Victor was starting to close the door.

"Where is Sister Anne?" he asked sharply.

"I don't see her," Paulus replied, his voice just as tense.

MacLeod heard a sharp intake of breath from the other sisters below. "Oh, Jesus and Mary, protect her," he heard one of them whisper.

MacLeod took a step toward the door, but Victor Paulus was already out and running. MacLeod looked at his co-workers and saw the concern on Azziz's face, the determination on Cynthia's, and he knew his next words would be unwelcome.

"You, too, Cynthia," he said, motioning with his head toward the hole.

"No," she answered. "Victor—"

"I'll get Victor—you get inside. Don't give him something else to worry about."

"MacLeod, you know they can't—"

"Inside," he snapped, cutting her words off again. He knew what she was going to say; he knew what Victor and Azziz did not.

Cynthia VanDervane was Immortal.

As such, the physical threat to her was minimal compared to the dangers a mortal woman might face. But slavery and concubinage were the same, regardless of mortality, and MacLeod was not willing to take the chance of that happening.

He looked at Azziz. The Sudanese man nodded. "Do not worry, MacLeod," he said. "She will be hidden. You go."

MacLeod darted one more warning look in Cynthia's direction. Then he turned and rushed through the door, following Victor Paulus with the hope of bringing both him and Sister Anne back—alive.

Chapter Two

Victor Paulus dashed quickly across the road and into the shadow of the nearest building. He was not as experienced as MacLeod nor, he knew, did he cut quite as dashing a figure. But in spite of his far less muscular build and the thick glasses that gave him a bookish appearance, these last six months had awakened the *hero* that had always waited in Paulus's soul.

It was true he had spent years traveling to war-torn areas of the globe, bringing famine relief and medical supplies. But it was also true that he spent even more of his time at rallies and conferences, raising public awareness and support, dealing with politicians and philanthropists, raising funding, and otherwise running the *business* of world relief.

Here in Sudan, his help was "hands-on" and immediate, and Victor Paulus found the experience quite extraordinary. It was not that he was unafraid; fear was a companion he lived with every day and with whom he had become quite intimately familiar. But each time it closed in upon him yet again, he reminded himself of the daily fears and dangers of the people he was here to help. That gave him courage to continue his efforts.

Fear was a snake coiling now in the pit of his stomach as he wove his way around the low sun-baked buildings. He listened to the growing rumble of automobiles in the distance, knowing that those automobiles carried men who wanted the death of himself and all others like him. Almost frantically his eyes searched the shadows for the crouching figure of the missing nun. Intent upon his mission, he did not hear MacLeod's swift, balanced footfalls until the man was almost upon him.

Then he spun swiftly around. He knew his fear was obvious on his face, but he did not have time to mask it. Relief flooded him when he recognized MacLeod. There was something about the man that inspired confidence, in him and in oneself, and Paulus was glad that in these last two months of working together, their friendship had deepened. He could well understand why, despite their differences, Darius had liked and trusted Duncan MacLeod.

A few seconds later, Duncan reached Paulus's side. "I don't see her and I'm not quite sure where to look," Victor said, keeping his voice low. It would make it much easier if he could just call Sister Anne's name and wait for a reply, but he could not take the chance of his voice carrying in the still, heated air.

"We came from that direction." MacLeod pointed to his left.

The two men began to run, working with an instinctive precision as each of them checked down opposite sides of the path MacLeod had traversed earlier. Still off in the distance—but oh, so much nearer—a sudden scream, a wail of anguish, rent the air. The sound cut through Paulus as if someone had stabbed a knife into his heart. He could not think of what might be happening; he must not let it distract him from his quest, though every muscle of his body, every corner of his soul, wanted to go with comfort and aid to the assailed.

Finally, he caught a glimpse of white down one of the alleyways between buildings. It was so small he almost missed it, just a little corner of fabric contrasting with the sand-colored houses around it. Not slowing his pace, Victor spun on his heel and rushed in that new direction.

It was Sister Anne, huddled in a doorway, her body shielding two small children. Their dark eyes were round with terror at the sound of his approaching footsteps. It took Sister Anne a few seconds to recognize him, and in those seconds Victor Paulus saw the ferocious spirit beneath the nun's gentle exterior. He knew that she would fight for the children, giving her life for their safety if she must.

As recognition dawned, the ferocity died in her eyes and was replaced by intense relief. "Thank God you're here," she said. "I heard these children crying and I had to find them."

Paulus nodded; he would not have been able to leave them either. "Let's get you all to safety," he replied.

Sister Anne stood, speaking soft reassurances to the children, who wanted to shrink away from the strange man in front of them. Victor wished he had time to win their trust but right now, if they were to live, speed was all that mattered.

Crooning a few soft words of his own, Victor scooped one of the children, a little boy he guessed to be about age six, into his arms. Then he turned in time to see Duncan MacLeod running toward him. Again, the sight filled Paulus with confidence. With Duncan carrying one child, himself to carry the other, and Sister Anne free to run on her own, there just might be time to get everyone well hidden before the raiders arrived at this end of the village.

"Here," Victor said as he thrust the little boy into Duncan's arms. He turned and picked up the other child, a girl. Without further words, all three of the adults began to run.

There were more screams heard in the distance, anguished wails and angry, shouting voices. Gunshots. Victor glanced at Sister Anne and saw her lips moving in silent prayer even as they ran. The shadows and stealth were less important than distance now. They ran openly, hoping that no one in the neighboring buildings would point out their house in a bid for clemency—or if they did, that the measures taken would be sufficient to keep the women and children from capture.

They could hear the automobiles' rumble again as they reached the safe house. The nuns and their children were down in the hiding hole, but Cynthia was not.

"She will not go," Azziz said in answer to the unspoken question as he closed the door behind the new arrivals. Victor lowered the little girl in his arms down into the opening and saw her quickly enfolded into loving and reassuring arms. Then he turned to face Cynthia.

"No," she said before he could speak. "I won't leave you to face this danger alone."

"You won't have to," MacLeod said behind him. "Victor is going down there, too."

Paulus spun around, ready to protest, but one look at the expression on MacLeod's face as he finished helping Sister

Anne to safety stopped the words in his mouth. It was not easy to argue with a man who looked like that.

Still, he knew he must try. Victor straightened his glasses in the automatic gesture he used so often when he was speaking from a podium or in front of a large crowd. It was a gesture that gave him a few seconds' respite to collect his words.

But after two months of working together, MacLeod must have recognized the gesture for what it was. Even as Victor was taking a breath to begin his argument, MacLeod cut him off.

"There's no other way," MacLeod began. "If Cynthia won't go down there without you, you go too."

Paulus shook his head. "I won't run out and leave the two of you." His glance took in Azziz, who had crossed the room and was standing impatiently ready to close the trap door in the floor and hide the evidence of the people below.

"Azziz and I will be fine," MacLeod countered. "But you the raiders would kill instantly. You *look* Western. And there is Cynthia's safety to think about. You two can help keep the children quiet. One sound could give everything away."

These were arguments against which Paulus had no answer. MacLeod was right; he did look Western—whether American or European, it did not matter. MacLeod, having adopted native dress, could easily pass for someone of Middle Eastern descent, like so many of the Muslim raiders.

Victor held out his hand to Cynthia. Wordlessly, she took it and together they went into hiding.

Moving quickly and in unison, MacLeod and Azziz lowered the trap door back into place and covered it with the rug. Over the rug went a low table and two worn cushions on which to sit. While Azziz brought out some tea things and bits of food, MacLeod's eyes scanned the room for any evidence of occupation other than theirs. Satisfied that all was in order, he sat down on one of the cushions. He and Azziz attempted to hide their nervousness beneath the mundane activity of a shared meal.

All the while, the noise of approaching automobiles grew closer.

" 'Thou shalt not fear the terror by night nor the arrow that flies by the day'," Azziz quoted to him softly. They were offered as words of comfort, and MacLeod knew that the people below could hear them too.

MacLeod gave the man across from him a wan smile. He saw the fervor shining in Azziz's eyes and knew that whatever might befall them, Azziz's faith would sustain him.

For MacLeod, it was not arrows—or their modern equivalent—neither were there mortal terrors he fought within himself. His Immortality protected him. His fears were all for the people around him and whether *he* could protect *them*.

His faith was not like Azziz's, or like that of the five nuns hiding in silence in that darkened hole beneath the floor. But he did believe, now as he had when he was a boy, that good must always triumph over evil. Somehow. Eventually.

The sounds of the automobiles had changed from a distant rumble to a close-range roar. MacLeod could hear how one of the engines coughed unevenly with a missing valve. That sound became the dominant one, as if the other vehicles had made a turn but this one kept coming in their direction.

It stopped outside the door. Once again MacLeod glanced at Azziz. The young Sudanese man gave a little nod; he was ready to play his part—as was MacLeod.

The door to the house was suddenly thrown open and three men with automatic weapons burst into the room. MacLeod and Azziz both affected surprise, scrambling to their feet in an attitude of innocence disrupted.

"Where are they?" one of the men asked in rapid Arabic. "We are told you are hiding women here—*white* women. Christians," he spat the word.

Azziz shook his head. "There is no one here but myself and my cousin, the son of my mother's brother."

The leader walked over to MacLeod and stared at him intently. "Who are you?" he asked.

"Hamza el Kahir," MacLeod replied, also speaking Arabic and using the name of his Immortal friend, now three centuries dead. He hoped that all Hamza had taught him, so long ago, would stay with him now.

"There are no women here," he repeated what Azziz had just said. "Search if you wish. We are honest men who serve the will of Allah. We have nothing to hide."

The man continued to stare at MacLeod as he motioned for his men to search the house. MacLeod met his eyes calmly, refusing to flinch at the sounds coming from the other rooms. *Are they being intentionally destructive?* he wondered as he heard the sound of glass breaking. *Are they trying to raise a reaction?*

MacLeod still did not move a muscle, not even to look over and see how Azziz was doing. He just had to trust that the younger man, so strong in his faith, would be strong enough in physical will—and well rehearsed enough—to continue to be steady.

The men came back from their search of the other rooms. MacLeod could see that the leader was not satisfied that they found nothing, but neither could he argue with the evidence of his own eyes. Wordlessly, he again motioned to his men and they headed toward the door.

Then the leader's eyes narrowed. MacLeod knew what was to come as surely as if aim had already been taken. His mind raced, searching for the means to reassure the man before Azziz's life became forfeit.

"The one true God is Allah," MacLeod said quickly the words he knew Azziz would never say, "and Mohammed is His prophet."

They were words of Muslim ritual, as familiar as invoking the Trinity in the Christian church . . . and their utterance, spoken in perfect Arabic, took the leader by surprise. He stared at MacLeod a few brief seconds longer, then turned and followed his men out the door.

The automobile engine sputtered to life again. The men drove off, but MacLeod knew the threat was not over. Victor Paulus and his companions would have to stay hidden for a while yet. This house would be watched; any unusual activity or the sound of voices other than MacLeod's and Azziz's could well bring death to them all.

Finally, when he judged enough time had passed, MacLeod nodded to Azziz. The young man went quickly to the window and looked out. Once he signaled MacLeod that all was clear, Duncan moved his cushion aside and knelt down to whisper through the floor.

"Victor," he called softly. "Is everyone all right?"

"Yes," Paulus's voice was muffled but understandable. "Most of the children are exhausted. They've fallen asleep in the darkness."

"Good," MacLeod answered. "You should all try to sleep. We'll let you out when we can, but it's going to be a long night."

"I understand," Victor said. "Do what you must. We'll be fine."

MacLeod stood, admiring the man's calmness and his courage. It would be very difficult, hiding in such a place for an unknown amount of time, unable to see, hardly able to hear, knowing that your existence depended upon other people—and that if things went wrong, there was no escape. MacLeod was not certain he could have done it; he would have wanted to take his chances and fight his way clear.

But Victor Paulus's presence would help keep the others calm; he and the nuns would take care of the children.

And Cynthia, Paulus's fiancee? Though he had worked with her for two months, she was something of an unknown factor to MacLeod. She was always by Victor's side, and so MacLeod had not had the chance to find out her history. How long had she been alive? Where had she come from and, when danger closed in as it was doing now, just how much could she be trusted? These were all questions MacLeod had yet to answer.

Somewhere in the back of his mind, the lack of knowledge worried him.

Chapter Three

The next few hours were some of the slowest in Duncan MacLeod's long life. He and Azziz waited in the house until long after the sound of the automobiles had faded from hearing. Only then did MacLeod venture out into the village to see what damage the raiders had done.

The wails that had torn through the air earlier had subsided. In their place they had left a silent grief that was all the more terrible to see, as people went about the business of mourning their dead or their captured. He passed one old woman, sitting splay-legged in the dust, cradling the body of her dead son. The cross around the man's throat proclaimed the reason for his death.

The scene was repeated over and over until MacLeod wanted to retch at the carnage. Victor Paulus would *not* remain here until his replacement arrived, as was the original plan. No one would remain in this village. Tonight they would all go out to meet the transport that would take them south.

As MacLeod walked back to the house that was safe no more, he readied the arguments he would need to convince Paulus. The man could be stubborn.

Well, so could MacLeod, when he knew he was right—and what he could not tell Paulus was that he had worked as part of such rescue operations before, starting back with the American Civil War. He knew the necessity of changing location once the safety of the "station," as safe houses were called during the days of the Underground Railroad, was compromised.

He just had to convince Paulus.

*   *   *

They waited until darkness had fallen and the village had quieted into troubled slumber before MacLeod and Azziz once more removed the table and rug from over the trap door, releasing the hidden occupants into light and fresh air. They came up blinking against the sudden brightness of even the soft candlelight. Azziz had food and drink waiting for them. While he helped the women get the children started on a meal, MacLeod pulled Victor aside.

"After the raiders left, I walked through the village," MacLeod began. "It's time to close this house up and move the operation to safer ground."

"I can't just abandon these people," Paulus answered.

"You're not abandoning them, Victor. You're moving on so that you can *continue* to help them."

"But how can I run—"

"Look, Victor," MacLeod cut him off. "The work you're doing here is important. But if you're captured or killed, the heart will go out of it. You're more than a single person who's free to follow his own wishes. For many of the people you work with, you've become a symbol—and that must be protected."

"But—" Paulus began again. Still MacLeod would not let him continue. Not yet; not until all his arguments had been stated.

"You have work to do that no one else can accomplish. That work is back in the States. But you have to be *alive* and *free* to do it. That means leaving here tonight. We'll all take the transport south with the nuns. We can set up another house near Tungaru or Ed Dibeikir. Azziz can run it. He's a good man, steady and reliable. If it makes you feel better, you can stay there a few days to make sure that word of the new location has begun to reach the people who need it."

MacLeod could still see the stubborn light in Victor's eyes, but it was beginning to fade. He pulled out his last argument and hoped it would turn the tide.

"And there is Cynthia to think about," MacLeod continued. "She won't leave you, and the next time the raiders come she might not be so lucky. She would make quite a prize as a concubine, with her blond hair and white skin, but the life she'd be condemned to would not be a pleasant one. You know I'm right, Victor."

Paulus's shoulders sagged just a little as he gave in, and he nodded. "I still feel like I'm running away," he said.

MacLeod reached out and grasped his shoulder warmly. "Sometimes it takes more courage to retreat than to go forward," he said. "You have to look at the strategy of the war, not just the battle."

Paulus gave MacLeod a wan smile. "Darius used to say things like that—when he was teaching me to play chess. It seems like a lifetime ago."

"Darius was a great man," MacLeod agreed, feeling the whisper of loss that came every time Darius's name was mentioned. "He understood that we live amid the greatest war of all—the war of good versus evil—and that every day, in every action we take, we choose the side on which we fight."

Duncan spoke these words as much to himself as to Paulus. The two men stood in companionable silence for a moment, each wrapped in his own memories of the priest who had touched their lives so profoundly.

Paulus had not known of Darius's Immortality. But he had recognized, and been shaped by, the timeless spirit of love and wisdom that had been the greatest part of Darius's presence in the world. Now he carried that same spirit onward.

To MacLeod, Darius had been a teacher as well, but most of all he had been a friend, in a friendship that had spanned almost two centuries. When Darius had been killed—murdered—by James Horton and his band of renegade Watchers, MacLeod had felt as if a bit of his own heart had been cut away. In a quiet place in his soul, he still mourned his friend's death—and he always would.

"All right, Duncan," Paulus agreed, bringing MacLeod's thoughts back to the problem at hand. "You're right. We'll leave as soon as everyone has eaten. The moon will be up soon and that will give us plenty of light to travel by. I'll go tell Cynthia."

"You're doing the right thing, Victor," MacLeod assured him.

"I hope so, Duncan. I truly hope so."

* * *

Traveling with the children, it took them almost two hours to reach the rendezvous point for the transport. It was a rickety old truck, but it did its job and by dawn they had reached the town of Waw. For a time they were safe. But that safety was precarious at best. If help did not come on an international level, there would soon be nowhere safe in Sudan for anyone who did not follow the banner of Islam.

The reunion between Victor Paulus and the other members of his rescue operation was poignant. Their fear for his safety was obvious in their great relief at his presence.

Waw was only a brief stop for MacLeod and the nuns—a chance for a meal, to feed the children, and to change vehicles—then it was on to Zaire. MacLeod had promised to see the nuns safely to a Chapter House in Duma. From there he would travel on to Kisangani, where he could catch a flight to begin the long trip home. Once back in the States, he would confirm with members of Paulus's World Peace Foundation that Victor would be there in a few days.

Once the nuns and the children were again settled into a truck, MacLeod turned to say good-bye to the mortal toward whom he felt both admiration and friendship. Azziz and Cynthia were with him. They both stepped forward to say their farewells first, so that MacLeod and Paulus had a moment alone.

It was Azziz who spoke, breaking the suddenly awkward silence. He enfolded MacLeod in a quick, brotherly embrace. " 'The Lord watch between thee and me'," he said as he stepped back, quoting the familiar verse from Genesis 31.

" 'While we are absent one from another'," MacLeod finished the quote. He smiled fondly at the man who had risked his life to claim him as a cousin these last months.

"Many people owe their lives to you, Azziz," he said. "I'm sure their prayers will bless you every day. You keep safe."

The Sudanese man gave a small, self-deprecating shrug. "I do not work for my own glory, but for God's. May He travel with you."

Cynthia VanDervane stepped up to Duncan and gave him a quick peck on the cheek. "Thank you," she said. Her voice was low and melodic, as always, with the trace of an accent MacLeod could never quite place.

He looked into her deep blue eyes. "Watch over Victor," he said, and they both knew what he meant.

Then both Azziz and Cynthia stepped away, and MacLeod turned to face Victor Paulus.

"What can you say to someone who has saved your life— more than once?" Victor asked as he held his hand out to MacLeod.

"How about—see you soon?" Duncan replied. He grasped the proffered hand warmly.

Paulus nodded. "As soon as possible," he said. "A couple of our people who were working around Nyala haven't reported in for several days."

"Victor—you're not planning to go after them yourself, are you?"

Paulus hesitated, but then he shook his head. "Part of me wants to," he admitted. "But you're right—I have other work to do. I just don't want to leave until I know what's happened to them."

"Don't wait too long. If I'm to call the foundation when I get home with your confirmation, you need to stick to the schedule you've sent them."

Again Paulus nodded. "The first set of meetings are in Sea-couver in one week," he agreed. "But somehow, traveling around, staying in hotels and comfortable houses, being chauffeured to appearances, eating and drinking with the well-to-do, won't seem quite real—and certainly won't seem right when I know the conditions people are struggling with here. It never does seem *right* for some to have so much and others so little."

There was no answer to that, or none that Paulus did not already know just as well as Duncan. MacLeod waited, letting the silence speak for him. Victor sighed and MacLeod could see that the mood had passed, at least for now. It would come again; MacLeod had no doubt that it was something Victor fought often in the work he did. But without someone like Victor Paulus to speak for them, the people here, and in so many parts of the world, would have no hope at all.

Behind MacLeod, the driver of the truck gently pressed his horn. There was a long drive ahead and they needed to get under way before the heat of the day became too oppressive.

"Travel well and safely, my friend," Victor Paulus said, ending their good-byes. "Peace be with you, Duncan MacLeod."

For just an instant, MacLeod felt as if he had stepped back in time. He thought he heard Darius's voice whispering over his protégé's. It was with those same words that Darius had sent Duncan off on his travels.

"Peace be with us all," Duncan answered softly.

As MacLeod boarded the truck, Victor went to stand beside Cynthia, slipping one arm around her waist to hold her close while together they watched the truck depart. The other arm he raised in farewell.

As it was thus they were still standing when MacLeod glanced back. As their figures grew smaller in the distance, words from a favorite poem filled Duncan's mind. It was by the poet Emily Dickinson, and her words seemed to embody not only what Paulus was trying to accomplish here, but all the people they were trying to help:

No coward's soul is mine
No trembler in the world's storm-troubled sphere
I see heaven's glories shine
And faith shines equal, arming me from fear.

Chapter Four

After the two months MacLeod had just spent in Sudan and the conditions in which he had been living and working, returning to Seacouver felt as foreign as the first time he had traveled to the New World. With all the changing planes and time zones, he also felt as if it had taken almost as long. Although his body cried out for a hot shower and some sleep, MacLeod knew there was one stop he needed to make before heading home. He needed to see Joe Dawson.

As MacLeod's Watcher, Dawson's duties should have taken him to Sudan with MacLeod. But he was also Duncan's friend, and to keep the mortal out of harm's way MacLeod had agreed to send the Watcher regular detailed reports of his activities. Now that he was back in the States, he wanted to go assure Dawson that all was indeed well. Besides, he had missed Joe's company.

MacLeod's black Thunderbird was waiting in the attended lot where he had left it. It started without hesitation, and in spite of the many weeks it had spent sitting, its engine sounded like the smooth contented purr of a big cat. He pulled out into traffic feeling glad to be back in this city by the sea. Jet lag would hit him later, he knew, but right now it was just good to be home.

A twenty-minute drive across town and he pulled into the parking lot of Joe's. It was nearly two A.M., local time, and there were not many cars left. Last call had probably already been announced, MacLeod thought as he walked toward the door of the blues club. Only a few more minutes and Joe would be able to lock the door. Then he and MacLeod could sit down over a "wee dram" or two and have the talk Duncan wanted.

It'll be good to talk to Joe again, MacLeod thought with a smile as he walked through the door just as the three-piece blues band in the corner was finishing their set. Those last few sweetly sad notes seemed to hang in the air, trembling slowly to a hush. There was a brief moment of silence, a tribute of appreciation, then the people at the tables broke into wild applause, a couple of them even coming to their feet.

MacLeod walked over to the bar, where Joe Dawson was beaming almost paternally at the band and patrons alike. This bar was his baby, and blues was the music of his soul.

"A new discovery?" MacLeod asked, taking a seat.

"Hey, Mac." Joe was all smiles. He held out his hand to MacLeod. "Welcome home. Yeah—they're good, aren't they? They just started here two nights ago and you should have seen the place earlier. It was packed, standing room only. Not bad for the middle of the week."

Joe didn't bother to ask MacLeod what he would like to drink. He just turned and grabbed the bottle of twelve-year-old single malt off the wall. With a practiced motion, he poured a generous dose and set it before his friend.

MacLeod smiled his thanks and lifted the glass toward his face. The pungent, slightly peaty aroma of the scotch filled his nostrils, sending a thousand memories skipping across his brain, ghost images of another home and of people centuries dead. This was *Uisge Beatha,* the Water of Life, the drink of the Highlands.

Why should he think of them now? he wondered, and had no answer except that memories were his constant companions: four hundred years of other times and other places, lives, and loves. He tried to live in the present and to look toward the future, but the past was always vividly with him.

He took a sip, letting the smoky liquid trickle down his throat, savoring its fire as he watched Joe come out from behind the bar and walk over to the corner stage. He shook hands with each of the band members before turning to the audience.

"I hate to say it, folks, but it's closing time," he announced. "I could listen to these guys all night, too, but the law won't let me. The band will be here for another two weeks, so be sure to come back and hear them again—and bring your friends."

MacLeod turned back around to the bar and, smiling, took another sip of the scotch. Behind him were the sounds of chairs scraping across the floor, glasses clinking, people speaking in sudden bursts of conversation as they finished their drinks and prepared to leave. Five minutes, maybe ten, then he and Joe could talk undisturbed.

As MacLeod expected, Dawson told the other bartender and the three servers to go home, that he would finish cleaning. Tired after a busy shift, they left quickly.

Joe held out the bottle of scotch and an extra glass to MacLeod. Duncan carried them over to a table while Joe again came around the bar to join him. He took a chair across from MacLeod and grinned broadly—"flashin' his pearly-whites," one of his favorite blues songs would say—letting MacLeod know how glad he was to see him back. In one piece—head intact.

Dawson took up the glass MacLeod had just filled and lifted it toward his friend in a silent salute. "I was beginning to worry when I didn't hear from you this week," he said after he took a sip. "When did you get in?"

"The plane landed about two hour's ago," MacLeod answered. "I haven't even been home yet. Once we'd decided I *was* coming home, there didn't seem to be much reason to write."

"So, you're done in Sudan?"

"For now," MacLeod agreed.

"What about Victor Paulus?" Joe asked. "I thought you went over there to protect him."

"I went over there to *help* him, Joe, not just to protect him. It's an effort that needs all our help."

"You know, Mac, I've been watching for reports in the news, and they've only been conspicuous by their absence."

"That will be changing soon," MacLeod told him. "Victor will be here in a couple more days to start a nationwide speaking tour on the subject."

"Are you going with him?"

MacLeod shook his head. "I have plenty of things to catch up on here. Besides, he'll have other company—his fiancée."

"His fiancée? She's there with him? That's a hell of a place to have a courtship."

MacLeod gave half a laugh as he nodded. "But she's as safe as anyone," he said, "and safer than most. She's an Immortal, Joe—Cynthia VanDervane."

Dawson's expression was thoughtful. "I don't recognize the name," he said after a moment. "Of course, with you guys that doesn't mean anything. Some of you change your identities the way most of us change our shirts. Sometimes that makes things tough on a Watcher."

"Yeah, poor you. Anyway, I thought your organization had us under such close observation, we couldn't make a move without it being recorded." MacLeod raised his glass to his lips to hide a smile.

"Hey, you think being a Watcher is easy? You have to go where your subject goes and do what he or she does, whether you like it or not. I've been lucky—you're pretty settled for an Immortal. Some of you move around like you've got firecrackers tied to your heels, and you've got centuries of experience in not being found out. If you really want to lose yourselves in a crowd or a country, you do—and we have to try to keep up with you anyway."

MacLeod's grin grew broader and Joe stopped, realizing he had just had his buttons pushed.

"Okay, very funny, Mac," he said. "So, tell me some more about Sudan and the work you did there."

MacLeod shrugged. "It's all in the reports I sent you—all the details of what's happening, all the statistics, everything I thought you'd need."

"Yeah," Dawson agreed, "and I really appreciate all the work you did on those reports. From the sound of things, that's not a place I'd want to be right now—or would anyone, for that matter. But you didn't tell me the personal stuff—like how you felt or what you thought, what impressed you and what repelled you. I think it's an important part of the Chronicles, when we can get it."

MacLeod knew what Dawson meant; they'd had this conversation before. It was a pet subject of Joe's, one that had grown out of their own friendship. Outside events had some-times strained that friendship almost to the breaking point, yet it had survived. Because of that, they had come to know and respect one another as men, as *individuals*, regardless of the gulf of mortality that separated them. Duncan MacLeod knew that the truth of who he was, good and bad, was safe in the hands of Joe Dawson. It was a shame more Immortals could not feel the same. So much bloodshed would have been spared, so much more truth recorded.

"Like you said, Joe—being a Watcher isn't an exact sci-ence."

"Yes, I know, Mac. There are just things about this business I'd change if I could."

Both men sipped their drinks in silence for a moment, each knowing what those changes would be. But the organization, as it stood, had been in place for centuries and if those changes came, if there was ever to be a more open relation-ship between Watcher and Immortal, it would be a long time coming.

MacLeod felt the whispered sadness that such thoughts al-ways brought tugging at him. It would be so easy, especially after all he had witnessed over the last two months, to give in to that feeling and sink into one of the black moods for which the Celts were—sometimes rightly—so famous.

But four hundred years had taught him the futility of de-pression. It sapped your strength and robbed you of the abil-ity to make changes—and change was the one thing that had to continue, or you were truly old, whether your age was counted in decades or centuries.

MacLeod turned his mind to the few positive aspects of his time in Sudan—especially working with Victor Paulus. Dar-ius would have been truly proud of his protégé.

"You know, Joe," MacLeod began as he sat a little farther back in his seat and lifted his glass to study the amber liquid. "I've been around for a long time and I've met a lot of peo-ple, mortal and Immortal. Few of them have impressed me as much as Victor Paulus. Working with him was almost like having Darius back again. I got the same feeling of, I don't know—total dedication, selflessness, love—that Darius al-ways gave."

"Darius—his death is one of the darkest spots in all the records. And to think that one of our own. . . "

Joe let the rest remain unsaid. That deed had begun a circle of pain for both of them that was best left behind.

"Tell me about Darius, Mac," Dawson said suddenly. "You knew him perhaps as well as anyone."

"Maybe," MacLeod agreed, "though there were times I wondered if I knew him at all."

"You know, but I can tell you that he was born in 50 A.D., that he was a Goth who met his first death in the year 95, leading his tribe in battle, and that his first teacher was Ahasuerus the Parthian. But those are just *facts* and there are little enough of them. There is even less about the *man*. The reports there are, are from the last few centuries—nothing at all about his early life, except legend. So much has been lost to us," Joe added sadly. "What was there about him that inspired the kind of emotion everyone seemed to feel about him?"

MacLeod shrugged as he finished his scotch. "It's hard to explain, Joe," he said. "Darius never talked much about himself or who he had been before."

"All the reports mention the sense of sanctity, the aura of peace that surrounded him."

Duncan smiled gently. "There was that," he agreed. "But there was often a sense of sadness, too. Especially the first time we met. Like Victor in Sudan, Darius was risking his life to help others—people he had never met and whom his countrymen would have called 'the enemy.' "

Chapter Five

June 18, 1815—The Battle of Waterloo

"Keep your bayonet up and your head down, you bloody fool," MacLeod shouted, not certain his voice could be heard above the pounding of cannon and musket fire and the screams of dying men and horses.

The stench of death was everywhere. It clung to the smoke from the guns that hung like thick fog over the battlefield. It rose from the blood-soaked mud, the trampled fields of barley and rye, and from the burning farms of Hougamount and La Hoye Saint that only yesterday had stood peacefully awaiting the summer harvest.

What had once been teeming with life was now an arena of slaughter.

And still the men fought on.

The man beside MacLeod went down, victim of a skirmisher's bullet. There was no time to do more than note his fall and close the square in around him. The square, with its outer rank of sharpened bayonets, was the only defense against the French Cavalry. The horses would not charge the wall of sharpened spikes; within the square, the Riflers shot and reloaded their weapons with deadly rhythm.

But while the square was protection against the waves of cavalry that thundered across the fields and up the ridge, it made the soldiers within sitting targets for cannon, howitzer, and musket fire. All they could do was close ranks around their dead and hold the square until the cavalry retreated. It did not seem like much protection, but MacLeod had seen what happened when a square was not formed in time and it was nothing short of slaughter.

The whole battlefield looked like a slaughterhouse. In over two hundred years of life, Duncan MacLeod, currently of the 71st Highland Riflers, had seen many battles, but not even the Scottish defeat at Culloden had prepared him for the carnage that was Waterloo.

The battle began in late morning and they had fought all through the day—advancing, retreating, advancing again only to once more retreat. This time of year, only three days from the summer solstice, darkness did not come early to end the suffering under the mercy of darkness—and neither had the Prussians, the British army's one hope of relief, arrived. All they could do was fight on and hold.

A rider and horse went down in front of MacLeod. The rider was silent, dead, the top of his head blown away. But the horse remained alive, screaming its agony. It tightened MacLeod's stomach to hear it. His muscles ached to go put the animal from its misery, but he could not break ranks. Not yet. Not while the French still charged. He willed his ears, and his heart, to close out the sound as it closed out the other sounds of death. He concentrated on helping those around him stay alive.

How long this charge lasted, MacLeod did not know. Ten minutes, ten hours; time had no meaning anymore. The only thing that could be measured was life or death, victory or defeat. MacLeod's eyes were red from squinting through the thick haze of smoke. His throat was raw and his lungs burned from breathing the acrid air. He would heal, but others—too many others—would not.

Damn that bloody Napoleon, MacLeod thought for the thousandth time over the last days. *God rot his black soul in hell for not staying on Elba.*

For over a year, the self-styled Emperor had lived in exile, and that year had brought a measure of peace to Europe after more than a decade of war. But in January, Napoleon had gathered enough money, ships, and support to escape. By March, he had reached Paris again, with an army at his back. The capital city of France had welcomed its Emperor home. After placating the French Parliament and finding that most of the country was still loyal to him, Napoleon renewed his plan to bring all of Europe under his control.

The Napoleonic Wars had not ended.

They would end today, MacLeod knew, one way or the other. If the British and Belgians could not hold, if the Prussians did not arrive because they had already been defeated, then Napoleon would win the day. His victory meant the defeat of European sovereignty and independence. From the Mediterranean to the Baltic, from the North Sea to the Straits of Gibraltar, the eyes of the Western world were focused on this battlefield.

The French were retreating, for now; they had not broken the squares, and for a few moments there would be a breathing space between attacks—at least on this part of the field. Time enough to get the wounded back to the surgeons and to give the dying a measure of peace.

MacLeod loaded his musket carefully, then stepped forward and finally ended the brutal torment of the horse in front of him. The humans would not be so lucky. Despite the best administrations of the army surgeons, many would die of their wounds, the pain-racked deaths of gangrene, blood poisoning, and fever. Others would survive, maimed and scarred, and even their survival would not come until after nearly unbearable pain.

MacLeod bent over the body of a man from within the ranks of his regiment. His face was almost unrecognizable under the mud and black powder residue, but MacLeod knew him by the bright red feather he had pinned to his lapel. Gordon Frazier, nineteen, from a farm outside Aberdeen.

The feather he wore had been given to him by his betrothed, just a week ago when she saw him off at the dock in London. Jenny was her name; Gordon often talked of her and of his promise to return once they had beaten "old Nappy." He had joined the army for the pay, to buy a piece of land where he and Jenny could settle down to raise a family.

MacLeod looked from the bright red feather to the deeper red staining the young man's middle, then up to the lifeless eyes that stared unseeing at the sky. There would be no farm, no wife and family, no future for Gordon Frazier.

As Duncan MacLeod gently reached out and closed the lids

over those sightless eyes, he heard a moan nearby. Within the moan was the whisper of his name. Ten paces away, another young man—*God, they were all so young*—reached weakly toward him. Duncan hurried to his side.

He recognized Charlie McKenzie. Just last night they had sat together in the rain, sharing the dubious warmth of a smoky fire and the last of their day's ration of rum.

"For the love of Christ, MacLeod, help me," McKenzie said, clutching at the front of Duncan's uniform. "Don't leave me to die like this."

"Hold on, Charlie," MacLeod answered. "I'll get you back to the surgeons."

Duncan ran a quick, assessing eye down Charlie's body. The blood from six wounds spread across his uniform like a crimson bouquet from an artist's brush dotting a canvas in brilliant color. Whether these wounds were from the deadly shrapnel charges of the howitzers or the roundshot loaded into the French eight-pounders, Duncan could not tell, but he doubted the surgeons would be able to do much for McKenzie.

Still, MacLeod could not leave him here to die alone. "Hold on," he said again as he lifted Charlie to his feet and began to half-carry, half-drag him back to safety.

McKenzie was silent, though his breathing was labored as he strove to keep in the cries of pain such movement was causing him. MacLeod was grateful. Though he was doing all he could to help his friend, he knew that this passage could not be easy.

Finally they reached the tents and wagons where the surgeons had set up their equipment. The smell of blood was even worse here than on the battlefield. MacLeod nearly choked on his own bile when he saw the piles of discarded limbs—arms and legs shattered by shot, trampled by horses, removed by the surgeon's knife and saw.

Men screamed as the doctors plied their trade, having nothing to dull the pain except a few extra swallows of rum and a leather strap on which to bite. The lucky ones lost consciousness as the pain began. But despite the horror of the scene, MacLeod knew the surgeons were doing the best they could to save the men brought to them.

He looked around for a place to lay his friend just as one of the doctors went rushing by. The man's haggard face, his bloodstained hands and clothing told their own tale of the day and the battle against death this man had fought. MacLeod was loath to keep him from his errand, but he had no choice. McKenzie was still bleeding from his wounds and had already fainted twice.

MacLeod stuck his musket out in front of the surgeon, barring his way. "Where do I put my friend?" he asked.

The surgeon looked at McKenzie, then up into MacLeod's face. Duncan saw the weariness in the man's eyes; the look of someone who had gazed on death too many times in a single day and who knew there was so much more to come. MacLeod saw no hope for McKenzie in those eyes.

The surgeon sighed and glanced around. "Over there," he said with a vague gesture to his right. "We'll get to him as soon as we can."

MacLeod lifted his musket and let the man go. He hurried away without a backward glance. Duncan took McKenzie in the direction the doctor had gestured, gently lowering his friend to lean against the wheel of a supply wagon.

"The doctors know ye're here now, Charlie," he said, slipping into the heavier brogue of his youth. "They'll help ye soon."

McKenzie nodded weakly. "Don't go, MacLeod," he said, his voice barely a whisper.

"I must, Charlie. There are others who'll need my help."

McKenzie was silent. He did not move for a long moment, and MacLeod wondered if he had lost consciousness again. But then he nodded once more.

"Aye," he whispered. "So ye must. Go, then, and I'll be here when ye return."

Be there he would, but alive or dead? MacLeod wondered. There was no help for it; MacLeod knew his duty lay in helping to retrieve the other wounded from the field before the French attacked again. He touched McKenzie's shoulder once in silent farewell, then rose and turned back to the battlefield.

Four more times, MacLeod made the journey from the battlefield to the surgeons' tents, carrying a wounded man. Each time he checked on McKenzie. Finally, on the fourth trip, the surgeon to whom he had spoken before came out to meet him. One look and MacLeod knew what he was going to say.

"Your friend has lost too much blood," the doctor began. "His wounds are too deep . . . there will be infection . . . I've done all I can. Take him back behind the lines where he can die in peace, away from . . . this," he gestured vaguely again. "Make room here for someone I can help."

MacLeod might have been angry at the seeming callousness of the man's last words had not the wounded been spread all around him. He nodded once and went to find McKenzie.

Charlie sat where MacLeod had left him, still leaning against the wagon wheel. His eyes were closed and face was so drained of color that if it had not been for the shallow rise and fall of his chest, MacLeod would have thought him already dead.

Duncan dropped to one knee next to him and put a hand lightly on McKenzie's arm. "Charlie-boy," he said, "can ye hear me, lad?"

McKenzie's eyelids fluttered open. "Aye," he said. "I'm glad ye're back, MacLeod."

"Come on, Charlie. The doctor said I should take ye where ye can rest more comfortably."

They both knew what was not being said, and they left it that way. McKenzie reached out an arm for Duncan to help him up, grimacing in pain at each movement as MacLeod draped the arm across his shoulders. Taking as much of the other man's weight as he could, he brought McKenzie to his feet.

Once more half-carrying, half-dragging his friend, MacLeod picked his way past bodies of the wounded, back farther behind the lines. There were wounded here too—the dying, the dead. MacLeod looked for a place less crowded with bodies, a place where there might yet be a bit of untrampled grass on which his friend might pass his last moments of life.

MacLeod saw a dark-cloaked figure in the distance, walking in his direction. As he neared there came the one feeling above all others Duncan did not want to feel.

He was Immortal.

Chapter Six

The cloaked man came closer. Duncan shifted McKenzie's weight slightly as he reached down and loosened his sword in its scabbard. It was not his beloved *katana;* it was the basket-hilted claymore of his uniform. But it was a good blade and Duncan, who had fought with many weapons, knew it would serve him well, if needs must.

"I am Duncan MacLeod of the Clan MacLeod," he said, drawing his sword so that a few inches of steel showed. He did not want to fight, but given no choice he was ready.

"I am Darius," the cloaked man said. He glanced down at Duncan's sword. "You won't need that."

It was then Duncan noticed that beneath his cloak the man wore the robes of a French priest. He was an Immortal, but he was also a holy man; McKenzie would not die uncomforted.

"Put him down here," Darius said, motioning to the dubious shelter of an overturned wagon where MacLeod could lay his friend. It was not such a place as MacLeod wanted, but glancing around, he knew it would have to do. It was as much shelter as anyone, living or dead, had known on this battlefield today.

Duncan gently eased McKenzie to the ground. All around them lay bodies of the fallen. Some few were dying; most were already dead. MacLeod tightened his lips in a grim line as inwardly he again cursed Napoleon and his obsession to rule the world.

Darius looked up from examining McKenzie and noticed MacLeod's expression. "Those wounds we cannot heal," he said of the dead men beneath Duncan's gaze. "We bury them to prevent disease. Infection kills more than all the English and French cannon."

Under Darius's careful touch, McKenzie moaned again. Duncan turned his eyes away from the dead and back to his friend. Then he looked over at the other Immortal's face and he saw the deep compassion in his eyes.

"The surgeon said he would die of infection," MacLeod said softly, "to bring him straight here."

"Well, perhaps I can save him," Darius replied.

"From the fevers?" MacLeod was unable to keep the amazement from his voice. "How?"

Darius moved swiftly now. He handed a tin cup to MacLeod. "Here," he said. "Fill this."

Duncan looked around for a source of water. The heavy rains of the last two days had swollen the small streams in the area. He crossed swiftly to one and filled the cup. Then he stopped at a small fire he passed to warm the water a bit before returning to Darius.

As he held the metal cup over the flames, he looked again at the Immortal priest. Darius was bent over McKenzie, examining him with a gentle, almost tender touch and a look as loving as a parent for a dearest child. Curiosity about who this man was and why he should care so much filled Duncan. He stood and hurried again to Darius's side.

"Here," he said, holding the cup out.

Darius did not take it. Instead he withdrew a small vial from a pocket in his cloak.

"There are medicines which have been lost to modern doctors," he said as he shook a small portion of the fine powder into the water. He then took the cup and swirled it, flashing Duncan a brief but confident smile. MacLeod felt oddly encouraged by the sight.

Gently, Darius raised McKenzie's head and held the cup to his lips. MacLeod was once again moved by the tenderness on the priest's face as he watched the soldier drink. A few sips, and with a grimace of pain McKenzie turned his face away. Darius lowered his head softly to the ground.

"Now we wait," he said. "It will take hours."

In the distance, cannons were thundering once again as attacks resumed and moved closer.

"Hours?" Duncan cried, knowing he could not stay away from his regiment so long. Another cannon blast rent the air. At its crash, so close, Duncan sprang to his feet.

"How goes the battle?" he asked, hoping Darius would have news he had missed while he carried McKenzie here.

Darius looked at him. "Why does that matter to you?" he asked. "Napoleon may lose a campaign, Wellington may win a great victory—but what have they really won or lost? Their reputations? These men have been robbed of their most precious possession . . . forever."

There was a sadness, incalculably deep, to his eyes and a weariness in his voice that spoke of too much knowledge of death. At his words, Duncan's gaze shifted out over the sea of bodies surrounding him and he felt the tragedy of the moment. But he was a soldier; he had seen such scenes before— in raids among the highlands, in battlefields like Culloden.

Darius came to stand beside him. "You shouldn't be taking part in this . . . tragedy," he said softly, sadly. His words were simple, heartfelt, and somehow he had chosen the same word that had echoed through Duncan's thoughts. But MacLeod's answer to him, as to himself, remained the same.

"I was raised a warrior," he replied. "I choose battles I believe to be just."

The weariness in Darius's eyes deepened. He lowered his head briefly, then raised it again and studied Duncan's face.

"Oh, I'm sure," he said. "You're quite loyal to your convictions and compatriots." His eyes swept out over the dead. "But I wonder what these men think about convictions and compatriotism now?"

Duncan had no answer. Darius turned away. He went to find the next wounded man who needed his help, leaving MacLeod alone to face the feelings his words had stirred.

Again, the cannons exploded. Musket and rifle fire shattered the spaces between bombardments and the moans of the dying raised a chorus of grief.

MacLeod stared in bewilderment at the retreating form of the man who had just left him. He saw Darius stop and kneel beside another prostrate soldier. There were no medicines to help this man; even from where he stood Duncan could see the gaping wound that had once been the man's stomach and the pallor of death spreading across his face.

Darius stayed there with him, whispering words of comfort, holding the man's hand so that he would not die alone. Duncan saw the look of peace slowly encompass the soldier's features as he closed his eyes a final time. Darius bowed his head, said one last prayer, then he stood and moved on.

MacLeod heard his name called. Looking toward the sound, he saw Rodney MacFergus, a lieutenant in the 71st Highlanders, his own regiment, beckoning him.

"Come on, MacLeod," he called. "We need you."

MacLeod glanced once again at Darius. The priest had also heard MacLeod's name called and he looked up to meet the eyes of his fellow Immortal. Once more, Duncan marked the sadness in Darius's eyes and the compassion—and with it, Duncan saw also an understanding he had never before encountered. There was an unspoken invitation to peace Duncan wished he could accept—but he could not, not at this moment.

He tore his eyes away. As he did so, he saw Darius sigh and turn back to his work. Duncan found himself sighing as well. Part of him wanted to stay, to hear more of this Immortal's words.

But he was a soldier. He was raised a warrior . . .

The battle continued for hour after bloody hour. Twice Duncan found the time to go back behind the lines and check on McKenzie. Each time, his friend was stronger. In Duncan's mind it was nothing short of a miracle.

Finally, the French Cavalry broke and their last retreat became a rout; finally, the darkness that, so near the summer solstice had seemed to hang back forever, descended, falling like a blanket—or a shroud—across the battlefield.

Bone-weary, MacLeod once more headed to McKenzie's side. Seeing that he slept peacefully, Duncan gently touched his forehead. There was no sign of the fever that could come so quickly and kill with so much agony.

Duncan stood and searched the area, straining his eyes for a glimpse of the dark-cloaked figure moving among the men. But Darius was nowhere to be seen.

Duncan hailed a soldier walking by. "Have you seen the priest who was here earlier?" he called.

"He left, during the battle," the man called back before continuing on his way.

MacLeod's disappointment was bitter, like the sudden bile that rose in his throat at the sight of the dead around him. He wandered away, not really caring where his feet took him but hoping to find a place free from the smell of blood and gunpowder where he could rest.

But he found himself wandering again to the surgeons' tents. As he neared, one of the doctors stepped outside and stood gulping in air hungrily; the man's face was ashen. Duncan walked up to him. He wished he could offer comfort and strength, but he had none to give.

"There was a priest here a few hours ago," he said instead. "Have you seen him?"

The surgeon looked at Duncan with tired, red-rimmed eyes. He blinked a couple of times, as if MacLeod's words had come in a different language he had to struggle to translate.

"I'm sorry," he said after a few seconds. "What did you ask?"

"There was a priest helping the wounded. I asked if you had seen him."

The surgeon closed his eyes, but he nodded. "I hear he's set up a hospital of some sort in a chapel a couple of miles from here. French, English—he doesn't care who's brought to him. He welcomes them all. Poor bugger, he has his work cut out for him. We all do."

The man took one more deep breath of outside air, then turned back to the tent and the horrors that awaited within.

Duncan stayed where he was. Although he wanted to move, his feet felt rooted to the ground—by the fatigue that had overwhelmed even his Immortal body and by the words of a priest that had unsettled his Immortal soul even more.

Without the constant barrage of cannon and musket fire, the other sounds of the battlefield magnified. Horses cried with the madness of agony from shattered limbs and gunshot wounds. Now and then, the single retort of a musket signaled the end of one's misery. The moans and tears of the wounded men were even more terrible to hear; their end could not be so swift or merciful.

Inside the tent, a man screamed as the surgeon plied his knife. With the sound, Duncan felt as if someone had cut him too—sliced him to the heart and was driving the knife deeper with each passing second.

He knew he had to get away at least for a few hours. In the post-battle confusion, while many of the British soldiers still chased their French counterparts or wandered the battlefield searching for fallen comrades among the dead, his absence would not be missed—and he would be back before dawn.

Two miles, he thought, knowing that of all the sounds in the world, what he wanted—needed—to hear were more of Darius's words.

Whether they would heal him or wound him more, he did not know. But he had to find out.

Shifting his grip on the musket in his hand, he began to walk.

Chapter Seven

The church turned out to be well over two miles distant, but Duncan did not mind the walk despite his weariness. Away from the battlefield the air was clear and it was a fine summer night. The sky, which last night had been a place of brooding heaviness as thick rain clouds poured their burdens upon the earth, tonight was alight with stars that twinkled and peeked through thin, gauzy strips of cirrus.

As Duncan walked, the last of the aftereffects of the battle left him. Little wounds, hardly noticed upon reception but a nagging pain afterward, healed, and lungs, charred from the hours of breathing the sulfur-laden smoke, now cleared again. His sore, stressed muscles loosened until he moved once more like a man in prime condition.

It was only the soreness of his heart and the fatigue of his soul that remained.

The ancient road down which he was walking curved gently with the lay of the land. As he followed it around a bend, he heard angry voices shouting—soldiers' voices. MacLeod began to run.

The church was a building of gray brick surrounded by a sea of trampled grass. Six soldiers stood near the entrance. They were English, though with their filthy bedraggled uniforms, MacLeod could not recognize their rank or regiment.

"Get some wood," he heard one of them shout. "If the priest won't give up the prisoners, we'll burn them out."

"Halt!" MacLeod shouted, putting two hundred years of authority, putting all he had learned as a chieftain's son, into his voice.

The soldiers quickly turned toward him. One man dropped

the wood in his arms guiltily. But the man nearest the door, obviously the leader of this little pack, eyed him with open contempt.

"What do you men think you're doing?" MacLeod demanded. "This is a church, not a battlefield. Have ye not had enough fighting this day?"

The ringleader swaggered forward. MacLeod recognized something of the uniform now—an Infantry sergeant, the kind Wellington called "the scum of the earth." Scum was what many of them were, too; in the army to avoid the prisons, enticed by the daily pint of rum but feeling nothing even remotely akin to patriotism or honor.

The man walking toward MacLeod was not a young man, nor was he a neophyte to battle. But as MacLeod looked him over, he knew that the scar that puckered his left cheek could have come as easily from a dockside brawl as from a military campaign. It was clear that the other men would stand or fall in accordance with this man's will.

"And who'll you be, to be givin' us orders?" the man asked in a heavy London accent.

MacLeod gritted his teeth. The sergeant still stood within the churchyard—holy ground—and unless MacLeod could draw him into the road, the only weapons he could use were his words and the power of the uniform he wore.

"I am an officer in His Majesty's army," MacLeod replied stiffly. "Your *superior* officer, Sergeant."

MacLeod saw the other men shift nervously at his words, openly looking to their leader for guidance. The sergeant scoffed.

"Superior? You're naught but a bloody Scot," he said. Behind him, one of the other men snickered.

"A dock rat's superior to you," MacLeod countered. He saw the man's eyes narrow with anger.

"Now, I'll ask you again, what are you doing here?" he said.

"There's French in there," the sergeant jerked his head in the direction of the church. "Wounded or not, they're soldiers, and I heard the Prussians are offering to pay a shilling each for every prisoner taken."

"If you believe that, then a dock rat's got more brains than you do, as well."

"Oh, yeah? Then why are you here? Want the reward for yourself, I say. Well, we was here first and them's that's inside is ours."

"You'll have to go through me to get them," MacLeod said.

The sergeant grinned as if he had just received an invitation to the Palace. "With pleasure," he replied. "I've wanted to put my fist through an officer's face for a long time now."

"I'll bet you have. Come and get me." MacLeod opened his arms wide and moved his fingers in small come-hither gestures, letting a little smile touch his lips.

The sergeant saw the smile and his own grin broadened. He swaggered forward. "I'm going to enjoy this," he said.

"No, I don't think you will," Duncan replied.

The other soldiers followed them and formed a circle around the combatants, a ring for their sport. Duncan undid the belt that held his officer's sword and dropped the weapon to the ground; he did not need it to overtake this jackanapes. As he did so, the men began to shout encouragement to the leader.

The sergeant dropped into the slight crouch so favored in street brawls. Again, Duncan smiled slightly. It was an inelegant stance he could have neutralized before the days of his Immortality. Now MacLeod had two centuries of fighting experience, including his most recent years in the Far East and the training he had received. The sergeant's stance looked as awkward and as easily toppled as a baby's first steps.

Then, out of the sergeant's sleeve a small dagger slid. Even at that, MacLeod's smile did not fade.

"And what harm do ye think ye'll do with that wee thing?" MacLeod asked, letting his highland brogue broaden to feed the man's prejudice. "Up in Scotland, we give our bairns bigger weapons than that. But then, we be real *men* in Scotland, not cowards who can't capture any but the wounded and dying."

With a snarl, the sergeant lunged, swiping widely with his blade. It was a movement of anger and gave MacLeod the advantage of control. He sidestepped easily away and brought his hand down with a chop to the sergeant's wrist, hitting the nerve. The man's fingers numbed and the dagger fell uselessly to the ground.

MacLeod spun, driving an elbow into the man's kidneys. He heard the sergeant mutter "Bloody hell" as he lost his balance and went sprawling in the dirt. MacLeod wasted no time. He put his boot to the man's neck, holding the sergeant in place as his eyes swept over the faces of the spectators.

"Leave here now," he ordered them, "and go back to your company. If I see your faces again, I'll have you shot as deserters."

He removed his boot from the sergeant's neck and let the man stand. Before he could slink away to join his retreating companions, MacLeod leaned close.

"Be careful what you say about Scotsmen," he said with a sneer. "The next one might not be so gentle."

The sergeant did not reply, save by the hatred in his eyes. Duncan did not care; he turned and retrieved his sword, then, after belting it on, he looked over at the church.

Darius stood on the porch. The disapproval and disappointment on his face was obvious, even from a distance. Wordlessly, he turned and reentered the building. MacLeod followed him, perplexed.

When Duncan stepped into the narthex, he found Darius kneeling beside a young man with a bandage around his eyes. The priest was holding a cup to his lips and speaking softly. MacLeod could not help but wonder what sort of brew was in the cup this time, hoping Darius would be able to help this young man the way he had helped McKenzie.

Surely he cannot help them all, Duncan thought as he looked around. Every area of the church—narthex, nave, and transept, except where the Communion rail cordoned off the altar, had people lying on clean pallets in neat rows. Yet, despite the wounded and torn bodies and the blood-soaked bandages, there was a sense of peace about the place. Instead of the smell of blood, it seemed a trace of incense clung to the air.

Darius finished with his patient. Speaking a few more soft words, he helped the boy lie back down, then stood and walked over to Duncan.

"If you've come to help," he said, "I can use an extra pair of hands."

"Aye," Duncan answered quickly. "I'll help you all I can. But I cannot stay over long—I'll need to be back to my regiment by dawn."

"Why?" Darius asked him. "Why must you go back to that place of slaughter? Have you not yet seen enough of battle?"

"I'll not be a deserter," MacLeod answered sharply. "My duty demands—"

"Ah, yes, a soldier's duty," Darius said with a sad smile. "But what does that duty really accomplish, except death? Wars come, young men die, wars end—only to start up again a few years later in another place."

"Should we give the world over to tyrants, then?" MacLeod asked. "Ah, Father, excuse me for saying so, but what can you—a priest—know of it? Your words work well in a cloister, but not in the world out there."

MacLeod saw the amusement grow in Darius's eyes. It was softened by compassion, but it was amusement nonetheless—the look a parent might give a half-grown child.

"There is nothing about war I did not know, Duncan MacLeod of the Clan MacLeod. I have not always been a priest—and there is no face of death I have not seen."

MacLeod had the feeling Darius wanted to say more. He waited, but the priest merely shook his head and turned back to his patients.

"You can help me apply fresh dressings to these wounds," he said, becoming practical. "There are many lives here we can save if we hurry."

"Aye, like you saved McKenzie. He was already much stronger when I left him."

The smile Darius flashed him this time was genuine. "I'm glad your friend will recover."

And Duncan knew that he was glad—not with some abstract feeling about life in general, but with a deep and personal concern. It made Duncan wonder about this strange Immortal all the more.

Was this true holiness then, true sanctity? MacLeod had felt something akin to it in the presence of Brother Paul, whose monastery offered rest and refuge to mortal and Immortal alike.

But there was a naïveté about Paul, despite his Immortal age, that Duncan did not feel from Darius. When the priest said he knew the faces of war, Duncan believed him despite the cloth and collar that he wore.

What else does he know? MacLeod wondered as he followed Darius through the rows of the soldiers, watching the priest smile at them, French and English alike. *And how did he come to be here?*

MacLeod had the feeling the story was a long one. Perhaps someday he would hear it all.

"Now, Duncan MacLeod of the Clan MacLeod," Darius said when they reached the corner where the priest had piled rolls of bandages, vials of powders, and pots of creams and ointments. "Let us put your hands to better work than holding a sword."

He handed MacLeod a small stone crock. Duncan unstoppered it; he turned his face quickly away from the sight of the gray mash and the sharp, unpleasant odor.

"Bloody hell," he whispered as he fumbled to get the cork covering quickly back into place.

Darius laughed. "Yes, it is pungent," he said. "But the ancient Persians knew the value of this mold and I have seen it pull the poison from many wounds already blackening with gangrene. Remember, Duncan MacLeod, it is not the appearance of a thing—or a person—that has value. It is what they do, what is in their heart."

Chapter Eight

Duncan stayed with Darius for several hours, helping as best he could. Most often that consisted of following behind the priest carrying supplies, emptying out basins of dirty water, or lending a hand to wash the soiled strips of cloth that served as bandages. And while he worked, Duncan watched Darius.

He had large hands, hands Duncan could well imagine holding a sword, yet these same hands touched the wounded with a gentleness MacLeod had rarely seen. His presence made this church seem like a place outside the mortal world, a place of timelessness where the barriers of humankind—tyrants and wars, national boundaries and personal prejudices—vanished like smoke on a windy day.

Even in pain, no one remained selfish in Darius's presence. Those who could not see helped those who could not walk; those with arms to carry a cup of water gave it to those who could no longer hold it for themselves. Uniforms were meaningless, the reason for the war unremembered in this place of compassion.

It was the sound of a cock crowing in the distance that reminded Duncan of his other duties. He sought out Darius, who was once again kneeling beside the blinded soldier Duncan had seen earlier.

"Will his eyes recover?" Duncan asked him.

Darius turned to him and smiled. "Oh, yes," he said. "Aldrich here will see again. His eyes were burned by some black powder that mischarged, but they will heal now—and without the scars that would claim his sight."

"Aye, 'tis wondrous what you do here, Darius."

"You could do it, too, Duncan MacLeod," Darius said. He stood and came to stand by Duncan's side. "You have good hands and, I believe, a good heart."

"I hope so," Duncan replied softly, "but I cannot stay. I must go back to my regiment and continue my service until I'm released from my oath. If a man cannot keep his oath, he has no honor."

Darius nodded, gravely, sadly. "You must do what you must," he said simply. "I hope I will see you again, Duncan MacLeod of the Clan MacLeod."

"That you will, Darius. I promise you that."

"And you are a man of your word," Darius said with a soft smile.

Darius turned back to his wounded as Duncan walked to the door.

Napoleon fled the field at Waterloo. He retreated to the relative safety of Paris, but this time the Parliament refused to be placated with promises of future glory. The battle was over; the allies had won the war and now the Emperor must be dealt with in a manner that allowed him no return.

Napoleon's second abdication came only four days after Waterloo—June 22, 1815. It was his intent to take a ship to the New World, but British ships surrounded the harbor, preventing his departure. He was taken prisoner at Rochefort and from there he was sent once more into exile. The place this time was St. Helena, a remote island in the South Atlantic from which there would be no escape, no return to threaten the peace again.

Duncan MacLeod's regiment had been among those who had trailed the Emperor's flight to Paris. After Napoleon's abdication, MacLeod put in his request to be released from duty. With the war over, many soldiers were going home; Duncan wanted to return to Darius.

Memories of those hours he had spent with the priest had haunted MacLeod ever since he had left Darius's side. His words of peace, spoken so simply, seemed somehow more real than the idealistic ramblings spoken by dreamers and mystics throughout the ages. There was something felt in Darius's presence, something that was both worldly and ethereal that Duncan was not quite certain how to define.

Could this be true holiness? his thoughts whispered to him time and again. Duncan had no answer—yet—but he knew he wanted to find out. When the papers finally came through granting MacLeod his discharge, he hurried back to the little church of St. Thomas, two miles from the killing fields of Waterloo.

Even before he reached the doors he knew the building was vacant. He did not *feel* Darius's presence and the building itself had a forlorn quality, as if with the Immortal priest's departure its vitality had been sapped away for good.

Duncan entered the building nonetheless, hoping for a message or a sign of where the priest had gone. The air still held a hint of the spicy smell of some of Darius's ointments. Other than that, the building showed no signs of its recent occupation. Even the floor had been scrubbed of all traces of blood and the other less pleasant evidence of wounded bodies.

Still, MacLeod had a feeling there would be something left for him. He walked from the narthex down the nave, his eyes searching for anything out of the ordinary. He reached the transept and looked up at the altar, his disappointment gathering into a crease between his dark brows.

Then, as he turned away, he saw it—a small stone resting on the Communion rail.

MacLeod picked it up and stared at it in confusion. It was a rune stone; he had seen similar marks on some of the ancient standing stones of Scotland. But he had no idea what the mark meant or whom he could ask for translation.

He put the stone in his pocket. He knew that somehow he would find Darius, even if it took him years to do so. He had time. He would return to Paris and start there. It was not the center of France, but Paris was its heart, and MacLeod could think of no better place to begin this new journey.

MacLeod found Darius almost by accident. He had been a week in Paris, and in the aftermath of Napoleon's defeat it had become a place of sadness, unrest, and for too many, of homelessness and despair. Paris faced the ages-old situation of what to do with the soldiers after the fighting was finished.

That so many of these soldiers were left maimed and angry at their defeat, living in a city—a country—still reeling from the aftereffects of revolution and occupied by their recent enemies, only exacerbated the problem.

MacLeod had taken rooms above a tavern he remembered from happier days a century before—*La Poule Aux Oeufs d'Or.* He somehow knew that Darius would not be serving a parish frequented by the rich or powerful, but rather by the people he felt needed him the most. Such people might also visit a tavern such as this one.

Duncan had been out in the city most of the day. He returned to the inn ready for a hot meal and the relative comfort of his bed, but when he walked through the door a snatch of conversation stopped him.

" . . . He's turned almost the whole church into a hospital, I tell you. And you don't need money. Take your brother there. I'm sure the priest will help him."

Duncan turned toward the table where two men sat over cups of the cheap red wine that was the tavern's main fare. The men drew back a bit as he approached, unnerved by the intensity of his wide-eyed stare.

"Where?" he asked them. "Where is this church and what is the priest's name?"

"The priest is Father Darius," the man Duncan had heard speaking replied. "His church is over on Rue St. Julien le Pauvre. It's not far. You go—"

"I know," MacLeod said quickly as he turned back toward the door. He called a thank-you over his shoulder as he headed out once more onto the streets of Paris.

Rue St. Julien le Pauvre was not far, as the man had said, but it was in the opposite direction from where Duncan had been searching. Using his memory as a guide, he had divided the city into large squares and had not yet reached the one containing Darius's parish.

Duncan's earlier fatigue left him as he hurried down the streets, occasionally cutting through an alley or across a city park. Although beggars, pickpockets, and prostitutes abounded, no one approached or tried to stop him. He hardly noticed them, hardly noticed anything until, at last, he stood across the street and in front of the church.

The church itself was of moderate size, built of large hewn stones like so many of the parishes in Paris. A fence of wrought-iron spikes rising out of a stone bulkhead enclosed the churchyard. To one side of the main church, a smaller building had been adjoined, a chapel no doubt dedicated to one of the parish patrons, such as the Virgin Mary or, considering the order to which Darius's robes belonged, a St. Joseph chapel. Back behind the church, Duncan glimpsed the roof of another building—perhaps the rectory or part of the old cloister.

How long had Darius been here, Duncan wondered, guessing the church to date from somewhere around the thirteenth century—and where had he been before this? Who had he been? Even as he thought it, Duncan realized he might never know. Mortals often had their secrets—past lives that were forgotten when new ones were begun. The centuries had taught MacLeod how much more true, and more necessary, that must be for Immortals.

The parish door opened and Darius stepped out. There was no doubt this was the same priest, for Duncan felt the Immortal presence of the man surge through him. Darius glanced quickly in Duncan's direction, but his gaze did not linger. He held the door open for an elderly woman who carried a small pot in her hands. Duncan watched Darius speak solemnly to the woman, no doubt giving her some final instructions on how the contents of the pot were to be used. It was only after she had left that the priest turned his attention back across the road.

Darius lifted a hand—in recognition, in greeting. Duncan began to walk forward, wondering as he did so why he should feel such a sense of homecoming. Why had a few hours in Darius's company left such an indelible mark upon him?

"Duncan MacLeod of the Clan MacLeod," Darius said as Duncan entered the churchyard and stopped before the little porch on which Darius was standing.

"I said I'd be back as soon as I could. It's taken me a while to find you."

Darius gave a little one-shouldered shrug. But then he smiled. "I had to come back where I belong. My parishioners need me."

"I've heard you've opened your doors to more than just your parishioners."

Darius looked out at the streets with a gaze of ancient sadness. "There are so many needs, so many wounds—and not just of the body," he said in a low voice, almost to himself. Then he turned back to Duncan and gave another soft smile.

"Come in, Duncan MacLeod," he said, his voice cheering. "I can use another pair of hands—and you, I think, can use some time where your sword will not be needed."

"Aye," Duncan replied. "Aye, that I can."

Chapter Nine

Duncan kept his room at *La Poule Aux Oeufs d'Or,* but he spent most of his time with Darius. The days turned into weeks and into months; summer passed into autumn and the whisper of winter was heard. But the changing of the seasons did nothing to cool the boiling unrest of the Paris streets.

Inside Darius's church it was easy to forget how much hatred was still in the world. He kept his hospital going, though the worst of the wounded from the war had already come and gone. There was always a need, he said, and the slow but constant trickle of bodies—some in need of healing, others who sought only a warm place to spend a night—proved him right.

Duncan knew Darius was right about so many things: the need for peace in the world, the futility of war. But, as wonderful as these ideals sounded, MacLeod also knew he could never be a disciple of Darius's words. He was often a weary warrior, but a warrior nonetheless. He could not put down his arms and stand aside when injustice or greed or oppression reigned, innocents still suffered under the hands of tyrants, and the weak were still at the mercy of the strong. This was the code of honor to which Duncan MacLeod had been born, the code he had never forsaken, and as long as evil existed he knew he must fight against it—not just with words and ideas, but with body and blood.

But their differences did not keep the two men from becoming friends. Their talks would often go on long into the night and Duncan learned many things about what Darius had done during the centuries he had been alive. There were enough allusions made for Duncan to realize Darius had once been a warrior and the leader of a great army, but the priest would not give specifics about those years. It piqued MacLeod's curiosity and he hoped that somehow, someday, he would learn more.

The late-November wind was cold as Duncan walked back toward *La Poule Aux Oeufs d'Or.* Tonight, Darius had brought out an old chess set, something he said he had not used in years, from one of his many cabinets. They had played four games and though MacLeod was no novice player, Darius had thoroughly trounced him each time.

MacLeod smiled as he walked along the river. The gaslights of the Paris streets sparkled on the Seine like captured stars. Overhead the sky was heavy with a coming storm. Soon it would drop its pellets of rain that could, this time of year, easily turn to snow before the night was out. Duncan picked up his pace. Dawn was now much closer than dusk and he wanted to be inside before the storm began.

He was now such a familiar face along the waterfront, the beggars and prostitutes who worked this beat had long ago ceased accosting him. He even knew several of them by name. But tonight he saw no one. The coming cold had driven even the most desperate of them to seek refuge elsewhere.

Then MacLeod felt it—another Immortal was close. Quickly, quietly, he drew his sword and searched through the gloom and the rising mist. From an alley up ahead he heard a scuffle and a grunt, then the sound of a body falling. MacLeod rushed forward.

There was no battle between Immortals. Rounding the corner, he saw a cloaked figure bending over a body. He called out his challenge.

The cloaked figure straightened and spun—and the Immortal who faced him was a woman. Even in the dim light MacLeod could see the heavy rouge on her cheeks and lips, the paint on her eyes. He had not doubt what trade she followed.

But in her hand she also held a sword. There was blood on the blade.

"What are you doing?" MacLeod asked sharply. "He's a mortal."

"He'll live," she answered. "I only cut him a little, enough to teach him a lesson. He wouldn't pay me what he owed—so I took it from him." She dangled a coin purse from her fingers.

MacLeod rushed past her to the man's side. He was more dazed than injured. There was a cut on his cheek and another, slightly deeper one on his arm.

MacLeod drew out his handkerchief and bound the man's arm. Then he stood, grabbed the girl and pulled her away. She started to struggle against him, but he tightened his grip.

She lifted her sword and brandished it with a childlike awkwardness. "You . . . you let me go," she said, "or, Immortal or not, I'll cut you. There ain't no man gonna take me without paying."

MacLeod sighed. With a single, swift motion he disarmed her. "I'm not going to hurt you," he said, "and I'm not after your . . . favors. Tell me your name and what you're doing here, like this."

"My name's Violane, Violane Armand—and where else am I supposed to be? Back in my village where they saw me die? They'd burn me as a witch."

"Don't you have a teacher, someone to tell you the rules of The Game and show you how to properly use . . . this?" He lifted her sword.

She shrugged. "Oh, I had a teacher, all right," she said. "'Twas him who brought me to Paris and put me on the streets. All he wanted was the money I could make for him. But I fixed him—I cut him good and ran away."

"Who was he, Violane?" MacLeod was angered by her tale.

"I'm not telling." Violane stuck her chin out. "You'll just tell him where to find me. I know what you're like . . . all of you. You just want what you can get from a girl. Well, no one's getting nothing from me . . . not no more."

MacLeod shook his head. He could not blame the girl for her thoughts. She was obviously young, both in years and in Immortality, and all she had learned from her own kind was how to be used. Well, he had a solution.

"Come with me," he said. Keeping his grip on her arm, he started back along the route he had just walked.

Back to Darius.

*   *   *

Still holding Violane's arm, Duncan went straight to the rear of the churchyard and the door to Darius's rooms. Violane had become very quiet when they neared the church but now, as she felt the unique sensation, that feeling of Immortality called and answered vibrating through the bones, she began to struggle again.

"Be quiet," Duncan ordered as he knocked on Darius's door. The girl obeyed, drawing back into the protection of his shadow.

Darius answered the knock quickly. "Duncan? What's wrong?"

"This," Duncan replied as he pulled Violane into the light.

"This . . . child?" Darius said. He stepped out onto the porch and put an arm around Violane's shoulders. "Come inside, daughter, and get warm. I've just made a pot of tea and I think we could all use a cup."

As he led the girl inside, he threw Duncan a look that seemed to say, "This must be a tale." Duncan gave a barely perceivable shrug and a weary smile, then followed the priest inside.

Darius led Violane to the table and bade her sit. In the brighter light of the room, her heavy cosmetics looked garish, almost clownlike, but underneath them Duncan saw that she was even younger than he had thought—perhaps seventeen, at best. As she followed the priest's movements with a frightened expression, she seemed far more vulnerable than she had in the alley.

Darius brought the pot of tea and three mugs to the table. "Now, my child," he said softly, "tell me who you are. You have nothing to fear here."

Violane looked from Darius to MacLeod and back again. Then, suddenly, all her facade of defiance left her and she started to cry.

Duncan turned away and went to stare out the room's little window, leaving Darius to console the girl. The priest let Violane cry for a few minutes, understanding her need to release all the pent-up feelings of loss, confusion, the anger and hurt she had held inside for so long. Then he began to speak to her in a low voice, both comforting her and slowly drawing out her full story.

She was every bit as young as Duncan had guessed. She had been sixteen when she had died her first death, and that was not quite two years ago. Her parents had been Royalists, supporters of Louis XVIII and not Napoleon as the rightful ruler of France. Napoleon's army had marched through their town, seizing what they needed to reprovision themselves and never offering a *sou* in payment. Most of the people had been too frightened to say anything. But not Violane's father. He had stood up to the soldiers when they came to the farm—and he had been shot where he stood. Violane and her mother tried to run to him . . . they were shot as well.

When Violane awakened from that first death, she found her home in flames. The soldiers were gone, except for one— Louis Ducharde, an Immortal.

"He brought me to Paris," Violane said. Her tears had subsided to sniffles now and her words were easier to understand. As MacLeod listened, his jaw clenched with anger.

"He said I'd have a new life. That there'd soon be money and new clothes and I could live like a real lady. But there wasn't no money at all—except what I made for him. I said no at first. I was a good girl once, Father, truly I was. But he beat me and he said he'd take my head if I didn't obey him."

"It's all right now, my child," Darius assured her. "We all have things in our past we wish we had not done. But that is over now and you are safe. No one can hurt you here or force you to do anything."

"You mean that, Father?" Violane asked, her voice heavy with disbelief. "You won't send me away, even knowing what I've done?"

"All you have done, my child, is stay alive the only way you knew how. As have we all. Now you must decide what you will do with the life ahead of you.

"But not tonight," Darius said, pushing his chair back from the table. "Come, and I will show you where you can rest and sleep in safety."

MacLeod heard Violane stand and follow Darius from the room. He waited, still not turning from the window, until he heard the priest return.

"That poor, poor child," Darius said now that he and Duncan were alone. "I am glad you brought her to me. She has many wounds to her soul that need to be healed."

MacLeod finally turned to face Darius. He saw the sadness, the deep compassion, which filled the Immortal priest's eyes. Duncan knew his own were still filled with anger.

"God rot the man who did this to her," MacLeod said fiercely. "Mortal or Immortal, such men are parasites."

"True, my friend, very true. But such men have always existed and I'm afraid they always will. Calm yourself. Come and have some tea while there is still some warmth to it. I make it from some flowers I grow in my little garden. It is very soothing."

Duncan let some of his anger fade—but not all of it. He knew that if he ever faced Louis Ducharde, only one of them would walk away from the encounter. But he could not hold on to such feelings for long in Darius's presence. It was more than the tea that was soothing—it was Darius himself.

Duncan sank into the chair he had occupied just a few hours before when he and Darius had bent over a chessboard. "What will you do with Violane?" he asked as Darius poured their tea.

"That depends on what she wants. There are many women in the parish who would be happy to take her in. Or, if she wishes to stay here, I can teach her what I know of healing. I can always use more help with the sick and wounded, as you know, and Violane would learn skills that would allow her other ways to support herself. There is always a call for good healers and midwives."

"She needs to learn more than herbs and ointments, Darius," Duncan replied. "She needs to learn the rules of The Game and how to defend herself from other Immortals—especially ones like Louis Ducharde. Will you teach her that?"

Darius shook his head. "I have not touched a sword in centuries. But you are not the only other Immortal I know. When the time comes, I will see that she has the right teacher."

Duncan nodded and sipped his tea. They sat in companionable silence for a few minutes. Then Duncan pushed back his chair and stood.

"I'm going to try once again to make it back to my bed," he said.

"You know you are welcome to sleep here," Darius replied, watching him. Duncan had the uncomfortable feeling that the priest knew his thoughts better than he did himself.

MacLeod shook his head. "It's more than sleep I want. It's a hot bath and a change of clothes."

"Is that all you want, Duncan MacLeod?" Darius said softly. "Do not go looking for battle, my friend."

At the priest's words, Duncan realized that a part of him had been planning to go in search of Louis Ducharde.

"Do I sit back and do nothing then, Darius?" he asked. "How many other girls must this man be allowed to use and to hurt before someone stops him?"

"I know your motives are noble, my friend," Darius replied, "but the world will never be changed by violence. Only love can do that—one soul at a time."

"Not even *we* have that much time," Duncan said.

Chapter Ten

The next weeks with Darius wrought quite a change in Violane. Without the cosmetics covering her features, she was a lovely girl, with dark hair that framed a small heart-shaped face, flawless skin, and large eyes the color of robin eggs. When she smiled, which still was not often, she went from pretty to beautiful, taking on a luminous quality as if someone had lit a bright candle within her.

Darius was also pleased with his new pupil, for Violane had chosen to stay and learn all she could from the priest. When Duncan arrived at the church one morning in mid-December, Darius took him back to the hospital rooms that still filled the old cloister. Violane was there, tending to a young mother and child who had come in from the cold.

Violane looked more at peace than Duncan had yet seen her, as she sat at the mother's bedside holding the child in her lap.

"She is a good student," Darius said proudly. "She has a quick mind and gentle hands. People respond to her. I think she will do very well in time. I tell you, Duncan, *this* is what we should be doing with our Immortality—using it to help people and to better the world they live in."

"Who's that Violane's with now?" Duncan asked.

"More of the many homeless filling the streets of Paris, I'm afraid. The child will be all right as soon as he has had some nourishing meals, but the mother has pneumonia. I think we have caught it in time for her to be healed, but she is very sick. I am trying to find homes for them so they do not have to return to the life they have had."

Duncan smiled. "More of one soul at a time?"

Darius gave his familiar one-shouldered shrug and the small, self-effacing smile Duncan had come to know so well.

"Have you decided what to do about a teacher for Violane?" Duncan asked as the two men slipped quietly away. "She still needs to learn the things you cannot teach her."

Darius sighed. "I know," he said, "and yes, I have two or three people in mind. Do not worry yourself, my friend. Just because I live on holy ground and because Violane is happy here now, I do not expect her to always stay—and I have not forgotten the ways of our kind."

Duncan said nothing more on the subject, but he did wonder how much Darius really knew about the city Paris had become. There was still so much anger, centuries' worth. It had boiled over, not so very long ago, into a revolution that had quickly degenerated into what was already being called the Reign of Terror, where the guillotine had worked its bloody business night and day under the guise of "justice for the people." But it was vengeance and greed that had truly fueled the fires. From those ashes Napoleon had risen, promising the people that with their country's New Order he could, and would, make France the most glorious and powerful country in Europe—in the world.

The people needed a strong leader. As a chieftain's son, MacLeod understood that—and so had Napoleon. He had given the people something, someone, in whom to believe. As his successes grew, they had even granted him the power and title Emperor, though they had just fought to throw off the shackles of a monarchy.

But now Napoleon was defeated, utterly, and all the dreams he had fed the nation had turned to disillusionment. With the onset of winter, that disillusionment had, for so many, turned to desperation, and those who had placed their hopes for a better life in him suddenly found themselves without bread to feed their children. Theft was common, murder growing more so, and the Paris police turned a blind eye to much of it, knowing there was little they could do among a populace of so many.

Duncan saw this, even if Darius did not, and he knew that it was not a problem to be solved one soul at a time. Or, perhaps, there was no solution; perhaps only time could heal

France's wounds. Duncan was not sure he had the patience to watch the process. He was struggling with a decision he was loath to make, but that he would have to face sooner or later.

He put off the decision through the Christmas season, turning his energies instead to helping Darius keep a kitchen open to feed the poor, and keep his little hospital going. Duncan gave Violane a Christmas present of a shawl that matched her eyes, and he gave Darius a new set of ivory and onyx chessmen. But not even their delight could quell Duncan's growing restlessness.

It was nearing the end of January. MacLeod came back from an evening playing chess with Darius to find that the little tavern he had come to think of as home had been ransacked. Tables and chairs had been overturned, some of them smashed. Broken glass was everywhere. MacLeod stopped as he entered, shocked by the sight before him.

But there was a worse sight still. Over in the corner, Madame Vernier sat upon the floor, cradling the body of her husband. In a glance, MacLeod saw the deep wound in his chest, the slack muscles of his body and the dull, lifeless eyes.

Pushing tables and chairs out of his way, MacLeod rushed to the old woman's side. He felt enraged that such a thing should have happened to the harmless, gray-haired couple who had run this inn for over thirty years. They were a kindly pair who often fed the beggars on the street and offered the destitute a place to get warm.

MacLeod knelt at Madame Vernier's side. She looked up at him and MacLeod saw on her face a grief that went beyond tears. He knew that the wound in her husband's body went less deep than the hole that his death cut in her soul.

"They killed my Richard," Madame Vernier said. "He had already given them the money, but they killed him anyway. I do not understand such men, Monsieur MacLeod."

"Nor do I, Madame," MacLeod agreed softly. He reached out and very gently closed Monsieur Vernier's eyes.

"Have you called the police?" he asked.

She gave a weary shrug. "I called, they came," she said. "They asked if I recognized who did this—as if I can remember the face of everyone who walks through the door."

Madame Vernier began to tremble. *The shock is wearing off,* MacLeod thought. He stood and quickly set one of the tables and a chair to rights. Then he went behind the bar and searched for an unbroken bottle of brandy and a glass. He brought these back to the table.

MacLeod knelt again by Madame Vernier. Gently, he reached to take her husband's body from her arms. She held on to it a moment longer, as if not quite willing to allow the final act of parting. Then, with a sigh that came from deep within her soul and held within it a future of age and loneliness, she released her burden into Duncan's care.

With a sad tenderness, he laid Monsieur Vernier's body on the floor and arranged his limbs into a pose of comfortable rest, respecting the life, the spirit, this body had once housed. Then he stood and drew Madame Vernier to her feet. She seemed to have shrunk beneath this new weight of grief, changed in a few hours from a woman in whom the years had dulled neither vitality nor humor into someone both weary and sad.

MacLeod led her to the table and had her sit, then poured a generous dose of the brandy and put the glass in her hands. She stared at it uncomprehendingly for a moment. Finally, she raised it to her lips and drank.

Duncan waited until he saw the trembling stop and a bit of color returning to her cheeks. "Madame," he said softly, "have you any family nearby? Is there someone you can go to or anyone who can be sent for?"

Slowly, Madame Vernier nodded. "My youngest son, Phillipe," she said. "He lives with his brother outside St. Denis. He will come and take his father's place here."

"Are you sure you do not want to close this place? Sell it and go live with your sons? It would be an easier life for you."

Madame Vernier reached over and took MacLeod's hand. "You are a kind man, Monsieur, to be so concerned about an old woman," she said. "But this place was my Richard's life. He loved it, and I will not sell it now that he is gone. I will stay here—and my Phillipe will come. He is much like his father. It will be a good life for him, as it was for us."

As she spoke, soft tears began to flow. MacLeod knew

from experience that such tears were the first step in the grief that would, eventually, bring healing.

MacLeod stayed at the inn for a few more days, until Madame Vernier's son arrived. During that time, the decision he had been putting off washed over him with undeniable clarity. He knew he could no longer stay in Paris. He was of no help here—he felt useless, and it was not a feeling he enjoyed. It was time to move on.

But where? he wondered. Home to Scotland? No, the wounds of that country, the memories of Bonnie Prince Charlie's defeat at Culloden seventy years ago, ran too deep. Nor did he wish to return to the East. The memories there were even more painful and more recent.

He would go to the New World, to America. It was a land of new hopes and new beginnings. Perhaps there he would find a place for Duncan MacLeod.

It took only a day to find a ship and book his passage. He said a fond farewell to Madame Vernier and her son, not telling them of the extra money he had left in his room but knowing they would find it. Then he set off for the most difficult task of all—saying good-bye to Darius.

The wind was bitter and MacLeod pulled the hood of his thick cloak over his head as he walked slowly toward the church, thinking of all the things he might say. But he knew that, in the end, none of them really mattered; Darius would understand the unspoken. He always did.

When he reached the little church of St. Julien le Pauvre, the narthex doors stood open—an unusual sight for this time of year. So many years a warrior, MacLeod stopped, his eyes and ears straining, his muscles on the alert.

From inside the church he heard angry words. "Take what is here and leave."

It was Darius's voice, but it was angry in a way MacLeod had never expected to hear from this gentle priest. He started to take a step forward, but he stopped himself. If he was on holy ground, he could do nothing to help his friend.

MacLeod hoped he was making the right decision.

"These are worthless pewter," came another voice, hard and strident. "Where is your gold?"

"Gold?" Darius answered. "I have none. Anyone in the quarter would have told you that."

For a few seconds there was silence. MacLeod's stomach tightened and he strained his ears even further, trying to catch any sounds from inside.

Two men scurried out, slightly bewildered looks on their faces. They wore filthy and torn uniforms of the French army. One carried a musket and the other a pike, both of military issue. It was obvious to MacLeod these men had been deserters. What was more, the wound that had killed Monsieur Vernier had been of the kind made by a pike thrust. MacLeod felt the rage he had known over the incident returning.

They stopped as soon as they spotted him. From inside the church came a small sound—*Oh, God,* MacLeod thought, *was that a body falling? Darius?*—and another man hurried out into the day. He wore civilian clothes that had once been fine, but now were so dirty and tattered MacLeod could only wonder from whom they had been stolen. In his hand was his still drawn saber. MacLeod saw the blood on its tip and was suddenly filled with a cold fury.

The leader, too, stopped and stared at MacLeod, but his confusion lasted only a moment. Then he laughed. He started to advance, slowly, swaggering.

"Another priest," he said. "We are blessed."

Duncan did not move. "Where is Darius?" he asked. His voice was low. It sounded calm, even to his own ears, but in truth it seethed with anger. Had these been the men who had robbed the inn, who had killed Richard Vernier and left his wife poor and grieving? How many other people had been their prey in the last months?

The brigand did not take his eyes off MacLeod, though he aimed his words at his cohorts. "The priests in this quarter are a surly lot, aren't they, boys?"

Bolstered by their leader's bravado, the two men in the torn uniforms raised their weapons and advanced a step. MacLeod gave a small snarl over gritted teeth.

"You've made a mistake," he said, quickly whipping off his cloak as he brought his sword, his beloved *katana*, to ready. "I'm no priest."

The chief brigand's eyes grew wide. He hesitated just a fraction of a second before giving his order.

"Attack," he cried.

But that brief second was enough for MacLeod. He side-stepped quickly, bringing his sword up in a parry that knocked off the musket's aim. The weapon discharged harmlessly. The man brought the handle around in a desperate swipe at MacLeod's head. MacLeod ducked easily underneath. One quick thrust of the *katana* into the man's side, and he fell away.

The second man had seemed frozen in place, shocked by the swiftness of the exchange. Now, as his companion crumpled, he stepped in, trying to spear MacLeod with his pike.

The man's movements were clumsy, his thrust too far forward. Once more, Duncan sidestepped, parried, and sliced. His controlled motion sent his opponent into a spin. MacLeod grabbed his head and slammed it into the wrought-iron rails of the fence. This man, too, crumpled to the ground.

Now MacLeod turned to face the leader. There was the smallest flicker of fear in the man's eyes, quickly masked. With a snarl, he charged.

MacLeod's smile was cold and deadly as he countered the man's swordplay. The brigand was not completely without skill, but his sword was no match for the hardened steel of MacLeod's *katana,* nor could his movements equal those of the masters with whom MacLeod had studied.

MacLeod let his smile broaden just a little as he ducked beneath a wide swipe. It was so easy to step inside and thrust. His *katana* connected with flesh; it pierced, and the man fell—back inside the gate, back to holy ground. The rage inside MacLeod was not abated, but he could not follow. On holy ground, the brigand was safe.

Darius came out of the church. He staggered weakly forward, holding his side. Beneath his fingers, Duncan knew a wound was already healing.

In the same instant, the other two thieves began to stir. Duncan turned quickly, his muscles still ready to fight. He reached toward the nearest man.

"No," Darius called. "Don't kill him. Let them go."

One of the men started toward their fallen leader. "Leave

him," Darius ordered, turning his head slightly but never taking his eyes from MacLeod's face and the rage he saw there.

The man looked up at the priest, then over at Duncan. He, too, saw MacLeod's expression and he scurried away, stopping only briefly to help his companion to his feet.

Duncan struggled to keep his muscles in check when his every instinct was to go after the men and stop them. It was only Darius's presence that saved them; the look on the priest's face kept Duncan where he was.

"He'll only kill innocent people," MacLeod said, glancing toward the man in the churchyard. "People who can't rise from the dead."

His words did not change the priest's expression. Darius came closer, growing visibly stronger with each step.

"Why have you done this?" he demanded. His eyes were filled with a pain that had nothing to do with the wound in his side.

Anger and frustration overwhelmed Duncan. How could he make Darius understand what he refused to see?

"What else was I supposed to do, Darius?" he asked. "Tell me that."

The words came out more sharply than he meant. Duncan looked away briefly and sighed, then he turned back to face his friend, this holy man.

"I can't be like you," Duncan said more quietly. "Maybe I'm not old enough or wise enough. I can't just stand by and let . . ."

Duncan's words faltered—but Darius understood. "You're leaving me," he said softly, sadly.

Duncan's eyes searched Darius's face. He saw the compassion there, and the forgiveness. The next words were even more difficult to say than he had imagined.

"Yes," he replied. "I'm going to America. The hatred's just run too deep here. Maybe in the New World it will be different."

Darius was silent for a moment. It was a silence full of things he would not say.

"I will not rob you of that hope," he answered at last.

Duncan reached out for the priest's hand. It was a grasp of friendship and a pledge for the years to come.

"Good-bye, Darius," he said simply.

"Good-bye, Duncan MacLeod."

The two men turned from each other—Darius to his church and Duncan to his future. MacLeod had gone only a few steps when Darius turned back around.

"*Peace* be with you," he called a final blessing.

Duncan looked over his shoulder and gave the Immortal priest a wan smile. He understood the gentle message within the words.

Chapter Eleven

Seacouver, present day

The plane carrying Victor Paulus and Cynthia VanDervane landed at Seacouver International Airport in the crisp light of early morning. Victor had hoped to have a couple of quiet days to reacclimate before picking up his work on this side of the world. But when he walked up the boarding ramp and stepped into the airport itself, he was greeted by the flash of bulbs and a cluster of microphones thrust in his direction. He felt Cynthia step close, and he put a protective arm around her as the clamor of questions began.

Victor had grown used to such receptions over the last few years and he recognized several of the newspeople. Some were from local television stations, others from newspapers, and he greeted them all with his friendly smile.

"Please," he said, holding up a hand to ward off the verbal barrage. "One at a time—and let's move out of the way here. There are other people anxious to get off the plane and go home."

A couple of the newspeople chuckled and they all willingly followed Paulus over to the waiting area. They knew he would give them a good interview.

"Now, one at a time," Victor said again.

"Mr. Paulus," came a voice from the back, "we heard that after your trip to Eastern Europe, you traveled to Sudan. Are you back now because your work there was successful?"

Victor shook his head sadly. "Until the last shot has been fired, until the last death has occurred, until the last woman has been raped, or has seen the loss of a son, a father, a brother, a husband, until the last child has grown up in poverty and starvation, fear and oppression, there is still work to do. While these things go on, my work will never be successful. Let us pray that someday it will be—someday we shall truly have world peace. And it is not just *my* work—it is the work of every decent person everywhere."

"What conditions did you find in Sudan?" came another question.

Again, a look of deep sadness flooded Victor's face. "Conditions I truly hope you never see," he said, "but of which the world must be made aware. Our foundation will be sending out full reports, complete with film footage and verifiable facts, to each of you. Those will tell you, in better words than I can give you now, all you need to know."

"You don't come to Seacouver that often, Mr. Paulus. We've heard rumors of a series of rallies and a speaking tour."

"That's right," Victor said, nodding. "I haven't been informed yet of the exact times and dates, but those will be included in the information that is sent to you."

"What are your plans in the meantime, Mr. Paulus?"

Victor gave a little laugh. "Well, first I plan to get some sleep," he said. "Then, soon, I'll be getting married." His arm tightened slightly around Cynthia's shoulders, and he smiled at her tenderly as lights once again flashed.

Then he looked again at the cameras and news crews. "A very great man, a teacher I once had named Darius," he said, "told me that even in the greatest darkness there is light to be found. This is Cynthia VanDervane, and in spite of all the darkness I have seen in the last months, having her by my side turned it to a time of light. Now she has consented to be that light always."

The questions came once more in rapid fire: "How did you meet?" "Will you be joining him in his travels, Ms. VanDervane?" "Has the date for the wedding been set?"

Again Victor Paulus held up his hand. "Please," he said, "no more questions. Our only plans are to rest for a few days, then continue our work. No date for our wedding has been set, but I promise I shall keep you all informed."

He gave the news crews his disarming smile again, then turned and led Cynthia out of the throng. No one tried to follow them; they all knew that he was as good as his word and they would be told of any newsworthy activities to come.

Behind him, Victor could hear the television people summing up their reports into the cameras. "I'm sorry, my dear," he said to Cynthia. "I didn't know they would be waiting for us."

"It's all right, Victor," she assured him, leaning her head onto his shoulder. "I didn't realize I was going to marry quite so famous a man. I thought prophets were supposed to be *without* honor in their own homes."

"I hardly qualify for that accolade."

"They seem to think you do."

"Maybe—or maybe, like the rest of the world, they're just hungry for some *good* news for a change. The work I do—*we* do—is something in which they can all take part, in one way or another. That gives them hope, and hope is a commodity that is sometimes in very short supply in this world. Now, let's get our luggage and go home. I don't know about you, but I don't feel that a couple of naps on the plane were nearly enough rest. I feel like I could sleep for a week."

Cynthia laughed. "Well, maybe not quite that long," she said.

There was no car waiting; Cynthia knew Victor had hoped to arrive without the notice a car and driver would necessarily bring. He hailed a cab, and after they were both inside he turned to her.

"Now, my love, have you decided which hotel you'd like? There's no need to worry about the cost. The foundation has a fund to cover such things."

"I thought we settled this weeks ago, Victor. I'm staying with you." She leaned close and whispered in his ear. "Or don't you remember the night I told you I was done with sleeping alone."

Sitting back, Cynthia thought how delightful it was to see a grown man blush, actually blush.

"Of course I remember," he said softly, reaching out to take her hand. "But now that we're back in the States, I thought you might have changed your mind. The house the foundation offered is nice enough, but after all you've been through lately I thought you might like to be pampered for a while—maids, room service, restaurants. And that you might like, well, some—space—for a while."

Now Cynthia did laugh, softly, gently. One of the things she truly liked about this man was his adherence to such outmoded ideas—and the way he almost stammered when he talked about them. For all his world renown, in many ways there was a childlike innocence that surrounded Victor Paulus.

And there was a part of Cynthia that would almost be sorry to see him die. Almost.

She leaned against him once again and softly brushed her lips across his ear. "In many times and places, being engaged was as good as being married, with all the same—privileges. I think my reputation is safe."

The cab driver cleared his throat, delicately reminding them that he still needed a destination. Once more Paulus looked embarrassed as he gave the driver the address of the house the foundation kept in Seacouver.

After the driver pulled his cab out into traffic, Cynthia looked up to see him smiling at them in his rear view mirror. Resting her head on Victor's shoulder, she returned the driver's smile. All was going well, just as she had planned.

Better than she had planned, really. Victor Paulus's death would be payment on a debt long owed. But she wanted more than his death. She wanted his pain. She wanted him to hurt in the same way she had been hurt. Toward that end, she had joined his organization and worked her way first to his side and then into his heart. He would know the little death of betrayal, as she had known, and the pain that turned the cessation of life into relief—which she had been denied.

Oh yes, she had planned carefully. She had won his love and his trust, and she had begun the steps to discredit him and topple his empire before she killed him. Once they reached Sudan, it had been so easy; a few words leaked here and there, so that the location of their safe houses became known, pushing the operation farther and farther south, building to the big moment when their entire network would be destroyed.

She, of course, would have survived, and she would have made certain Victor did as well. There would have been scandal, rumors and innuendoes followed by carefully fabricated "facts," all pointing to Paulus's complicity in the deaths of his associates in return for his personal safety. Once that was accomplished and Victor felt the full burden of it, then she would have his life—carefully making it look like the suicide of a guilty man.

Then Duncan MacLeod had arrived in Sudan and changed everything. Well, she would have his head, too—soon. She owed him that for spoiling her plans, but she wanted it for another, more personal, reason. He had robbed her of the one man in all the centuries who had truly understood her. For that, he would die.

She would still have Paulus's death—the last, the final act against Darius in a debt that spanned the ages. Duncan MacLeod would die as payment for Grayson's life. It had taken her a long time to find out who had killed Grayson, and where. But once she had found out, she had vowed to be that Immortal's death.

And yes, revenge would be sweet.

Joe Dawson stared at the screen of his laptop computer. His eyes were red-rimmed and weary from the long hours of work he had just put in, but now he sat back with a sigh and picked up his cup of coffee.

It was just as he had thought; he had read through all of the Watcher reports over the last few months and the only ones coming in from Sudan were his own, supplied by Duncan MacLeod. Whoever this Cynthia VanDervane really was, she did not currently have a Watcher assigned to her case.

Joe grimaced as he took a swig from his coffee. It had gone cold again, and he hated cold coffee. It reminded him of the army—long marches, torrential rains, always being too hot or too cold, bad food, cold coffee, bugs, snakes . . . and those were the *good* memories.

Oh well, he could use a stretch while he made a fresh pot and got the afternoon paper. Then he would start going through the files of female Immortals whose names began with the letter "C." That was something he had noticed; when Immortals changed identities, most of them tended to stick to names similar to their original ones.

Whether that was for vanity or convenience, it certainly had made his job a lot easier over the years, he thought as he headed toward the kitchen and the coffeepot. Once it was on, he went to the front door to get the paper.

News of Paulus's engagement had made the front page. Joe Dawson smiled as he looked at the article and its accompanying photograph. He had MacLeod's description of what Cynthia VanDervane looked like, but this was better. Much better.

Dawson tucked the paper under his arm and headed for the kitchen once again. He decided he would make himself a sandwich to go with his coffee and then get back to work. With luck, he would know Cynthia's past identity before the day was out.

Cynthia stretched lazily upon her bed, enjoying the movement of her long, supple muscles, the sensual feel of the sheets sliding across her soft skin. When she looked at mortal women she wanted to laugh; they were so worried about whether they were twenty-eight or twenty-nine this year, lying about whether they were forty or forty-two. *She* was over sixteen hundred years old. Her poor mortal sisters aged and died—and she remained in her prime, with a face and body forever in their early twenties.

God, she loved it!

Beside her, Victor Paulus slept on. He did not toss or snore; he was, in fact, as fastidious in slumber as in everything else. Cynthia lay there quietly, being careful not to disturb him. He had, after all, earned his rest—she'd made certain of that.

Yes, he was a thorough lover, careful of her pleasure. But sometimes she missed the passion, the abandon, she had known with others. Over the centuries there had been only two of any importance and she thought about them now with a familiarity that was never far from her mind. To them she owed everything she was now—*everything*.

One had taught her the ways of love, the other the way of the sword. . . .

Chapter Twelve

Central Europe—A.D. 409

They came out of the north and swept across central Europe like great packs of ravening wolves, hungry for all they could conquer. Wave upon wave, army after army they came, intent upon a kingdom that stretched from the Caspian Sea to the Mediterranean and, perhaps, beyond.

The Visigoths—great and terrible; dressed in skins and furs against the harsh northern weather, with long braided hair and unshaved faces, their enemies called them barbarians, a plague of death. But they knew themselves ordained to rule. Though they were strong and swift, they were not without mercy or honor. Those who surrendered were treated well; those who resisted felt the power of their swords.

With the armies came wives and children to occupy the conquered lands. Many of the warriors, finding towns and farmlands that pleased them, were content to settle. But two of the greatest leaders continued their relentless march south toward the heart of the empire that had ruled the world for too long and now lay crumbling under the weight of its own corruption.

They marched toward Rome.

Nothing less than Rome itself would satisfy Alaric, called The Great. He marched not just at the head of an army; he led a nation thirty thousand strong. He had tried twice to deal peacefully with the Roman leaders—Stilcho, the general, and Honorius, the Emperor. Alaric wanted lands in Italy for his people to settle, Roman citizenship for himself and his family. And he did not come empty-handed: He offered Rome the wealth his people brought, and his protection.

Alaric had petitioned the Roman Senate, yet the olive branch of peace they had seemed to offer had only hidden the blade of betrayal and deceit. Now Alaric wanted vengeance. He would *take* the lands he meant to occupy, and destroy Rome itself in the process.

Alaric and his people made their winter camp along the Danube north of the Loibl Pass. In the spring, the way through the Julian Alps would open again and his army would begin their southern march of Death. They would not march alone.

Darius was coming.

Some called him Darius the Mad, and Alaric, who had fought by his side, knew the name to be well justified. Never had Alaric seen a man go so wild in battle. Darius fought like a berserker, heedless of wounds or danger. He was unstoppable—and Alaric wanted such a man by his side when he attacked Rome.

The camp along the Danube had spread out like a city of tents and carts and roughly marked corrals. During the day, the surrounding forests rang with the sound of ax and hammer. Soon semipermanent stables would be erected for the livestock. At night, the campfires were so numerous it looked as if a piece of the heavens had fallen and the stars had settled down amongst the trees.

It was a good camp and a good place to dwell for the winter. There were fish in the river and plenty of game in the forest. There was wood for heat and water to drink. The children would be able to run and play; it was as permanent a home as many of them had ever known.

Yes, it was a good place—but Alaric wanted more for his people. He wanted the sunshine of Italy. He wanted warmth and fertile Mediterranean soil. He wanted houses of wood and stone, not tents of animal skins. And, though he spoke these words aloud to no one, he wanted peace.

For his children, yet unborn . . .

For his children's children . . .

For himself.

But first there would be war. First he would crush all those who had denied him peaceful recourse to his dream.

Each morning while his people went about the chores of the camp, Alaric mounted his big black stallion and traveled down on the road he knew Darius's army must follow. They had fought together many times before, spent many winters in each other's camps, and Alaric knew that Darius would come—if not for Rome, then for the brotherhood of arms they shared.

Darius would come because Alaric had asked. Darius would come for the call of friendship; Darius would come for the call of battle.

Darius, the warrior, the general, *The Mad,* lived for battle.

Today, as every day, Alaric rode to the crest of the hill three miles from camp and waited. The wind that whipped his dark hair around his face whispered of snow that would soon fall. Alaric pulled his thick bearskin cloak more tightly around him as his eyes scanned the horizon and his ears strained for the sounds of an army on the move.

For two hours he sat unmoving, a black-clad silhouette against a sky darkening to the pewter gray of storm. The third hour came and still he did not move; something in his bones had told him today would be the day. It was a warrior's instinct he had learned to trust.

The wind grew colder, reddening his cheeks and puckering the scar that ran from his left temple down to his chin, disappearing into his thick beard. Darius had saved his life the day he received that scar. Darius had not failed him that day. He would not fail him today.

As the snow began to fall, he heard it—the sound of horses on a road, the thin creak of cartwheels, the faint call of a voice. Alaric smiled briefly, grinning around the gaps of the teeth he had lost in battle. Then he turned his horse and put his heels to its flanks. Darius was coming; tonight they would feast in celebration.

At the camp, one other had been awaiting Darius's arrival with an eagerness she could barely contain. Alaric's sister, Callestina, saw her brother galloping toward the camp, and she felt her heart soar. Alaric's haste could mean only one thing.

Darius was coming.

For years Callestina had loved him, and now, at twenty-two, she was eager to show him how a young girl's infatuation had changed into a woman's passion. Alaric wanted Darius the Mad by his side, but Callestina wanted Darius the *Man*—and she meant to have him.

She waited until Alaric reached her and jumped from his sweating horse. "Two hours, maybe three with this weather," he said, knowing she would understand. "Have the hunting parties returned?"

"Two of them," Callestina replied. "They've brought in three stags and a boar. It's not enough."

"Do not worry, sister," Alaric said, once more showing his gap-toothed grin. "God is with us—I feel it. Tonight there will be meat at every fire."

Alaric turned away and began to stride through the camp, calling to the men he passed. As ever, they came running at the sound of his voice. Soon more hunting parties would leave the camp. For once, Callestina would be glad to see them go. She had her own preparations for Darius's arrival and she did not want her brother around while she made them.

Like most nomadic tribes, the Visigoths were a communal people, with families sharing their tents and possessions by will or whim. But Callestina had long ago demanded a place of her own and it was there she headed now. While the men were hunting, living their rituals of death and life, Callestina had her own rituals to perform.

This was Woman's Magic, old before the coming of the one male God in whom her brother believed, powerful with the force of life that had governed her people long before the pantheon of male deities had obscured the place of the Mother-force. It was a divining of blood and fire, and Callestina wanted no man's presence to taint its outcome.

Her tent had been erected next to her brother's. Between them, on the great fire pit that was kept perpetually lit, a large cauldron of water had been set to boil. Callestina did not bother to ask its purpose; more water could easily be brought from the river to replace what she would take. She quickly drew out the bucketful she could use for washing, then entered her tent, taking care to close and tie the flap behind her.

A smaller fire burned within, most of its smoke drawn up by the hole in the top of the skins. Beneath her feet, the ground was covered with furs for added warmth. Going to stand near the fire, Callestina quickly stripped. She unbraided her hair so that it fell in a golden cascade past the small of her back. Then she began to wash. She must be cleaned, purified, before she petitioned the Norns, the Goddesses of Destiny.

Callestina washed herself carefully, scrubbing until her skin turned pink. From her scalp to the soles of her feet, there must be no dirt to defile her or her request. As she washed, she slowly formed the words she would present before the goddesses, for such a petition must be performed correctly. One wrong word could mis-seal a fate and bring disaster.

After she had washed, Callestina wrapped herself in a robe of silver fox and ermine, for these colors were pleasing to the goddesses. Then she pulled away the furs from one corner of her tent and slowly poured out the water she had washed in, chanting her gratitude to the Mother Earth goddess as she watched it be absorbed back into the ground.

Next, Callestina found the small silver bowl her mother had given her before she died. It was her mother who had taught Callestina the ritual she was performing, as it had been taught her by her mother, who had been taught by her mother before that—back through the generations.

Callestina filled the bowl with honeyed wine, symbolizing the sweetness of life. Rummaging through her clothes, she found her red woolen shawl and from that she cut three lengths of yarn. Red was the color of blood, of both birth and death, over which the Goddesses of Destiny ruled—and it must be yarn, not fur or leather, to honor the craft of the goddesses, the weaving of time. Callestina cut a lock of her own hair, which would symbolize the offering of herself into the goddesses' care. Finally, she pricked the tip of her finger with a silver pin and let the blood drip into the bowl to mingle with the wine—life and death, sweetness and pain. It was not her woman's blood, which was the most powerful, but it was blood of her body and she would trust that it would be acceptable to the goddesses.

Callestina now went and sat before the fire, letting the robe fall from her shoulders so that the warmth of the flames bathed her body. Fire was sacred of itself, a gift from the gods to their mortal children. Callestina closed her eyes, clearing her mind of all but the divine caress of the heat. She let the sensation seep inward, filling her body until, at last, she knew she was ready.

Slowly, softly, Callestina began to chant the names of the goddesses.

"Mothers of Destiny, I come before you. Great *Urd*, your thread binds the fate of the world; Great *Verdandi*, your thread secures the path of the present; Great *Skuld*, your thread weaves the course of the future. Great and powerful Mothers, without your skill all is chaos. To you, Great Mothers, I bring my petition. You alone can be my help."

Callestina took the first thread and dipped it in the wine. Then she threw it on the fire, and as its smoke rushed upward she asked her first boon.

"Great Mother Verdandi, holder of the present, show me the way to make Darius love me as I love him. Help me awaken his desire and his heart."

Again Callestina took a red thread, dipped it in wine and threw it on the flames.

"Great Mother Skuld, keeper of the future, weave my life and Darius's together. Let the path of our futures be bound by your unbreakable thread."

A final time Callestina repeated the ritual.

"Great Mother Urd, Mother of Fate, I do not ask for riches or power—only for love, and for the passion of that love to be the force that decides the fate of my life."

Now Callestina placed her own hair in the bowl, spreading the strands out to cover the honeyed wine. She passed the bowl three times over the fire, once more chanting the names of the goddesses. Then she poured the liquid onto the flames. Pungent smoke filled her tent and she lifted her naked arms upward into it.

"Great Mothers of Destiny," she sang out to them. "You hold all that is and all that is to be. I place myself within your care. I pledge myself to your service. Only hear the cry of your daughter and grant the requests of my heart and all that you ask of me I will do. Whatever path you lay before me, Great Mothers, I will tread without fear or wavering."

Callestina sat back now, energy spent. She could feel her heart pounding, her blood racing with anticipation. She was certain she had performed the ritual correctly—surely the goddesses would hear her and look on her with favor.

By tonight, Darius would be hers.

Chapter Thirteen

Many of Alaric's people turned out to cheer as Darius's army approached the camp. Unlike the nation of Visigoths under Alaric, few of Darius's followers were women and children; none of them were wives. The men who followed Darius were warriors, killers, who took joy in their skill and their mobility. There were a few camp followers who satisfied the quick lusts of the men, but even these women carried swords and spears. They rode a horse as well as any man and counted themselves among Darius's chosen.

When the two armies combined under Darius and Alaric, there would be forty thousand to attack Rome.

Darius motioned for his army to halt and begin pitching their tents while he rode on toward Alaric's tent at the center of the camp. Only one man rode by his side, one man who was always by his side.

Grayson, Darius's second-in-command.

They had been together for forty-five years and Grayson alone knew the secret of Darius's ferocity, his unbeatable skill in battle. Grayson knew because he and Darius were of a kind.

Immortal.

The truth of their lives gave them a power mortal men could not understand. It freed them from the fears that ruled lesser men—fear of pain, of wounds, of illness, of death. They were free to go from glory to glory, century to century, until the world lay at their feet.

Grayson of course knew of The Game; Darius—his teacher, his mentor, almost his personal god—had neglected no part of his education when he had discovered Grayson awakening from his first death. Even now, Grayson shuddered to think of it: the sword slicing through him, weakening him; his fall as the horses came galloping toward him; their hooves trampling him, smashing his body until the pain gave way to the oblivion of death.

And then—Darius sitting on the ground waiting until life once more coursed through Grayson's body.

Grayson remembered the smile that had greeted him when sight returned to his eyes, the hand that reached out and drew him to his feet, the strong arm around his shoulders, steadying him at a time when existence had just twisted to a crazy new shape and angle.

It was an irony Grayson had long ago come to appreciate, that the very hooves that had crushed him belonged to the horses of Darius's army.

His mortal life had ended that day on the trampled field in Dacia, but he had been reborn into something far greater. He had left behind his plows and his crops and his old name of Claudianus. He had taken his new name for the gray wolf's skin Darius wore in battle. He was now *Grayson,* Son of the Wolf, and at Darius's side he learned the art of war. Together they were unstoppable.

Grayson felt all the power of his Immortality as he and Darius rode side by side through Alaric's camp. It was a sea of mortal bodies and Grayson saw them only as tools, as fodder for the machinations of conquest.

Darius's conquest; *his* conquest.

From the back of his horse Grayson looked down on them, both in body and in spirit. He returned their cheers with a slight, sardonic twist of his lips he knew they would mistake for a smile—weak, blind mortals that they were.

As the riders neared the center of the camp, Alaric himself came out to meet them. By his side walked his sister. Grayson felt a wave of hunger crest through him; here, finally, was someone worthy of his attention.

With the hunger came the whisper of another sensation. It was the merest glimmer of what he and all like him would someday feel in her presence, but it was enough. Callestina, Alaric's younger sister, was Immortal. She did not know it yet, for no first death had claimed her, but the truth was apparent to Grayson.

Grayson glanced at Darius. For the briefest moment their eyes locked, and Grayson knew that Darius had also felt it. Or, as often as they had shared winter camp with Alaric's people, perhaps Darius had known for years. Darius always seemed to know—everything.

"Darius, my friend!" Alaric's booming voice cut into Grayson's thoughts. The leader of the Visigoths stepped forward, arms outstretched, as Darius dismounted and handed his reins into Grayson's keeping.

Grayson let his eyes rake over the man as Alaric enfolded Darius in a welcoming embrace. Alaric was a bear of a man, suited to the black fur he wore about his shoulders. He had not the height of Darius, but he had greater girth, with a barrel chest and thick arms that came from wielding the battle-ax he preferred over a sword.

"Always you keep yourself a little apart, Grayson," Alaric called as he released Darius and turned toward the mounted man. "Come—let another see to the horses. They'll be well cared for, I promise you. Come into my tent. There is a feast being prepared. The whole camp celebrates your arrival."

Slowly Grayson dismounted. He threw the reins of the horses to a boy who rushed out to take them. Hiding his reluctance with a sigh, Grayson turned and strode to Darius's side. As Alaric embraced him as well, Grayson tried not to grunt in disgust. Then the leader of the Visigoths turned and led the way into his tent.

"You must look more pleased, Grayson," Darius said to him softly as they followed Alaric. "Being pleasant to one's allies is also one of the arts of war. As long as they are useful, you must flatter them and make them feel they are your equals—especially if, in truth, you know they will never be so."

Grayson inclined his head slightly so that Darius would know he understood. Even after all these years he was still learning from the master.

Then Grayson straightened his shoulders slightly, put on a false smile, but one that he hoped was convincing, and walked with Darius into Alaric's tent. As he entered, his gaze fell again on Callestina. At that moment, his smile became true.

Callestina barely returned Grayson's smile and she gave no more of one to Darius. She was polite and yet aloof. In the time between the ritual in her tent and Darius's arrival, a plan had formed in her mind and she would do nothing to jeopardize it. She was certain it was a gift from the goddesses.

She had dressed with special care this evening, laying aside comfort and warmth for beauty. If all went as she planned, she would have Darius's arms to warm her tonight and the slight discomfort of these hours would be forgotten in the pleasure of his touch.

She had left her hair unbound, and brushed it until it shone like strands of golden silk. The gown she chose was deep blue, a color not easily achieved in dyeing, and was woven of the finest lamb's wool. It clung to every curve when she moved, outlining the fullness of her breasts, the roundness of her hips and thighs, the long supple line of her waist. She did not sit at Alaric's side, as was her right and her usual wont, but kept moving about the tent, serving the men herself and letting the magic of a woman's body work its own eternal spell. She could feel Darius's eyes following her. That gave her body warmth enough without the fur robes she would otherwise have worn.

Grayson watched her also, but of his obvious desire she thought not at all.

Callestina ate sparingly herself; she found that the excitement she felt left little room for food or drink. Nor did she participate in the men's discussion of conquest. Throughout the winter months ahead there would be many hours to hear her brother's plans for what was to be—and, in truth, it mattered less to Callestina where she settled than with whom.

She went to refill a pitcher of mead, not bothering to grab her cloak before leaving the tent. The air outside was cold and crisp and Callestina filled her lungs with it. The ground had a light covering of snow, but both it and the wind had stopped and now the night seemed to sparkle, as if the air had been freshly washed.

Around her were the sounds of the camp in celebration—

laughing, singing, greeting old friends—yet Callestina felt oddly alone, as if the noise eddied and swirled but passed her by, leaving her in a pool of calm.

But she was not calm. Now that she was alone, her heart pounded almost painfully against her ribs. Would she have the courage to carry out her plan tonight, to act without fear of consequence?

Yes, she told herself, lifting her head higher. *This, too, is war. It is a conquest and I am as much a warrior as my brother.*

Callestina walked to the wagon where the casks of mead were stored. As she lifted a lid and prepared to plunge the dipper down into the golden liquid, she felt a presence behind her. She turned quickly and found Grayson watching her from a few feet away. On his arm he carried her cloak of silver fox.

"I saw you leave without this," he said as he stepped nearer. "It is too cold a night to go about uncovered."

With a swift motion, he shook out her cloak and draped it around her shoulders. For an instant their bodies stood close to each other, almost touching, and Callestina could feel the heat of him. His hands were on her shoulders. Even through the thickness of the fur, she could feel how his hands shook, as if he did battle with some enemy.

Slowly, Callestina lifted her eyes to Grayson's face. Like Darius, he was clean-shaven, Roman style, though tonight a fine stubble accented his high cheekbones and the slant of his jaw. His hair, too, was Roman style, swirling in a dark blond mass no longer than his ears. This was also Darius's influence. Beards and braids could give an enemy a handhold, Darius said, and many of his army went without them.

Finally, Callestina looked up into Grayson's eyes. They were the pale blue of a sky just lightening to dawn. She saw the desire that filled them and knew that his own feelings were the enemy he fought. Grayson did not want to love or to keep a woman. He wanted nothing in his heart but himself, Darius, and the world that they would rule.

Callestina lowered her eyes in triumph. She did not care about Grayson's desire except for the feeling of power it gave her. Darius was not so cold a man as his companion. If

Grayson had been thus affected by her presence, surely Darius . . .

She would waste no time; she would go to his tent tonight. "Thank you, Grayson," Callestina said calmly, turning back to her task. "It's true—I had not thought it would be so cold."

She nearly laughed as she said the word. Cold. Her body burned with heat. It was a fire Darius alone could quench—and feed.

Grayson stepped back and let Callestina return, unhindered and unassisted, to filling the pitcher in her hand. As she walked away, his eyes followed her movements but he took no step to join her. He stood with his jaw shut tight, his hands clenched by his side. He was furious—at himself and his own weakness.

It had been all he could do to keep from crushing Callestina to him, feeling the softness of her body pressed against his, tasting the sweetness her lips promised. Why hadn't he? his thoughts raged. Any other woman and he would not have hesitated. He was not a man who ever hesitated over what he wanted.

Through all the times they had shared Alaric's camp, Grayson had seen Callestina change from girl into woman and never given her more than passing notice. Until tonight. Tonight she had seemed made for a man's passion and his body responded of its own accord, filling him with the desire, the need, to be near her.

But, in truth, her beauty daunted him. That very quality that had drawn him to follow her out into the night, had kept him from taking what he wanted. It was more than the fact she was Alaric's sister and Alaric was an ally. That would not have stopped him had he felt the least bit of yielding in Callestina herself. But he had not. She had seemed a creature of fire, standing next to him in the darkness—and also of ice. And he had known it was not his touch she wanted.

Darius. The name came unbidden to his mind. It was for Darius that Callestina burned so brightly. Grayson nearly laughed out loud. He knew that he was thought cold and aloof, that Darius was imagined the more passionate of the two. But Grayson knew the truth: Darius merely played his part with greater ease. He'd had centuries more practice. If Callestina thought she would find love in Darius's arms, she would find only disappointment.

Grayson had no doubt his mentor would be amused by Callestina's infatuation. He might even spend the winter taking his pleasure of her, though to do so here in Alaric's camp might well prove dangerous. Yet danger was never something Darius avoided. He thrived on it and he had taught Grayson to do so as well.

No, if Callestina wanted love, she would not find it in Darius's heart. He loved only his sword and his battles. This love, too, he had taught Grayson to share.

Fly to him, my little dove, Grayson thought as he watched Callestina's retreating form. *Let him melt the ice I felt beneath your fire. And when he has taken what he wants of you and grown bored with your charms—as he has with all other women—where will you go? To whom will you turn for comfort?*

Perhaps I shall be waiting, he thought as the distance and darkness veiled her from his eyes. *And then again, perhaps not.*

Chapter Fourteen

The feast went on long into the night. Callestina thought she would go mad waiting for the celebration to end and for the men to grow weary enough to let sleep or drink overtake them.

Darius, she noticed, drank sparingly. Even here in a friend's camp there was a part of him that remained wary, watchful, that would give an enemy no weakness to exploit. Callestina was glad of his sobriety. She had no desire to give herself to a drunk and clumsy lover.

But she knew she had no fear of that with Darius. The aura of power and of control he exuded was part of what drew her to him.

Alaric, by contrast, drank deeply. By the time the earlier storm clouds had finished their pass and the moon had risen over the trees, Alaric was deep in his cups. His words were slurred and his eyes had grown heavy-lidded. Soon he would stumble to his sleeping furs and pass the night in snoring stupor.

It was obvious that Darius also realized the time of intelligent conversation had passed. Callestina watched him lean and whisper something to Grayson, who nodded silently.

"Well, my friend," Darius turned to Alaric, "we have traveled far this day and glad as I am to be in your company, I shall be gladder still of my tent and a night's sleep."

"Aye, well, let us drink one final toast, then," Alaric said, reaching for the pitcher of mead. He started to fill the cups, but his unsteady hand caused him to spill a large amount on the ground. With a slight smile, Darius took the pitcher from his hand and filled the cups himself.

"One more toast, then, my friend," he said. "Shall we drink again to our success in Rome?"

"To the conquest of Rome," Alaric agreed loudly, raising his cup high—and spilling more wine in the process.

After the toast was drunk, Darius and Grayson both stood. Alaric, too, came unsteadily to his feet. He pounded his companions on the back as the three of them made their way to the tent flap.

"Now that you are here," Alaric said, "I know we shall succeed. Tomorrow we will begin to plan our attack. I have maps," he added proudly.

From the corner into which she had retreated, Callestina watched as an amused look again crossed Darius's face, as if he knew what his friend's head must feel like tomorrow.

"I think tomorrow should be a day of rest for us all," Darius said. "My people and I must look to our camp if we are to stay here all winter. You and I have plenty of time to study your maps and plan our strategy."

Alaric nodded, then brightened. "But you'll take your evening meal here, of course—you and Grayson both."

"Of course," Darius replied. "Now, good night, my friend. And good night to you, Callestina."

These were the first words, aside from a brief greeting, Darius had spoken to her all evening. His overt attention had been with her brother—the two leaders of two great armies sharing a meal of brotherhood—but she had felt his eyes following her and had been content with that.

Now, looking into Darius's eyes, Callestina wondered what she saw. His usual look of amusement was there; Callestina had never seen that leave his eyes for long. But what else she saw, she was not certain. His feelings were not so easily interpreted as his companion's. Grayson's face still showed his desire for her—and his disgust at himself for being at the mercy of his own feelings.

"Good night Darius, and you, Grayson," she said, surprised to hear her voice come out so calmly. Inside she was shaking. She lowered her eyes and turned before her own expression could give her away.

As she began to gather up the platters and cups that had been used and put them aside for the morning wash, she listened to the sound of Darius's footsteps slowly disappearing in the distance. Her mind began to race. He must want her. He *must*! Surely the goddesses would have shown her if it was not to be.

And she would make him love her. She was Alaric the Great's sister. If he could lead a nation and conquer a city, the greatest city in the world, then she could certainly conquer one man's heart.

No—she would not waver in her plan. She would go to Darius tonight.

Alaric wasted no time stumbling to his sleeping furs. He fell quickly into a drunken stupor; Callestina could hear his snores even before she had crossed the short distance to her tent.

Once inside, she was filled with restless energy. She began to pace. She knew she must give Darius time to reach his tent, time for Grayson to leave him, but how long must she wait? Every second that she paced felt as if it stretched to eternity. Soon the walls of her tent seemed to mock her with their confinement.

Finally, Callestina could stand it no more. She turned abruptly on her heel and, breathing one more prayer to the Goddesses of Destiny, she stepped out into the night.

It was not difficult to find her way through the camp. There were still fires burning low to give light to her travels and deep shadows through which she could walk unseen. Her heart pounded with excitement and she could feel the blood rushing through her. Was this akin to the thrill of battle her brother spoke of from time to time? she wondered. It was a heady sensation, a feeling of fire in the veins, of knowing nothing had the power to stand between her and her goal.

She reached the camp of Darius's army. Tents had been pitched to shelter them for the night, but without the sense of order that would grow in the next few days. Far fewer fires burned and the darkness was much deeper. Callestina proceeded with greater caution, stopping often to listen for the sounds of voice or movement.

Like Alaric's tent, Darius's was erected at the heart of his camp; the leader surrounded and protected by his men. Callestina knew it was his tent as soon as she saw it. But she did not approach it right away. She stood in the shadows, listening for the sound of his voice.

He was talking to Grayson. Though Callestina could hear their voices, their words were indistinct. Then she heard Darius's low laughter and a moment later Grayson came out of the tent. He stopped and looked around, staring at the shadow in which Callestina was hiding. She could see the anger that burned on his face. She held her breath, waiting, praying that the night was too black and he could not see her.

Finally he turned away. A few steps and he was gone. Slowly, careful to make no sound, Callestina released the breath she was holding. She waited for a moment longer, wanting to be certain Grayson was gone before she stepped out of the shadow and crossed to Darius's tent.

A sudden fit of trembling gripped her as sudden doubts assailed her mind. What if Darius did not want her? What if he sent her away? *No*, she told herself. *I won't think that way. I have promised the goddesses my faithfulness. I must prove to them that I am worthy of their favor. Such thoughts are the enemy and I will conquer them.*

Taking a deep breath to calm herself, she quickly stepped across the area that separated her from Darius's tent, put her hand to the fur that closed the tent from the night and lifted. Then she stepped inside.

A small fire burned in a stone-lined pit in the corner and the air inside the tent was warm. Darius had removed the cloak he had worn all evening. He stood naked to the waist; Callestina gasped at the sight of him.

His body was perfect, like looking at the image of a god. He had wide, strong shoulders and arms of both grace and power. The mat of hair that spread thickly across his chest narrowed to a thin line that ran down the rippling flatness of his stomach. It drew Callestina's eyes with it, down to his narrow hips and the muscular thighs she could see through the doeskin britches that clung to him like a second layer of skin. She knew he had been wounded in countless battles, but she could see no scars to mar his perfection.

As her eyes traveled down his body, she felt a heat begin to build within her own. With it came a kind of trembling she had never felt before. She had to struggle to keep her breath even.

"I wondered how long it would take before you came to me," she heard Darius say. She looked up and saw again the amused expression dancing in his eyes.

"You knew that I would come?"

A smile touched his lips; Callestina found her eyes drawn to them. They looked full and soft, and Callestina wanted to feel them on her mouth, her body. She wanted to run her own lips along the strong line of his jaw, to twine her hands into his hair and pull his face to her.

"Did you think that I am blind, my little Callestina?" She heard his words as if through a fog. "Or that I could not feel what is between us?"

No more preamble was needed. Callestina walked the few steps that separated them. She watched her hands come up of their own accord and her fingers spread themselves through the thick hair on his chest. It tickled her palms and sent sensation shooting up her arms.

Silently, Darius unfastened the broach that kept her fur cloak in place. It fell to the ground as he lifted her and carried her to the soft pile of sleeping furs.

He laid her down and stretched out beside her, gazing down into her eyes as if waiting for some further word or sign from her. She raised one hand to touch his cheek, glad that he wore no beard to hide his face. She had no other word to say but his name, and she whispered it softly as their lips finally touched.

His lips stayed on hers as his hands slid down her body. He raised the skirt of her gown until at last he reached her skin and began to stroke his fingers across her flesh, leaving trails of fire beneath his touch.

His kiss became gently insistent. With his tongue he parted her lips and teased the inside of her mouth, and his hands grew bolder on her body. He raised her gown farther until he was able to cup one full breast in his hand. Callestina felt herself moan softly with the sudden ecstasy of the touch and the taste of him.

Darius drew away as he pulled her gown over her head and tossed it aside. She did not want to part from him for even that brief time. She lay there naked, bathed in the golden firelight and the warmth of his gaze.

"You are truly the goddess of love, lying there," he said, his voice as caressing as his touch had been.

Goddess to his god, she thought, feeling that all the deities were within their union this night.

Darius removed the rest of his clothes also, then lay back down beside her. Once more he kissed her, but his lips only brushed hers briefly. They moved down her neck, slid across her collarbones, down farther still until they reached her breasts. His mouth closed on one nipple and suckled softly. He began to tease her with his tongue, moving his mouth to the other breast—back and forth until she was no longer aware of the furs on which she was lying or the tent in which they rested. She felt nothing but Darius.

He did not stop with her breasts. Using his hands, his lips, his tongue, he explored the rest of her body, lingering across the soft plain of her stomach, the round fullness of her hips and thighs.

Finally, gently, Darius opened her legs. He brought his face down to that part of her no man had ever seen, ever touched, and kissed her there. With his tongue, he parted the soft golden curls and touched the sensitive flesh beneath them.

Callestina shivered at the touch. Her hands clutched at the sleeping furs beneath her as Darius's tongue continued to bring her a pleasure she had never dreamed existed. She dwelt in a place without thought, without time, where all that she knew were the waves of fire and passion cresting through her body.

Still it was not enough. She wanted to discover, to know his body as he was knowing hers. Gently she pushed him away and onto his back, and she heard his soft chuckle as he rolled to oblige. For a brief second she wondered what to do, what would bring him pleasure. But her own body told her, for all the secrets of womanhood were within her and had waited until this moment to be unleashed.

She ran her fingers across the tautness of his muscles— neck, arms, stomach, all within her reach—and followed that touch with her lips. She buried her face in the hair on his chest, breathing in the scent of him. She moved her mouth to his nipples and heard his sharp intake of breath as they hardened beneath her tongue.

Gently now, her hand caressed that most male part of him, fingers trembling with wonder and anticipation. She bent her head and kissed him as he had kissed her. Once again she heard his soft gasp of pleasure. The sound emboldened her. She ran her tongue down the hard flesh beneath her lips, tasting the slight saltiness of his skin. Again, a shiver of anticipation raced through her as her body began to ache with the need for their joining.

Darius lay still for a moment as Callestina's mouth continued to caress him. Then he gave a single moan that was harsh, almost savage in sound. He drew her up to him and, putting a strong arm around her waist, he rolled her onto her back. Callestina looked deeply into his eyes. She twined her fingers into his hair and pulled his lips to hers as she opened herself to him.

She felt none of the pain she had heard other women speak of when he entered her. He did not rush their joining. His movements were slow and controlled, filling her more and more deeply with each thrust of his hips. The fire that had smoldered like embers in her belly burst into flame. The heat of it filled her until she felt like a creature of fire.

Not losing the contact between them, Darius rolled her on top of him, guiding her now in the movements that brought her even greater pleasure. He sat up and raised his face once more to her breasts. Lips, teeth, tongue, he caressed them, never ceasing the slow, steady rhythm beneath her.

Callestina felt as if she teetered on the brink of oblivion, filled with sensation too intense for mortal being to bear. Darius had brought her there; now he kept her there. She could hear the little cries of pleasure she knew must be hers, but she had no more control over them than over the mounting waves of honeyed fire that tightened her muscles and arched her back.

Once more, Darius turned her beneath him; once more his body covered hers. His mouth was insistent now, demanding, as the rhythm of his body changed. His lips crushed hers. His tongue probed and filled her as his hips moved faster. Callestina wrapped her legs around his thighs. She raked his back with her fingers. Her hands moved to his buttocks, felt his power, his strength, and she raised her hips to meet him.

Again, her back arched. She passed the brink where she had teetered. A thousand lights exploded within her and carried her into another realm where the universe was filled with the union of their bodies. For a long, timeless moment she was held there; then, slowly, she floated back to the world that was.

Darius, too, was spent. He kissed her tenderly once, and moved his head to nuzzle her ear. Then he turned on his side and pulled her to him. She lay there contentedly, listening to his heart beat.

She knew this was only the beginning. She wanted him again. Tonight. Tomorrow.

Forever.

Chapter Fifteen

It became a time of wonder for Callestina. The days Darius spent with Alaric—planning their conquest of Italy and Rome or hunting in the nearby forest or seeing to the comfort of his people. But his nights were spent with her. His tent became a world within a world to her, the only place where she was truly alive.

The goddesses had not failed her, and at dawn after that first night, she had given them thanks.

Once, in the midst of their passion, Callestina had spoken of her love to Darius, but he had only laughed and kissed her, not returning the words Callestina longed to hear. It did not matter; the words would come. Darius, she knew, was her destiny.

The only dark spot to her joy was Grayson. He rarely spoke to her, and then with only the briefest words. Callestina knew his eyes often followed her with a look that wavered between hatred and desire. His presence was heavy and brooding and it was always a relief when she could leave his company.

But Callestina did not let her thoughts linger on Grayson. She had Darius. He filled her thoughts, her body, her world—her life. What did anyone else matter?

The weeks passed. Snow fell heavily upon the ground, covering the winter landscape with fairyland beauty. Trees of the surrounding forest bent beneath their frozen weight until, boughs breaking with a sudden crack that echoed through the countryside, they dropped their burdens into drifts that stood tall as a man.

But the camp had been chosen well. It stood on raised

ground and was sheltered from the worst storm winds. There had been enough time now for semipermanent structures to be erected to give cover to the horses and livestock. Wood had been gathered and stockpiled, items of comfort added to family tents, and large communal fire pits dug.

Most important of all, the two armies were slowly merging into one. Old friendships were strengthened and new romances begun, babies were born and livestock traded. It was a good time, a time of family and community. During the long months ahead the leaders would be worrying about roads and passes, about messengers and tactics, as they planned routes and counted supplies. But the rest of the people would be mending old clothes and making new ones, sharpening weapons, repairing equipment, and looking to the hundred little things they had put off in the summer months just past.

For Darius, however, these winter months soon palled. He had little interest in the common life—it was only something that must be endured between battles—and Alaric, although a good fighter, a competent strategist, and certainly a beloved leader of his people, possessed a mind Darius quickly found to be pedestrian. In truth, Darius was bored most of the time—except at night, when Callestina came to him.

It was a day of bright winter sunshine, four weeks after Darius had arrived in Alaric's camp. During the night another storm had passed, leaving a fresh wash of white across the landscape, but by morning the clouds had disappeared. The sky overhead was a brilliant blue and the slight breeze, although cold, smelled of mountain lakes and pine trees. Darius knew he could not remain bound to camp on such a day.

He saddled his horse, took three hunting spears from the communal stores, and headed for the forest. Perhaps a hunt would stave off his boredom. The excitement of the chase, of running a stag or a boar to ground, of watching its blood run crimson over the snow, would make him feel alive again. It would not be as good as a battle or, better yet, a Quickening—but then, nothing was, and the only other Immortals nearby were Grayson and Callestina. Darius had no desire, even in his boredom, to kill either of them. The former was both brother and son to him; the latter was the only spark of true pleasure amid the interminable wait of winter.

Darius had just passed beneath the shelter of the trees when he *felt* a presence behind him and heard the sound of hoof-beats. He did not need to turn to know that Grayson was joining him. Darius smiled and pulled his horse up to wait; Grayson was probably more bored than he was.

A few seconds later, he heard the hoofbeats slow—and then Grayson was beside him. As always. At his right hand.

They said nothing as they began to walk their horses beneath the trees. There was no need for words between them. For nearly half a century they had been together and often it seemed they could read each other's thoughts.

"How can you stand to spend each day in that man's company?" Grayson asked, suddenly breaking the silence.

"Alaric?" Darius said. "He's useful."

"He's a boor. He's loud, he stinks, and he drinks too much."

Darius chuckled. "All true," he replied.

"He's drunk so often, I'm surprised he has any head left for battle."

"Ah, but he does. I have fought with him—as have you. You know what a formidable warrior he can be when the blood lust is upon him. Alaric is often a fool, that is true, but he is also a tool, and a useful one."

"Why don't we have done with these mortals, Darius?" Grayson asked, a slightly petulant quality to his voice. "You know what army I think we should raise. I still say *you* could do it."

Darius laughed. "Come, Grayson, we've been through this before," he said. "An army of Immortals—such a thing can never be."

"Such a thing has never *been*," Grayson countered. "But you could do it, Darius. Men follow you willingly."

"Mortals," Darius replied. "Such men need a leader to follow. But our kind?" Darius shook his head.

"There is more than one game we play, my friend," Darius continued. "In The Game between Immortals the rules are clear: In the end there can be only one. The game we play with mortals is much more subtle, for they do not even know such a game exists. Mortals are only tools, Grayson—never forget that—but like all tools, they must be carefully studied in order to wield them properly. Learn their strengths and their weaknesses. Properly handled, they will lay the world at your feet and think it is their own idea. But come now, this army is not truly what bothers you."

Darius turned to look at Grayson when he did not answer. His expression was hard and shut, but his eyes betrayed the inner battle he waged over whether or not to speak.

It was always thus with Grayson, Darius thought. The younger Immortal had a tendency to imbue Darius with almost godlike qualities, to grant him a wisdom and infallibility he did not possess. It was useful, this near worship, but it made Grayson hesitate to say anything that might be construed as correcting his mentor—a trait Darius sometimes found irritating when he wanted to get to the point of their conversation.

Still, as he had said, tools must be handled carefully—even Immortal ones.

Darius smiled. "Out with it, my friend," he said pleasantly, almost gently.

Still Grayson hesitated. Darius watched his hands tighten on the high pommel of his saddle.

"She loves you, you know," Grayson said at last.

"Callestina?" Darius nearly laughed. "I suppose she thinks she does. It will pass in time."

"She's not like Alaric and the others. She's one of us—Immortal. She deserves to be treated better."

Little by little the anger was coming out in Grayson's voice. It amused Darius to hear it.

"My friend, women of any kind are of even less importance than mortal warriors. They are playthings—pleasurable, certainly, but of no real use. If you want Callestina, take her. She means nothing to me."

"She doesn't want me," Grayson answered.

"Ah, well, that is a problem, then. But don't worry, my friend—she has years, maybe centuries ahead of her. Women are petty, fickle creatures. She'll no doubt change her mind. And when she does, she will come to you well taught in the arts of love. I promise you," Darius added with a laugh, "it will be worth the wait."

Grayson said nothing and Darius let him brood for a moment. Then Darius smiled and slapped him on the shoulder.

"Come, my friend, and put these thoughts away. Women are passing, much the same whether mortal or Immortal, but a good hunt—ah, there is something worthy of your attention. Surely there must be a stag or two in these woods."

It took another moment, but finally Grayson returned his grin. The expression was a bit strained, but Darius accepted it for what it was and what it symbolized. Darius slapped him again on the shoulder and pointed to a stand of birch trees in the distance.

"A race?" he said. "Give the horses a chance to stretch their legs."

Grayson's smile turned earnest now. With a nod, he urged his horse forward. It crashed through the trees, lengthening its stride with each step, answering with well-trained precision the silent commands of Grayson's hands and knees.

Darius followed, but he did not push his horse as hard or as fast as Grayson. The greater contest, the one for Grayson's unswerving loyalty, he knew he had already won. But as he bent low over his horse's neck, to avoid the slap of branches, he knew he had not told his companion the whole truth about his feelings for Callestina.

He did not love her; love was something for which he had no time in his life. It was a weakness he would not allow himself. In the centuries he had been alive, he had seen too much of the damage love could do; he had seen otherwise strong men turn into mewling babies at the thought of losing a woman's touch. No, that was not for him. It would never be for him. As he had told Grayson, women were merely instruments of passing pleasure. Nothing more.

But he had not tired of Callestina yet and he would have been sorry to see her go. Her passion and her lack of virginal inhibition had given him a pleasant surprise that first night. Since then, she had only grown more skilled. Darius knew he looked forward each night to their hours together.

What was more, it amused him to lie with Alaric's sister in the mortal leader's own camp and to have him unaware. Alaric, who was a follower of the Aryan branch of the Christian faith, demanded a certain morality among his people Darius found contradictory in a man so skilled at killing.

Darius himself paid little homage to any god, Christian or

otherwise. The tribal totems of his youth were slowly disappearing, and Darius's own faith had died with his mortality. There was only one will by which he lived—the will of Darius, and that was divine enough for him.

He urged his horse a little faster, drawing up close to Grayson's. It would not do to let the other man think he had won too easily; Darius must keep all his playthings happy—at least while he had need of them.

Grayson's mind, too, was far from silent as his horse shot forward beneath the trees. He had smiled at Darius, signaling his acceptance, his acquiescence to all his mentor had said. But there was a part of him that whispered Darius was wrong. Not all women were the same. Some were worth more than passing attention.

Callestina was worth more.

But Grayson would not argue with Darius—Darius, who had taught him everything, had made him who he was. Before Darius's army had attacked his village, Grayson had been a farmer and the son of a farmer. His world had been made up of crops and soil, an iron plow and the back end of an ox. Glory was something scarcely dreamed of on long winter nights.

Then Darius had come and taught him the truth of who he was and all that he could be. Grayson had abandoned all he had known before, all he had believed before, and put his faith in his sword—and in Darius. Together, the world he had only imagined stretched before him, waiting to be taken.

Surely that was worth even the woman whose name his heart whispered in the night. Even Callestina.

Wasn't it?

Chapter Sixteen

Winter deepened. The long night of the solstice passed and little by little the days crept toward spring. As the hours of light slowly lengthened, Darius found the restlessness in him increasing. He began to spend less time with Alaric and more time drilling his army, checking their weapons or leading them in groups to take their horses out for exercise. They were already formidable warriors, but by the time they crossed over the pass into Italy, Darius wanted his army to be a killing machine against which no legion of Roman troops could stand.

Of Alaric's army, he did not care. Their skill—and their survival—were not his responsibility. But the mortal leader, either inspired or shamed by Darius's example, began to drill his warriors as well. Soon a healthy competition grew up among the men to see who could endure more, fight longer, or wield a weapon with greater accuracy.

Darius did not share this competitive spirit. With centuries more experience than anyone else in the camp, including Grayson, he had no need to prove his prowess. The fact that he was still alive after three hundred sixty-five years of The Game was proof enough. He was surprised, therefore, when one afternoon Alaric challenged him.

"It's all in sport," the mortal leader said, grinning at him. "Good for the men to see us joining in. It reminds them what kind of fighters they're following."

Darius was tempted to say that his men needed no such reminders, but he did not. Perhaps, he thought, Alaric himself needed the lesson, the reminder of just who he was facing when he drew sword on Darius.

The Immortal glanced at Grayson, noting that his own amusement over Alaric's challenge shone clearly on his friend's face. Then Darius turned back to Alaric.

"Very well," he said. "For sport only."

Darius unfastened the silver broach that held the wolfskin cloak around him. He carefully folded the fur and handed it to Grayson.

"Are you sure this is wise?" Grayson asked him softly. "If you are injured and they see you heal—"

Darius grinned at him. "You worry too much, my friend. If I am cut, it takes only a bit of cloth to hide the truth from mortal eyes."

"What about Callestina's eyes—later?"

Darius remained unconcerned. He gave a slight shrug. "Callestina will know the truth soon enough. Quit worrying, Grayson. I've no intention of letting Alaric close enough to draw blood. It's just sport, remember?"

"Even sport can be dangerous."

Darius laughed and clapped Grayson on the shoulder. Then he drew his sword and turned to face Alaric. The mortal leader, too, had removed his outer cloak and stood waiting, sword in hand. Although Darius knew that in battle Alaric's preferred weapon was an ax, he did not make the mistake of assuming the mortal lacked proficiency with a sword as well.

The men had drawn back, clearing a battlefield on which the two leaders could fight. They began to circle each other. Alaric crouched low and Darius watched his footwork, the way he shifted his balance, the grip of his sword, the way he moved his eyes, his shoulders, his hips, his hands.

Darius walked casually upright, swinging his sword with seeming nonchalance. But, in fact, this stance was as calculated a defense as Alaric's low crouch. Darius knew it threw an opponent off and weakened his first blow with overconfidence. As he walked, he counted the seconds, watched Alaric's muscles for that sudden, betraying tension, and prepared.

There—Darius saw the slight shift of weight in the lead leg and the fingers tightening on the sword. Alaric's arm lifted and swung, and Darius's sword was there to meet it as the Immortal twisted easily from harm's way.

Darius brought the hilt of his sword around and tapped Alaric lightly in the kidneys. A cheer went up from Darius's men. They knew, as did Alaric, that in real combat that could have been a death blow. Alaric took the strike in good spirit. He grinned at Darius, acknowledging a foray well played— and as Darius inclined his head in a slight bow, he knew there would be no such blatant opening again.

They circled each other once more. Then, as if a spark burst suddenly into flame, their swords began to flash in the bright sun. The clash rang over the mounting cheers of the men as they shouted encouragement to their leaders.

While Darius fought, Grayson watched the faces of the crowd. This was a friendly competition, true, but still the blood lust was there. The men looked on with their eyes shining, their faces flushed, their mouths all but slavering.

And Grayson watched them, fascinated. They wanted destruction; they breathed it, tasted it, lived for it.

The women, too, were gathering around, drawn by the sounds of excitement. Grayson watched their faces as they began to add their voices to the general clamor. A few, not many, watched for a moment then turned away. They quickly went back to their duties of hearth and home with a calm certainty that, for now at least, their man, their mate, was safe.

But Grayson was not fooled. He knew that in each of them was the heart of a she-bear who would kill if pushed far enough or in the right way. They were far more deadly than their sisters who stood shouting beside the men, for they hid their claws until the moment came to strike.

It was then Grayson saw Callestina push her way through the crowd. Inside the circle, the two combatants slashed at each other, grinning amidst their battle. Grayson knew that Darius was toying with Alaric and that he could have ended the contest in two or three moves. This certainty was there in his mentor's eyes.

But Callestina did not know. Mock battle though this was, her face was a gray mask of terror as she watched her brother and her lover strike and parry, lunge and counterlunge.

For whom is she more afraid? Grayson could not help but wonder. *Is she afraid Darius's control will slip and he will kill her brother? Then her knowledge of Darius is small,* his thoughts turned almost to a sneer. *His control never slips. Never.*

Does she fear for Darius? Grayson nearly laughed aloud. He had yet to see the man, mortal or Immortal, who had the skill to best Darius in a fight. And that man was certainly not Alaric the Visigoth.

Unconsciously, Grayson stroked the wolf's fur draped over his arm. His eyes narrowed slightly as he continued to stare at Callestina. There were high spots of color on her cheeks and her eyes were bright, as if with fever.

Even from here he could see that her slender body trembled. For an instant he wanted to go to her, to put his arms around her and lead her away. The feeling was unwelcome. It whispered of another emotion Grayson refused to acknowledge. He had loved only once in his life, years before his first death.

He had been eighteen and the woman—his wife—had died of a fever during the first winter they were together. Nothing he had done had saved her. He had vowed then he would not love again.

And he had kept that vow; the only devotion he felt was to his sword—and to Darius.

But now, with Callestina, love threatened again. It was more than the hot spark of desire that seared through him each time he looked at her. In the past, such lusts as gripped him were quickly satisfied with women toward whom he felt nothing. He had, over the last weeks, tried to eradicate his desire for Callestina by lying with any woman in camp who made herself available to him—and there had been many. None of them satisfied him. The momentary lust was gone, but the desire, and the emptiness, remained.

As he continued to stare at Callestina, he struggled to draw indifference like a protective cloak around his heart. When indifference would not come, he turned to anger.

She does not truly fear for Darius's life, he told himself, *or for Alaric's either. She just does not want to lose the lover she takes each night to her bed. You need not fear, Callestina. You will not lose the stallion that you ride.*

A shout went up around him. Grayson quickly shifted his

eyes back to the center of the circle, grateful to draw his thoughts away from the dangerous ground on which they were treading.

Darius stood over Alaric, sword to his throat. "I yield," the mortal cried with a smile, holding up his sword.

Darius, also grinning, stepped back. He transferred his weapon to his left hand and held out his right to help his opponent to stand.

"Well fought," he said to Alaric when the Visigoth was again on his feet.

Alaric nodded. "A good fight," he agreed, somewhat breathlessly. "But remind me not to make you an enemy."

Darius laughed. He slapped Alaric companionably on the shoulder. "I'll do that," he said as he walked across the circle, back to where Grayson was standing.

"You see, my friend," he said softly, lifting his wolfskin cloak from Grayson's hands and setting it once more across his shoulders. "Your worries were for nothing and everyone is happy. It takes so little to please them, Grayson."

Darius turned. He put an arm casually around Grayson's shoulders as he gestured toward the slowly dispersing throng.

"You see how they smile, my friend? They have just been reminded of the skill of their leaders. In battle, they will remember and fight with greater confidence. It is a little thing that has great rewards."

"Your warriors need no such reminders."

"Oh, indeed they do. We have fought many battles together, that is true. But you must always remember, my friend, that mortal memories are short—and weakness of the body comes so quickly to them. It is because of their own weaknesses that they need to know their leaders are still strong. Alaric, for all his annoying habits, understands his men. He is not a better fighter than you are—but he is a better leader. You would do well to learn from him."

Before Grayson could respond, Darius turned away. "Alaric, my friend," he called out, striding toward the Visigoth with his arms outstretched. "Such a fight is thirsty work. Let us find some wine and talk of battles to come."

As the two leaders walked off together, Grayson looked again at the men. Many of them stood laughing and talking—

many more had taken up their own weapons and renewed their drills with increased vigor.

Darius is right, Grayson thought. *They are happier now.*

Then Grayson noticed that Callestina still stood where she had before. She watched the departing figures of her brother and her lover. The expression on her face and in every line of her body shouted how much the sight hurt her. Darius, for whom she had run here, fearing for his safety, had passed her by without a look, a word, a gesture. He had walked past as if she did not exist.

It seems, little Callestina, he thought, echoing Darius's name for her, *we have both learned a lesson this day. I wonder if you will remember yours as well as I will remember mine.*

Chapter Seventeen

The snow began to fall less often, then warmed and fell as rain. Streams and rivers swelled. The frozen ground began to thaw, turning the roads to ribbons of mud that refroze each night, more slick and treacherous than before.

Spring had come.

Each day riders were sent from the camp up into the mountains; each night they returned with reports on the conditions of the routes the armies might take into Italy. The date of the invasion drew closer.

Callestina saw less and less of Darius. His hours with his army increased, as did the time he spent with her brother. They were together each evening, examining Alaric's precious maps, discussing the merits of various routes, arguing over which cities to capture for the best advantage during their long march toward Rome. Darius's interests were purely military, while Alaric was looking for lands on which to settle his people.

Callestina heard their voices, raised and strident, cutting through the stillness of the night while she sat alone in her tent waiting for the time when she and Darius could be together. Often sleep claimed her before that time arrived. Her body, and her heart, began to ache with the need for his touch.

It seemed to Callestina that Darius hardly noticed their separation. He appeared happiest during the hours he was with his men. Callestina often watched him from a distance and she saw the way his face glowed as he called out orders or encouragement.

When, in the evenings, she brought food and drink to her brother's tent, Darius hardly spared her a glance. There were no caressing looks, no gentle words she longed to hear; no silent signals passed between them. As the snow melted in the outside world, the ice transferred itself to Callestina's heart and gripped her with unrelenting fingers.

She made a hundred excuses for Darius's inattention. *Commanding an army is difficult and serious work,* she told herself time and again. *So many lives depend on each decision he makes, Darius must—MUST—give all his thoughts and energy to what lies ahead. I will be patient. I will encourage him with my silence and be waiting when again he turns to me. I will show him I understand what his responsibilities demand of him—and of the one who would share his life. . . .*

But in the silence of her own tent, her determinations often failed her and the doubts, born out of the hours of loneliness, still whispered.

One night, when Darius was once again staying long in Alaric's tent, Callestina's patience failed her. Loneliness was like a fire in the pit of her stomach and she knew that if she did not put it out, it would consume her. Grabbing up a cloak, she headed out into the darkness.

She did not care who saw her as she marched through the camp. This time there was no surreptitious movement from shadow to shadow. She was going to Darius's tent to wait for him. She would show him that, tonight at least, she needed him as much as his army.

There were those who would have asked her why she was out alone in the night, but one look at her face stopped them. Tonight she would answer no questions, stay at no man's word. As she passed by campfires where those who were still awake were gathered over cups of wine and small ale, she paid no attention to either the silences or the whispers that followed her. In her mind, she was already in Darius's arms.

As she neared his tent, she saw a figure step out from inside. He turned and looked at her. *Grayson.* Over the last days and weeks, she had grown jealous of his constant companionship with Darius. Grayson was like Darius's shadow; they were always together—laughing and talking, sharing the hours Callestina was denied.

Why are you here? she wondered, knowing that Darius was still in her brother's tent. *I don't want you here. Go away.*

But he did not go. Folding his arms across his chest, Grayson waited.

Tonight, Callestina would not let his presence stop her. She was here to spend the night, at least this night, again in Darius's arms. She took a deep breath and stepped forward.

"Darius is not here," Grayson said coldly. "He won't be here for hours yet."

"I'll wait," Callestina replied. She started to step past Grayson, but he grabbed her arm.

"Don't be a fool," he hissed through gritted teeth, "waiting around him like some pathetic dog hoping for a few crumbs to fall your way. There is more ahead in life for you, Callestina. Much more."

Callestina tried to pull away, but Grayson tightened his grip. His fingers dug painfully into her flesh. He leaned closer until she could smell the wine on his breath.

He's drunk, she thought, suddenly realizing she had never seen Grayson drunk. Her brother was drunk frequently, and she had even seen Darius drunk once or twice—but never Grayson. She wondered what had happened, why he was drunk tonight.

His face was so close, she thought for a single instant that he was going to kiss her. But instead he just smiled a dark, humorless smile. It was like a wolf's snarl.

"Poor Callestina," he said. "You think he loves you, don't you? Well, he doesn't. Darius doesn't love anything except Darius. You're just a plaything to him, a toy for his amusement. The whole world is just a plaything to Darius."

"How dare you!" Callestina was angry now. "How dare you talk about him this way. You—who say you are his friend."

Grayson's smile grew a touch broader. "I am his friend," he said. "If any other man were to say these things, I'd cut his tongue out and make him eat it. But, believe it or not, little Callestina, I'm trying to be your friend as well. Go back to your own tent. Forget your dreams about a life at Darius's side. It won't happen."

Callestina jerked her arm away, and this time Grayson let it go. "My dreams are my own," she said, "and my future is no concern of yours."

Grayson inclined his head slightly and stepped aside, giving her free access to Darius's tent. She brushed past him, head held high. But as she started to step inside, his voice followed her.

"You have been warned, Callestina," he said. Callestina dropped the tent flap behind her, cutting off anything else he might say.

Inside the tent the air was cold, but warming quickly from the fire that had been recently lit. On the small table in the corner, a pitcher waited. Callestina went over and sniffed its contents. It was ale, strong and black. She found a cup and filled it, then drank it down quickly. It was bitter and it burned as it hit her stomach, but not as bitter as the words Grayson had said to her.

He was drunk, she told herself again as she poured a second cup of ale and sipped it. *And he's jealous because I want Darius instead of him. His words don't mean anything. Darius does love me.*

The fire was continuing to heat the air and the ale Callestina had drunk so quickly made her cheeks feel hot and her head feel a little dizzy. She stretched out on the sleeping furs to wait for Darius.

Lying there, the memories of his kiss, of his touch, enveloped her. *He does love me,* she thought again. *After we defeat Rome and Alaric forces them to give us land and citizenship, there will be no more reason to fight. The armies can disband and Darius and I will be together every day— and every night.*

Callestina smiled a slow, languid smile as she gave her thoughts over to imaginings of how her life would be. She pictured days of warmth and sunshine, nights of ecstasy. Darius was with her, loving her, giving her a family. She did not notice when her eyelids closed and her self-willed imaginings gave way to sleep-filled dreams.

Callestina awoke to the sight of Darius's face bending over her. With a little cry of joy, she threw her arms around his neck and pulled his face to hers. His kiss was warm and real and for that instant all of her dreams became reality.

A moment later, Darius drew back. He stretched out beside her and gently brushed the sleep-loosened hair from her face.

"I could not stand another night without you," Callestina said. She would not hide her feelings from him. "I've missed your arms around me."

Darius gave a low chuckle. "Is that all you have missed, my little Callestina?" he asked.

Callestina moved her body closer. "You know it is not," she answered as her hands pulled at his clothing, eager to reach the skin beneath.

Again Darius laughed. As he pulled his shirt off and tossed it aside, Callestina turned her attention to the fastenings of her own clothing. Soon the two of them were naked. Darius's hands began to move knowingly across her body and his lips sought those places that gave her the greatest pleasure. Callestina closed her eyes. She let herself be carried on the mounting waves of passion.

She did not need Darius's words to tell her of love. Love was in his breath upon her skin. It was in his lips, his tongue, his touch; it was in the weight of his body covering hers. What else could matter but these things?

She almost laughed when she thought of Grayson's warning. Poor Grayson—he did not know. How could he know what passed between herself and Darius when they were together? How could anyone, anywhere, know joy such as this?

There was only one Darius—and he was hers.

Chapter Eighteen

It was summer in the valley before the passes were deemed clear enough. Despite weeks of preparation, it still took many days to break camp and for the combined armies to be on the move.

Behind the armies came carts and wagons, the extra horses and supplies, the women and the families of the warriors. As always, the men would lead and their passage would widen the trail and clear away any obstacles that might impede the progress of those who followed.

Even with the armies clearing the way, the passage from the lower Danube Valley into northern Italy was slow and arduous. Once in Italy, they built a temporary camp near the city of Cremona. Here the families would remain while the warriors began their march of devastation southward.

But Alaric would not be called a barbarian. He offered one final chance of peace to Rome. While the new camp was being established, he sent a messenger with his terms to the Roman Senate. Alaric demanded lands within the Italian province for his people to form their kingdom, four thousand pounds of gold in tribute and, above all, the full privileges and recognition of Roman citizenship. If these terms were met, his message said, he and his people would not only live peacefully on their lands, they would turn their aid and their weapons to the defense of the Roman Empire.

Alaric worded his message carefully so neither the threat nor the promise within could be misunderstood; he would meet the answer from the Emperor Honorius outside the city of Ravenna.

To show that his word was good, Alaric ordered the army

to march peacefully between Cremona and Ravenna. There would be no sacking of the northern towns, no burning of the farms and villages they passed—for it was here in the fertile lands of the north that Alaric hoped to settle his people. It would be foolish, he said, to destroy what they would soon possess, and unnecessary. The presence of so great a fighting force would be enough to strike terror in all who saw them, and their peaceful passage would lay the responsibility for any future destruction on the shoulders of the Senate in Rome.

Darius's men, not as intent upon Italian settlement, grumbled over the lack of booty. But Darius saw the wisdom of Alaric's plan. A Visigoth kingdom on the Italian peninsula would provide a power base for future expansion. It would also give his men, mortals that they were, a place to think of as home when the years began to weigh heavily. For these reasons, Darius supported Alaric's orders, and because it was Darius's will, his men obeyed.

The night before the armies were to march, Callestina lay again in Darius's arms. Their lovemaking had been even more passionate than usual, for she could not bear the thought that she would not see him, would not touch him again for weeks. Now, in the aftermath of that passion, she lay with her head on his shoulder, running her fingers through the hair on his chest and listening to his heartbeat slowly quiet.

"I will be waiting for you when you return," she said softly.

"I know," Darius replied, absently running his fingers along her arm. She could hear the closeness of sleep in his voice and she was not yet ready to let him go.

"You are coming back, aren't you?" she asked.

Darius gave a small sigh. "We've been through this, my little Callestina. I will not make such plans for the future. If I come back, then I come back—that is all I will say. It takes only the fall of a sword to change all plans, no matter how carefully laid."

"But no sword can fell you, Darius. My brother says you are nearly invincible."

Darius laughed. "Not even I can control all the Fates," he said. "Enough now, Callestina. I wish to speak no more of this."

Callestina was silent. But as she lay there her mind began

to form a bold and daring plan. It frightened her to think of it, but it excited her, too. If she had not been bold, not been daring, she would not now be in Darius's arms. *Perhaps,* she thought, *life only consists of what we are strong enough to take.*

She nestled a little closer to Darius's body. *I will be strong enough,* her thoughts continued. *Nothing will keep me from being with him forever.*

It was not yet dawn when Callestina felt Darius rise from his bed. The sudden absence of his warmth shocked her awake; she could not let him go—not yet.

She opened her eyes. The only light in the tent came from the glowing embers of last night's fire, but it was enough for her to see the outline of his body as he stretched to shake sleep's hold over his muscles. The sight awakened the hunger deep inside of her, the desire his touch seemed to feed rather than satiate.

He reached for his clothing. "Wait," she said softly. "Not yet."

At the sound of her voice, he turned. Even in the dim light, Callestina could see the familiar smile that tugged at the corners of his lips and the amused look that came back into his eyes. She did not mind that she amused him as long as that amusement fed his desire for her.

Could love be born of laughter? her heart wondered briefly. *Yes,* it answered itself in that same instant, *if the need for laughter is great enough.*

I'll make him need me, she told herself.

"Are you awake, then, Callestina?" Darius's voice silenced her thoughts. "I thought to leave you sleeping."

"Did you think I could remain asleep knowing you would soon be gone?"

She held out her arms to him, but he shook his head. "There is no time for that, Callestina," he said.

She listened for a moment to the sounds of the camp. All was silent.

"There is no one moving about yet, Darius," she said, keeping her voice low and soft. "Even the horses are still. There is no reason you must go now."

"I must prepare for my men. I will not have them think me lazy as we go off to battle."

It was Callestina's turn to be amused. A low chuckle escaped her throat.

"Do you think you are the only warrior in camp who has spent the night in a woman's arms, knowing that at dawn he must again take up the sword? And do you also think that I am the only woman in camp who seeks the solace of a lover's touch one last time before that dawn comes?"

"No, my little Callestina," Darius said as he came back to the bed and to her side, "I do not think these things." He pushed the hair back from her face and kissed her once, gently. "But a commander cannot act only as he wishes."

"Then, for a while yet, forget you are a commander. Be only a man whose woman has need of him."

As Darius's hands began to move almost involuntarily across her body, Callestina knew that she had won. For a while yet, he was hers.

And later? Later, she knew what she would do. They would be together again sooner than he thought.

Callestina stood among the women of the camp, watching while the men rode away. Although many stood dry-eyed, she alone had a smile upon her face. Her body still glowed with the sweet exhaustion of making love, but it was not this that made her smile. It was the thought of what was to come and of her own courage.

She watched the women around her turn away from the sight of the men and back to the everyday tasks of children and cooking fires. She noted the subtle changes that had come over them. Their voices were lower, their movements a trifle slowed, as if with the departure of husbands and fathers, sons and lovers, a certain measure of their life force had been drained away.

But not Callestina; she felt *alive*. Her thoughts and her heart already rode with Darius, and soon her body would follow. She knew she had to choose her timing or her brother would merely send her back here. But if she was careful and did not reveal herself too early, then her return to camp would cause more trouble than letting her stay with the army.

Oh, Alaric would be angry. He would yell and bluster, as was his way. Callestina did not care. She had stood up to his anger before and would do so again unflinchingly. *Darius* would understand. He would see that she was willing to fight for what she wanted from life, to reach out and take it heedless of the cost, and he would approve. He would see that she was worthy, was strong enough, to share not just his bed—but his life.

For Grayson she spared not a thought.

The long, dark line of the army could still be seen in the distance, but Callestina did not care. Hugging her secret to herself, she turned away from the sight. She would go back to her tent now and begin to gather the things that she would take. Then, as on the day Darius arrived, she would make a prayer to the Norns, asking the three Goddesses of Destiny to give their aid to her undertaking.

Tomorrow, before dawn, before the camp was yet awake, she would ride away.

At the head of the army, Darius rode his great stallion. To his left rode Alaric, looking ursine in his great bearskin cloak, and to his right—always to his right—rode Grayson.

Darius smiled to be on the move again, to feel his horse beneath him and hear the sounds of his men at his back. Soon they would face an enemy and his sword would sing in the summer sunlight.

Unlike Alaric, Darius harbored no vain hopes of peaceful settlement with the leaders of Rome. For three centuries he had watched the Roman Legions march across Europe. He had fought them many times and in many places and he knew what they thought of "the barbarians from the north."

No, the Roman Senate would not accede to Alaric's demands. There would be fighting. There would be death.

And much of it would come from Darius's sword.

It was difficult to keep to the sedate pace at which they were traveling, but it was a steady rhythm that would cover the miles without overtiring either the men or the horses, a pace every army had learned through centuries of experience. Yet Darius was tired of control and necessity. He wanted to gallop forward, to revel in the sense of freedom he felt. His horse felt it too, for beneath him the creature pranced and sidestepped. The long winter had been hard on both of them, as winters always were, and he was glad to leave it behind.

Callestina's name whispered itself in his ear and Darius felt the briefest pang of regret, but it passed almost before he felt it. She had been pleasurable, certainly, but of late her presence had a cloying edge. She sought to possess that which he would not give—his love, and his freedom.

No, he was glad to be leaving her behind with the winter.

Darius turned to Grayson and found the man watching him with eyes narrowed against the bright sunshine. It was hard to read the expression in them.

But then Grayson smiled at him. "You seem even more eager than usual at the beginning of a march," he said.

"I am, my friend, I am," Darius replied. "It feels good to be on the move again, to be doing what we were born to do."

"And after," Grayson asked. "Have you decided?"

Darius gave one curt nod, knowing that was all Grayson would need to understand. They would fight beside Alaric in his conquest of Rome, as much for the glory of battle as for any call of friendship. But they would not remain after the fighting was done. There were other places, other battles, awaiting.

There was a world ahead to conquer. And someday, Darius knew, it would all lie at his feet.

Chapter Nineteen

The army marched from Cremona to Ravenna, passing villas and farmsteads, temples and hovels. Everywhere they passed, the people fled before them. When the army turned no hand to destruction, the more overtly brave—or overtly curious—returned to watch their passage.

The attitude of the men changed as they neared Ravenna. Everyone, including the leaders, grew more watchful, more wary. Within the stone walls of the city, the Roman Legions and their first battle could be waiting.

The city gate was closed against them. Alaric called a halt five hundred yards from the walls; he and Darius would ride forward together while the men stayed in their formations, ready to spread out at the first signal.

Side by side the leaders rode, their great horses prancing with matching steps. They knew that, of themselves, they were a formidable sight and with the army at their backs they were enough to fill even the coldest heart with fear. As they neared the city, the gates opened slightly and a single rider emerged.

"Now we will hear Honorius's reply to my terms," Alaric said to Darius without taking his eyes off the approaching rider.

The Immortal made no reply. *Let Alaric have his hopes,* he thought. *They will not last for long.*

Darius's eyes saw what Alaric's did not. Darius saw the bundle that hung from one side of the messenger's saddle, and he had no doubt of its content—he had sent many such gruesome replies himself.

The rider stopped a mere twenty feet away. For a moment

there was silence. Alaric sat easy on his horse, still dreaming his dream of Roman citizenship. Darius kept his eyes on the messenger's face, yet peripherally he watched the man's sword arm and concentrated on noticing the slightest movement. It was a talent he had long ago trained in himself and it had saved his life on more than one occasion.

The man made no move. He waited for the Visigoth to speak.

"Hail, Roman," Alaric said at last, shouting over the distance in his great rumble of a voice. "You bring a message to me, for I am Alaric, leader of the Visigoths. Speak—what words does the Emperor send to my people?"

"No words," the man shouted back, his voice as clear as the summer air. "The great Honorius, Emperor of the Roman world, sends this to speak for him."

The messenger loosened the bundle from his saddle and threw it. It landed with a sickening thud. As it rolled toward Alaric's horse, its covering fell away and staring up was the severed head and sightless eyes of the man Alaric had sent to Rome.

The Visigoth gave a cry that was half anger, half anguish. He dug his heels into his horse's flanks. As the animal shot forward, he drew his ax and began to swing. He was on the Roman before the man knew what was coming. The Roman barely had time to raise an arm, no time at all to draw his sword, before Alaric's ax bit deep into his flesh. His blood shot a crimson geyser that sprayed the Visigoth's face like fierce war paint.

Alaric paid no heed. He hacked again and again. Behind Darius, a slow rumble grew as the men saw their leader attacking. The sound mounted. It became a shrill cry as, to a man, the army surged forward to siege the city.

Grayson brought his horse close to Darius's side. "Shall I stop them?" he asked.

Darius shook his head. "No," he said. "Let them go."

"But you've given no order for the attack."

"It doesn't matter—not today. Today they fight with their hearts, not their heads, and their passion will carry them to victory. Tomorrow and all the days after that we will have order."

Darius made no move to join the fray. This was a *mortal* battle and, as he said, a battle of passion—a passion he did not feel. He would fight, and in plenty, in the days to come, especially when they reached Rome.

But not today.

The army flowed around him and Grayson like a great river swerving around a rock. He was a boulder of calm in the midst of their roaring madness. Not even a great city like Ravenna would stand for long against such numbers and such ferocity. By tonight, the gates would be broken and the city within reduced to flame and rubble; most of the young men would be dead, the women ravaged, art destroyed, gold and jewels confiscated.

Darius would not ride into the city. While the mortals ate and drank and celebrated their victory, he would be looking ahead to the battles that would serve a greater purpose than this petty revenge.

Callestina traveled carefully, not too close to the army but neither too far away. She did not want her presence to be discovered—not yet, not when it would be so easy for her brother to send her back to the camp outside Cremona.

She had never traveled alone before and the first night on her own she found terrifying. The night noises were so different here than in her homeland and each one of them, as they built upon each other throughout the night, seemed magnified by the darkness. Callestina had sat awake, huddled between her fire and her horse, waiting for the dawn to come.

But sometime during the days that followed, a change took place. She began to revel in the feeling of freedom. She had no one to think about but herself, no one whose needs must be met but her own. She ate when she was hungry, slept when she was tired, and thought only of her own plans and dreams. In some ways she felt like a flower that had finally found the warmth of the sun and was able to blossom at last.

It was not that her brother was unkind or her life unpleasant. But life within the Visigoth camp for a woman, any woman, was a life of looking after the needs of the men. They were the warriors and the hunters and it was, as they often proclaimed, through their prowess that the people survived and were strong.

Until now, Callestina had accepted that life without question. These last few days, however, as she snared rabbits and small birds for food, drank water from the streams she passed, and made her own camp at night, she began to doubt that she needed a man for anything. Except love.

And for that, she had Darius.

She was wearing men's clothing, and she found she liked the freedom they gave her as well. The doeskin breeches and short tunic were a welcome change from the heavy weight of a wool gown. When she finally did reveal her presence to the army, Darius would see that she was capable of riding by his side. She would persuade him to teach her to use a sword— something Alaric never thought she had needed to know— and then she and Darius would never be separated. She would be able to ride beside him even into battle. . . .

And so Callestina's thoughts continued as she followed the army. These dreams were her close companions, filling her hours with sweet company.

It was the sounds of the siege that disrupted her idyll, ugly sounds of destruction and death. The brightness of the day was suddenly dulled by the crash of swords, the screams of the dying, the smell of smoke and blood. Callestina drew her horse far off the road and under the trees where she could wait out the hours away from the battle.

But the sounds followed her. All through the afternoon and into the night she could hear them. She tried, at first, to stop her ears—but no, she told herself firmly; this was Darius's life and if she was going to be with him, she must become as inured to it as he was.

She unstopped her ears, hardened her heart, and waited for the long night to be over.

Grayson found himself slightly disgusted by the events of the day. It was not the killing itself he minded; he had killed more times than he could count or remember. What disgusted him was the lack of order, the disregard for discipline that was present in Alaric's army today.

Yet the men merely reflected the attitude of their leader and

Alaric's reaction to the severed head of his messenger had given them all the inducement they needed. This siege had been nothing less than a rout; even after the city had surrendered, the killing had gone on.

It was not only the men of the city who had been killed. The old, the infirm, the children—anyone who had been in the way of a sword or who had not been kept alive for some other purpose, all now lay like abandoned trash in the streets.

And for what? Grayson wondered as he walked his horse through the death-choked scene. *What did we gain here? Nothing done this day has furthered us toward our final aim.*

This, above all, was what annoyed and disgusted Grayson. He did not shun battle, but killing was meant to serve a purpose. Darius had taught him that long ago, just as Darius had taught him the need for order and discipline—both within his own life and within their army.

Order, discipline, and purpose: Those were the three elements that had made the Roman Empire the power it was, Darius had told him one night many years ago, when Grayson had first been with him. Grayson had been eager to go out and test his new Immortality, but Darius had other plans—as Darius always did. Even while he was honing Grayson's skill with a sword and teaching him a hundred different ways to kill an opponent, he was training Grayson to use his mind as the greater weapon.

"Order, discipline, and purpose—above all, purpose," Darius said until it was ingrained into Grayson's every thought and action. It offended him now when *purpose* was not served.

Not that he always understood *Darius's* purpose. But Grayson had learned that Darius put great thought into everything he did.

And today? Grayson wondered as the smell of blood choked his nostrils. Off in the distance more than one woman's scream could be heard, and Grayson could well imagine what they were suffering. *What was Darius's purpose in letting our army behave like Alaric's rabble? Now that they have broken discipline, how will they behave tomorrow?*

Grayson's horse rounded a corner in the city streets and he had his answer. A group of young men stood together, men

Grayson recognized as his own. On their faces he saw the same look of disgust he knew his own wore.

He knew they would not break discipline again.

They saw him and raised a hand in greeting. Grayson returned the salute and they walked toward him, picking their way around the rubble and the dead.

"You're not celebrating your victory," Grayson said.

One of the men turned and spat on the ground. "This was no victory," he replied. "Women, children, old men—there was hardly a man here worthy of battle. They had already surrendered—there was no need for . . . this." He waved a hand in a curt, expressive gesture.

"Where's Darius?" another of the group asked.

"Outside the city," Grayson answered. "He took no part in today's . . . campaign."

"Nor will we again, unless Darius orders it," the first man said.

There were answering nods from within the group. They turned and began to walk toward the city gates, back over the path Grayson had just traveled.

Grayson watched them go. Darius's position as their leader had already been exalted, but now Grayson knew it was impregnable. Any doubts or questions that might have grown in their minds over the long winter had been wiped out today.

Grayson nearly smiled. Darius was always clever, always understood what his men needed—he knew them better than they knew themselves. He had silently let them go and now, just as silently, he would watch them return—more loyal, more committed, more willing to serve him without question.

Grayson knew he still had a lot to learn.

But, perhaps, so had Darius, an inner voice whispered. Why could he not see the *greatness* that an Immortal army would bring? Darius had won the hearts, perhaps even the souls, of his mortal followers; Grayson believed—*knew*—Darius had the power to do the same with those whose lives were Immortal.

It was a dream Grayson would never abandon, no matter how often Darius rejected the idea. Someday Grayson would convince him, and then they would establish a kingdom that would truly cover the earth. It would show the Roman Empire for the petty concern all things *mortal* must be.

He moved his heels against his horse and it resumed its slow walk. There would be other groups to meet and tell that Darius awaited them outside the gates. Eventually the word would begin to spread on its own. Before the moon had begun its downward arc, Grayson was certain that the army of Darius would stand free from the debacle of Ravenna.

And tomorrow they would march toward Rome.

Chapter Twenty

Blurry-eyed and hungover, Alaric emerged from the ruined city shortly before dawn. Slowly, straggling in small groups and looking no more alert than their leader, came the men of his army. Their sallow skin and glassy-eyed stare told of a night spent in drinking and other, more dubious pleasures.

They were, indeed, a sorry sight.

With them they brought much of the city stores—food and wine that would be consumed during the journey, or outside Rome if the siege of the city turned long. They also brought treasures to be divided later. Many wore necklaces draped around their shoulders, jeweled broaches pinned to their cloaks, and earrings that shone brightly in the rising sun. But these did not offset the blood and gore that still covered their hands and stained their clothing.

No tents had been pitched for the night. Darius and his men had slept on blankets around small fires that had been more for light than for warmth. When Darius saw Alaric approaching, he stood and went out to meet him. Grayson, as always, followed; as always, he watched Darius's back. Even here, even now.

Alaric greeted Darius with a wan but genuine smile. "This is a cold place for warriors to sleep when there is a conquered city but a few paces away," he said.

A thousand retorts, all of them insults, hammered at Darius's lips. He uttered none of them. Neither did he smile at Alaric's words, as was his usual wont. He stood in stony silence while behind him he could hear his men rolling up their blankets and falling into ranks.

As if shamed by the sight, Alaric turned and waved his own

men forward. Looking at them, both leaders knew the march today would be slow. It was still almost two hundred miles to Rome—two hundred miles in which the Roman Legions, the most renowned fighting force in the known world, might yet be waiting for them. If they were in today's condition at the time, the Roman Legions might also defeat them.

The rebuke, unspoken, hung in the air between the two leaders as Alaric turned once more to face Darius. There could be no repeats of Ravenna during the long march south. The destruction of this city and the condition of Alaric's men today had won for Darius the point he had so often argued during the winter. This was not a campaign to conquer Italy, city by city. That day still might come, but it was not now. If Alaric wanted Roman citizenship for himself and his people, then Rome was all that mattered and they must save their strength until they reached her.

Order.

Discipline.

Purpose.

By nightfall the tension between Alaric and Darius had dissipated and they sat together around a small cooking fire. Though both of them drank sparingly, it was enough to ease Alaric's pounding head and loosen his tongue. He was once more talking expansively.

"I say we can reach Rome in a week," he was saying. "The men have rested and grown strong all winter. They'll handle the march—you'll see."

"And we will arrive at Rome too tired to fight," Darius countered.

"No," Alaric said, putting down his cup. "I have a plan." He picked up a stick and began to scratch out a drawing on the ground where Darius could see it.

"Here is Rome," he said. "Remember, I have been there. I do not need maps to remind me that Rome is not built on flat terrain. Just as she is built on hills, there are also hills around her. Through these, the roads wind. We will take our positions in the hills, covering them with our men and surrounding the city."

Alaric's drawing was crude but effective enough for Darius

to see his strategy. Darius nodded. "From there we will have full view of the roads so that none of the legions or guards can come upon us unaware and neither can the Emperor escape the city," he said.

"That's it, exactly," Alaric agreed, smiling broadly. "Then we will once more send a message to the Senate, giving them a final chance to surrender and our men a chance to rest while we await a reply."

"There is still the water route that the Emperor might use to flee."

"True," Alaric agreed, "but we will have men stationed here and here," he pointed on his map, "who can warn us of any sudden or unusual activity in that quarter. Then we attack at once, regardless of what the Senate has or has not said."

Alaric sat back and picked up his cup once again, waiting for Darius's approval. The Immortal slowly nodded.

"Very well, my friend," he said. "One week to Rome. It will not fall as easily as Ravenna. We must be prepared for a long siege."

"Perhaps," Alaric agreed. "Or, perhaps, they will see they cannot stand against us. Either way, Rome will fall."

Alaric held his cup high and shouted these last words again. All through the camp his shout was returned. Only Darius and Grayson remained quiet.

"And when Rome falls, then what?" Darius asked as things grew quiet again.

"Then we will have our place in the empire—and in history," Alaric answered. "Had Honorius treated fairly with us before, I would have been happy to settle my people on farms and been done with fighting. Now he will find it takes much, much more to still my sword."

"What is it you desire now, Alaric?" Darius asked.

With a smug smile, Alaric lifted his cup to his lips. "You will see soon enough," was the only answer he would give.

Darius looked over at Grayson. In the silence, Grayson could almost hear Darius wondering what foolishness Alaric might have planned. Then Darius smiled his slow, amused smile and Grayson knew that whatever the Visigoth was going to do, Darius would find it an entertaining diversion.

But Grayson was tired of this particular band of brothers.

He stood and walked away from the campfires and out into the clean air of the night.

He felt a presence come up behind him and he did not have to turn to know who was there. A moment later, Darius stood by his side and the older Immortal put an arm across his shoulders.

"You must learn to laugh more, my friend," Darius said softly. "I have told you often, you must learn to see the absurdity in these mortal lives and mortal plans that they take so seriously. Without such laughter the centuries become very long indeed."

Grayson said nothing; he and Darius had had this conversation too often in the past for more words to be necessary.

"Come back to the fire, my friend," Darius said. "Come—drink some wine and laugh at this game we play with other men's lives. Never forget that for all their blustering, they are only pawns. They are born, they love, they fight, they die—and we go on. *This* game we win just by being alive."

Grayson let himself be soothed by Darius's words. Together they walked back to the fire where Alaric still sat, drinking his wine and shouting jests with his men.

Absurdity. Suddenly Darius's word filled Grayson's mind and it seemed so very, very right. There was Alaric, full of bluster and bravado, leading his great army of uneducated barbarians against an empire that had stood for centuries. The absurd part, Grayson realized in that instant, was that they would prevail. The unwashed masses would topple the tower of reason and civilization.

And then what? Then the cycle would begin again: human history built on the short spans of mortal lives and the equally short span of mortal memory. And he and Darius would watch it all.

Someday, perhaps, they would control it all.

Grayson threw back his head and roared his dark, sardonic laughter into the night.

As the army resumed its march south, the novelty of her freedom began to pall for Callestina. The days were not so bad, riding in the warm summer sunshine. But at night the loneliness set in. It did not help that in the distance she could hear the men talking and singing and laughing with each other. Each day she found herself edging a little closer, instinct driving her to the comfort of companionship.

Still, she tried to be careful where she made her camp. She looked for little hollows in the land or sheltering stands of trees that would hide the small fire she made to cook her food and keep the empty night at bay.

As the army neared Rome, the places she could hide grew fewer. Traces of organized civilization and too many people spread like grasping fingers outward from the city. Callestina had to trust to luck and hope the army would be too intent upon looking forward to notice one small fire twinkling behind.

Her luck held until the army was one day's march from their goal. She had snared a rabbit for her supper, then cleaned and skinned it, built a fire, and set it to roast on a spit. She was so bent upon her work that she did not hear the footsteps behind her.

Suddenly, rough hands grabbed her and she heard the hiss of a sword being pulled from its sheath. Callestina had no time to scream as she found herself on her feet, arms pinned behind her and a blade at her throat.

"By the gods, 'tis Alaric's sister," the man in front of her said. His companion, the one who held her arms in a viselike grip, swung her around to look at her face.

At first his eyes were wide with surprise, but then a slow grin spread across his face. It was not a pleasant sight and Callestina felt her insides go cold.

"So it is," he said. His eyes raked down her body, lingering hungrily over the way her breasts strained against the fabric of the tunic she wore. "Even dressed in men's clothes, she's a sight. It's been too many days since I had a woman."

He started to pull her close. Callestina prepared herself to scream, to fight in any way she could, but the other man moved faster. In an instant, his sword was between her and her would-be rapist.

"Hold," he said sharply. "She's been Darius's woman all winter. Take her now and that's who you'll have to face."

Callestina watched her captor's face blanch. *So they're*

Darius's men, she thought as her heart filled with pride in her lover. Even his own men feared him.

Callestina pulled her arms free. She turned to run, but the man with the sword caught her once again.

"Oh, no," he said, "you'll not get away. Darius will want to see you—and Alaric. Get her horse, Torvald, and we'll take her to camp."

Callestina was silent. She would not give these men the pleasure of hearing her beg for her freedom. And this moment might still be used to her advantage, if she was careful. She would have had to reveal her presence to her brother—and to Darius—soon. But she had planned to wait until after they attacked Rome. She had *planned* to show herself only when she could greet Darius as the conquering hero she knew he would be.

Now *destiny* had changed her plans to one of its own. Callestina knew she must continue to trust the goddesses who wove time within their threads. She was their sworn servant and they would not fail her entreaties.

"You need not hold me like some prisoner," she said, pulling her arm against her captor's grip. "I'll not run away. Release me and take me to my brother's fire."

Both men laughed. "You're in a fine position to be giving orders," the man who held her arms replied. "I'll take you to Alaric's fire, all right, but prisoner you are and will remain until I'm told you are not."

I'll make him pay for this a thousand times over, Callestina thought as the man holding her began to walk, pulling her along. Behind her, the other man laughed again.

I'll make them both pay. I'll see that Alaric has them whipped for treating me this way. And Darius—he'll be angry, too. He'll see to it that they're punished. I know he will.

Buoyed by that thought, Callestina walked a little faster.

Chapter Twenty-one

"Callestina!" Alaric shouted at her. He had come to his feet at the sight of her, spilling his wine and his dinner onto the ground. Now he stood glaring at her across the fire.

"You were told to wait at Cremona. How dare you defy me. This is no place for a woman."

"Why shouldn't I be here?" Callestina shouted back. "Does not the same blood flow in our veins? I have every right to be a warrior, too," she added, lifting her chin to stare at him defiantly.

She heard Darius's chuckle and she whipped around to face him.

"You have women in your army," she said to him. "They are warriors. I have a warrior's heart—I can fight as they do."

"No doubt you can, my little Callestina, after a few years of practice with a sword," he said quietly.

The laughter in his eyes caressed her. Callestina felt for a moment as if her insides melted. She wanted to run to him, to throw herself into his arms and kiss those smiling lips until his amusement turned to desire.

"No!" Alaric roared. "No, you will not fight."

Callestina tore her eyes away from Darius. She turned to face her brother once more.

"You are *my* sister," he continued. "The sister of Alaric the Great, leader of the Visigoths and soon to be the conqueror of Rome. There are other things ahead in life for you than wielding a sword."

"*Your* plans for my life, you mean," she said.

Alaric stepped across the fire and grabbed her arms. His

fingers dug so cruelly into her flesh that Callestina almost cried out.

"Yes, *my* plans," he said, towering over her, "and you will obey them."

Rage burned in his eyes. Callestina bit back a retort. For now. But he would find that her obedience was something she did not surrender easily. She had plans of her own and she would not give them up just to please her brother.

If the war she was given to fight was one of wills, she would use every weapon she possessed.

She lowered her eyes in false demur. "As you say, Alaric," she answered, making her voice low and sweet.

Alaric's grip loosened. The fire died in his eyes. *He is so easily fooled,* Callestina thought.

"Now, sister of mine, what am I to do with you?" Alaric said more quietly. "With Rome almost within my grasp, I cannot spare an armed escort to take you back where you belong."

"Alaric, please . . . I want—"

"Be quiet," he snapped before she could finish. "I don't care what you want."

"I'll take care of Callestina," came a voice from the other side of the fire. "I'll make certain she's safe."

Callestina turned toward the sound. It was Grayson, sitting half in shadow; Callestina had not noticed him before, but where else would he be? She was grateful for his intervention—and she was sure that when the time came, she could persuade him to do as she wished. He would take her to Darius.

She smiled at Grayson, briefly, then her eyes sought Darius once again. Just the sight of him made her tingle all over; they had been apart far too long.

Why hadn't Darius offered to protect her? She felt the question pass quickly through her mind. But no, she answered it herself; his place was leading his men and fighting by her brother's side. She would not deny him the glory of it. His strength and his leadership were part of what she loved about him.

"Hmmph, well," Alaric blustered, obviously relieved to have the problem solved. "You can't very well sleep among the men, Callestina. I'll have a tent set up here, next to my fire. It's nothing but trouble you're causing, girl. See that you don't cause any more. If you were one of my men, I'd have you beaten for such disobedience."

Callestina once more lowered her eyes meekly. "Thank you, Alaric," she said.

She kept her eyes lowered as he left to arrange for her quarters. Only when she was certain he was gone did she look up again. Then she found Darius's eyes and smiled. With a defiant toss of her head, she sat in her brother's place and lifted his cup to her lips.

Her action was rewarded by Darius's hearty laughter.

Darius did not come to her during the night. Although Callestina burned for his touch, she had not expected him. The next morning it was Grayson, not Darius, who met her as she emerged from her tent.

"I said I would keep you safe," he said to her, "and I mean to do just that. Come with me."

He turned and started walking away. Callestina saw she had no choice but to follow. She hurried to catch up.

All around them, the men of the army were preparing for the day's march—the final day's march to Rome. Amid the ordered chaos, Callestina could feel the excitement in the air; she could hear the eagerness in their voices. Grayson, however, was as taciturn as ever.

"Why?" she asked when she reached his side. "Why did you say that?"

Grayson turned and looked at her. It felt as if his eyes were boring into her with a look that held neither love nor loathing, but something more intense than either. Yet what it was, Callestina could not name.

The long stare seemed to last an eternity. Finally—*finally*—Grayson turned away. "Come," he repeated as he began to walk once again.

They walked to where the horses were staked. Grayson led her to her own and indicated she should mount.

"If you give your word to ride peacefully, I'll not have you tied to the saddle, as your brother suggested," he said. "And don't think you can fool me with your meek words and soft looks. I know you well, Callestina of the Visigoths. Better, in fact, than you know yourself."

Callestina wondered what he meant by these words, but one look at his face and she kept her questions to herself. *It doesn't truly matter what he thinks anyway,* she told herself as she swung into her saddle. *I'm here, near Darius, and that is all that matters.*

"You will ride, at least for now, at the front of the army with your brother, Darius, and myself. If we run into any resistance, you will do exactly what I say, without hesitation and without argument. If you do not agree to this, then we will stay here. I am loath to leave Darius's side this close to battle, but I have given my word and I intend to keep it.

"Well?" he said sharply when Callestina did not answer immediately. "Do you agree?"

Callestina nodded, but that was not enough for Grayson. "I want your word," he said. "Swear by whatever you hold sacred. I don't care by what, but swear you will obey and cause no more trouble."

"I swear," Callestina said, searching her mind quickly for a belief he would accept and that would give her the freedom to do what she needed. "I swear by the destiny I follow."

Grayson shot her a quizzical look, but he said nothing further. After a moment he nodded, then he turned away to mount his own horse. He reined it in until it sidestepped close to hers. With his free hand, he motioned toward her saddle.

"There's bread and meat in the bag and fresh water in the skin," he said. "We eat as we ride."

Callestina did not argue; she would say and do nothing now that might jeopardize her nearness to Darius. Today she would do as she was told in quiet acquiescence.

Tomorrow was another matter.

Camp was made that night within sight of Rome.

Rome, the Eternal City. Nestled among its seven hills, Rome spread in glory and poverty, opulence and decay. The sight of it had nearly taken Callestina's breath away; she had never realized it was so *big.* How could any army, even one as large as theirs, hope to breach those walls?

At a word from her brother, the army had spread out,

swarming over the surrounding hills like a great horde of locusts. By nightfall they had encircled the city, and now, in the darkness, their campfires dotted the landscape. All who lived within the Roman walls knew that the Visigoths were only waiting upon the dawn to attack.

And thus, *Fear* was their first weapon.

"She's like an overripe plum—near to rotten and ready to fall," Alaric said, gesturing with his wine cup in the direction of the city. His spirits were high and he seemed to have even forgiven Callestina for her intrusion upon this male domain. At least he had neither glared nor growled at her all evening.

"I tell you, we shall sleep tomorrow in that city of dreams and she shall be ours," he continued.

Darius laughed. "That is well said, my friend," he agreed.

Callestina looked at the men. She could see nothing but confidence in their faces—even Grayson was smiling. Was she the only one, then, who felt awe at this city that had stood for a thousand years? Was this merely the bravado men needed to prepare themselves for the battle ahead, or did they see something she did not? Rome looked impregnable to her.

The sound of men's voices filled the darkness. They were talking and laughing, even singing around some campfires. *How many of them will be dead tomorrow?* Callestina wondered.

Suddenly, she could not bear to sit here another instant. She was tired of thoughts of death. She stood and walked away from the fires. A few steps, and then the cool, welcoming darkness embraced her. She stood still, trying to block out the voices, trying to hear her own breath, her own heartbeat. She did not want to think about tomorrow, but the thoughts followed her.

Tomorrow men would die—perhaps some she had known her whole life. Perhaps her brother . . .

Perhaps Darius . . .

Darius.

The thought nearly choked her. She found it hard to breathe around the constriction that began at her heart and went up into her throat.

Darius—no, he must not die. Whatever else happened tomorrow, he must remain unharmed.

"Death is part of life—for mortal men." Grayson spoke suddenly behind her.

Callestina whipped around. How could he have known what she was thinking? Then the strangeness of his words hit her. All men were mortal; only the gods did not know death.

She could see nothing more than his silhouette, a deeper shadow in the darkness. Even when he stepped close to her, she could not read his expression.

"You must accept that, Callestina," he continued. "Mortal men die—in battle, of sickness, of old age. What does it really matter how? Short, pitiable mortal lives. At least those who die tomorrow will go out as warriors."

"And that makes a difference?" Callestina forced the words out.

"To them, yes."

"And to you?"

She could almost hear Grayson's sardonic smile. "Ah, I am another matter entirely—as you will learn soon enough."

He turned and started to walk away. "Come, Callestina," he said. "There will be time enough for fears and worries tomorrow. Tonight you must have the courage to put them aside for the sake of those who must soon face battle."

Callestina made no move to join him. His words unnerved her and she did not want his company. But Grayson was relentless. He stopped, and though he did not turn around, his next words were pointed.

"I never thought you a coward," he said.

"I am no coward," Callestina retorted. "I am here, am I not?"

"Yes, you are here—cowering in the darkness. If you truly believe you have a warrior's heart, then come back to the fire. Do not think of the death that might come to the men around you, but of their bravery and their strength. Tomorrow, send them on their way with your smile. *That* is the courage all sisters and mothers, wives and lovers must possess—and it is, perhaps, the greater battle."

Grayson's words surprised her. She would not have thought him capable of such depth of understanding. But then, there was much she did not know about Grayson and the life he had lived. Had he ever loved, ever wanted and needed someone,

as she loved Darius? There seemed to be much more to
Grayson than she had ever valued before.

*Perhaps, when this is over and Darius and I have a home
together, I will have time to learn more about this man whom
Darius calls friend,* she thought as she began to follow him
back to where the others were waiting for their night to pass.

Chapter Twenty-two

The army was moving before dawn. Trees, felled last night, had their branches cut away, leaving only stubs for handholds and turning the lifeless trunks into siege weapons. With these, they hoped to shatter the gates.

The branches were lashed together into crudely shaped ladders by which the men would try to scale the walls. Their greatest weapons, however, were their numbers and, if necessary, their patience. Rome, that great and overpopulated city, had little within her walls to sustain her for long. If she could not be taken by force of arms, she could be starved into submission.

Alaric did not hurry the men in their work; he knew that, as with the campfires last night, the sound of the army's activities was a weapon itself. By the time the actual attack on the city came, the nerves of those within the walls would be fraying and mistakes would be more easily made.

The sun had almost reached its zenith when the order to march finally came. Grayson's face wore a grimace of anger that was close to pain as he watched the men, watched Darius, mounting their horses. Damn Callestina for her willfulness in being here and damn himself for his own stupidity in promising to keep her safe. His place was with Darius, watching Darius's back, as he always did—not cowering in camp with some woman.

But there was no help for it. He *had* given his word—perhaps in a moment of weakness, true—and keeping his word was part of the discipline that gave order to his life.

The attack on Rome would go on without him.

Forty thousand men, on horse or on foot, came down out of

the hills. Grayson felt the earth shake with their passage; his heart pounded with their war cries. Even from where he stood, he could hear the answering cries from within the city.

Or were they screams?

Grayson strained his eyes to watch, to keep Darius in view as the army reached the city walls. He hardly noticed when Callestina came to stand beside him. No word was spoken; they both knew whom they watched, and why.

The leaders of the Gothic army remained mounted, riding in all directions to shout orders and encouragement to the men. The gray wolfskin on Darius's back shone like silver in the sun, making him easy to spot.

A great pounding began to rend the air; the battering rams had reached the gates. The noise from the city increased as though in answer. Even from where Grayson stood, it sounded like a war within a war.

Suddenly, from over the wall, poured a tide of spears. Gothic warriors fell, some wounded mortally, and others stepped into their places so quickly that the hole in the ranks seemed to disappear almost before it was made. Nothing would stop them today. Nothing.

Grayson's stomach churned as he watched fireballs, the dreaded weapon the Romans had learned from the Greeks, catapult over the walls. Horses reared, some throwing their riders; men screamed in agony as bits of the phosphorous fire fell on them. But still the Gothic army did not stop.

The ladders went up to the walls. Men swarmed like ants up an anthill, like bees covering a hive. Soldiers, the great Roman Guards, massed at the top of the walls and fought them.

And the tide of the Goths kept coming.

The sound of the battering rams continued pounding, pounding, like the giant heartbeat of the earth itself.

Suddenly, one of the gates opened. It was not shattered—it was opened from within. The army began to pour into the sudden gap like a dark river. Grayson looked around frantically, trying to spot Darius. The Immortal leader was near the gate, sword held high. In a moment, Grayson knew he would be through the opening and out of sight.

Grayson felt his own sword thrust into his hands. He turned

and found Callestina staring at him with eyes as bright as any fire, fierce as a wild animal about to strike. She looked like a warrior's goddess.

"Go to him," she ordered, not bothering to say the name they both knew. "Keep him safe."

"But you—" Grayson began. She shook her head.

"Go," she ordered again.

Grayson needed no further urging. He ran to his horse and, with a single leap, he was astride.

He glanced once more at Callestina. She stood where he had left her, the sunlight making her blond hair look like a mantle of gold draping a fair and perfect statue.

Then the statue moved; Callestina raised her arm in a salute, a farewell, a benediction. Grayson raised his sword high in return. Sunlight sparked along the blade as he drove his heels into his horse's flanks and galloped toward the battle.

Callestina did not move as she watched Grayson ride into the crush of men. Her heart was pounding with the words she had spoken. *Go to him, keep him safe,* it repeated over and over. The words, the plea, were in her breath; it was part of the blood that rushed through her veins.

Keep him safe . . .

Darius . . .

Callestina saw Grayson ride through the gate and into Rome itself—and she felt like someone suddenly blinded. Outside the walls the battle still raged, but she did not care. Everything—everyone—she cared about was within the city now and cut off from her.

She began to pace restlessly, needing movement to stay sane. There was nothing she could do but wait—and waiting was an enemy against whom there was no weapon.

Bright afternoon turned to starlit evening and still the sounds of battle raged from within the city. Callestina made a fire and tried to cook some food, only to let it burn while she stood watching the distance, waiting for a rider to bring her news. It seemed, however, that she was forgotten. No word, either good or bad, came her way as the hours dragged on. Uncertainty was near to driving her mad.

Finally, Callestina knew she could bear it no longer. She *must* know that Darius still lived. Frantically, she began to search through the belongings the army had left behind. Somewhere, she knew, there would be an extra sword she could carry. She did not fool herself with the thought of giving great battle, but she would not enter the city helpless and unarmed.

She found a short sword wrapped in a bedroll. Barely longer than a dagger, it was an ornate weapon, with gold wash upon a hilt set with rubies and lapis lazuli and etching that ran down the length of the blade. Callestina guessed it was a prize taken at the destruction of Ravenna.

She lifted it, turning it this way and that, slicing through the air to feel the weight in her hand. It was too light and short a weapon for a man to carry into battle, but it fitted both her arm and her strength. With a smile, Callestina slipped it through her belt.

She was ready.

Quickly now, she braided her hair and tied it back with a scrap of leather. Then she ran to her horse and mounted it quickly.

"Oh, great goddesses," she prayed, "whatever awaits, guide me to my destiny."

Though brief, her prayer was fervent and she knew the Norns had heard. With the eyes of her soul, she could almost see the threads they were weaving and the shining strand down which she would ride. Gathering up her courage, she turned her horse toward Rome.

She rode down the hills without incident, for the battle had taken itself inside the walls. But once she passed through the gate, it was like entering a madman's nightmare. Rome was a holocaust of fire and blood.

Callestina had seen the aftermath of battles before; she lived among a warrior people. But she had never entered a destroyed city, not even Ravenna when she was following the army. Somehow, seeing the dead litter the city streets and hearing the screams of the living echo off city walls made a more horrible scene than the same dead in an open field or forest.

These dead were not only warriors, though the bodies of the Roman Guards were numerous; these dead were everyday people who, from the looks on their faces, had been unprepared to die. Women, children, landowners, slaves—unarmed and unprotected—lay side by side with the soldiers whose bloodstained weapons had not saved their lives or their city.

Light from the fires that raged through the buildings gave the night a surreal cast painted in hellish shades of orange and red. Smoke muddied the air. Off in the distance, deep in the heart of the city, Callestina could hear the sounds of battle still ringing in the clash of swords, the war cries and shouts of men, the screams of wounded horses and the higher screams caused by wounded human flesh.

She drew out the sword that she had found and moved forward, gritting her teeth to keep from screaming as a woman dashed in front of her carrying a long knife. The front of her dress was soaked in blood. Her eyes were hollows of madness. Callestina saw the slave collar around her throat and wondered, briefly, from whom she had escaped—and how. Had death bought her freedom?

Callestina rode on, urging her nervous horse forward when its instinct, like hers, was to turn and run. Nearer and nearer they drew to the sounds of fighting. It was only her need to know of Darius's safety, to see him with her own eyes, that kept her moving.

The bodies of the dead gave way to the bodies of the dying. Some made pitiful mewling sounds as she passed, reaching out to her for succor. Others screamed or cursed as they tried to drag their shattered bodies farther out of harm's way.

The stillness of death had also disappeared; slaves and beggars dashed about. Freed from the constraints of society, many had their arms loaded with wealth they had known only in their dreams. Others carried makeshift weapons or stolen swords by which to claim bloody payment for each past moment of pain, indignity, and injustice.

Suddenly, a man grabbed the reins of Callestina's horse. She moved by instinct and brought her sword down, slashing with all the strength of her fear. The man's hand came away at the wrist. He fell back with a scream, his blood gushing crimson.

Callestina drove her heels hard into her horse's sides. It shot forward; she struggled to stay astride, despite the bile that rose in her throat. Her horse, finally given its head, charged ahead. Callestina struggled to stay astride, though trembling shook her body and her stomach threatened to disgorge its contents with each movement. Her horse ran and she hung on, uncaring of the direction.

The battle was up ahead—or was it a battle? Callestina could see that some still fought, but many busied themselves with loot and rape.

Where is Darius? her heart screamed as her horse continued its wild gallop. Her eyes searched frantically through the mad, twisted scene. Still, she did not see him.

Her horse shied and reared as a javelin whizzed past its head. Callestina held on, pressing her arms against the horse's neck to regain control and urge it forward, into the fray. The fighting closed around her, enveloped her, and she began to use her small sword once more.

Then, up ahead, she spotted him. Darius lifted his head with laughter as his sword drove through a Roman Guard. The look on his face was one Callestina had never seen. It was a look of lust gone bestial.

His arm came up again. He hacked and stabbed, howling a war cry that made Callestina's heart freeze. How could this be the man she loved?

And yet it was. It was.

She felt the pain shoot through her, sudden and hot as fire. Callestina looked down and saw the arrow in her chest. Her eyes widened with disbelief; she felt her strength draining. So fast . . .

"Darius," she screamed once, using the last of the energy left in her body.

The darkness closed in. . . .

She fell. . . .

Chapter Twenty-three

Callestina did not feel the arms that caught her, that lifted her body and carried her away from the battle. She felt nothing.

There is no feeling in death . . . .

With a sudden gasp, air forced itself into her lungs. Once. Twice. She was breathing . . .

She opened her eyes slowly, afraid to see what strange afterlife awaited her.

There was a ceiling high over her head, decorated with blue and white mosaic tile, like clouds drifting in a summer sky. A male figure, bright with gold and wearing a crown of thunderbolts, filled the center of the scene.

Callestina opened her eyes a little farther. She turned her head to see . . . Grayson. He sat upon the floor a few feet from her body. His head was bowed and his shoulders slumped as if he carried a great burden.

Where is this place? she wondered. It did not fit the description of any afterlife she knew. And why was Grayson here? Was he also dead? Was . . .

"Darius?" She breathed her question in his name.

Grayson looked up. He scurried quickly to her side and gently lifted her hand into his own.

"He is unharmed."

Grayson's words sent a flood of relief through Callestina. She closed her eyes again and let the feeling warm her. Darius was safe; whatever awaited her now, she could face it with this knowledge.

"Where?" she asked softly. She did not want to move yet, not until she knew what was to come.

"This place?" Grayson glanced around. "A temple to Zeus, I think. Holy ground—you're safe here."

"Safe? But the arrow . . . I'm . . ."

"Dead?" Grayson shook his head and with a small, ironic smile said, "No, Callestina, you're not dead. No arrow can kill you."

Callestina brought her hand up to her chest. The arrow was gone, but more—the wound itself was no longer there. Blood still stained the front of her tunic, but the skin beneath was whole and firm and her touch caused no pain.

Her fingers trembled as she took them away. "I . . . I don't understand."

Grayson gave another small smile. It was softer this time. "No, of course you do not," he said. "But you will.

"You are Immortal, Callestina—as am I, as is Darius. We live among mortals, that is true, but our destiny is different."

"Our *Destiny*," Callestina repeated. Then she started to laugh.

Grayson felt bewildered and helpless as he watched Callestina laugh. She kept laughing until tears streamed from her eyes and her breath came in short, ragged gasps.

"The Norns," she said at last. "The Norns did this to me. The Goddesses of Destiny—it is their way of answering my petitions."

Callestina sat up and looked Grayson full in the face. There was a fierce light burning in her eyes that made him wonder if she teetered on the edge of madness.

"They say the gods have no humor, Grayson," she said to him, "but that is not so. They play with human lives as best amuses them."

Grayson had no idea of the meaning behind her words. One god or many, he had left such beliefs behind long ago.

"Don't you see?" Callestina continued, black laughter threatening once more in her voice. "I prayed to the Norns, the old goddesses my people served before the Christian God, and I made sacrifice to them in the ancient Women's Way. I wanted my destiny to be joined with Darius. Now they have changed me into—this."

Grayson shook his head. "They have changed nothing," he said. "You were born Immortal, Callestina. We all are."

"Who? Alaric? My people? Who is this *we*?"

Again, Grayson shook his head. "No, Alaric is not Immortal," he said. "But there are others. Not among this army, but in other lands, other places. And there is much you must learn if you are to survive."

"Survive? You said I was Immortal."

"Against such things as arrow wounds, yes," he said. "Against old age and illness. But there is one way of death, and of that you must learn."

Grayson took a breath. He wished Darius were here to better explain. Grayson knew he did not have Darius's way with words or with people. But Callestina had to know—and he had to tell her. He had given his word to keep her safe in her mortal life—but he had failed; he would not fail her now, as her Immortal life began.

"We are born Immortal," he said again. "No one knows how or why, but it is true. Death comes to us only one way . . ."

The Game—Grayson explained its rules and its reasons. He told Callestina about the need for a sword and why she must carry one, about holy ground, their only true refuge of safety. Finally, he explained that in the end there can be only one— one Immortal to claim all Power; one Immortal who would rule throughout time.

As he talked, Grayson watched the emotions play across Callestina's face. First came the shock and disbelief, then the question whether he might be insane to speak such words. But she could not deny that she was alive, and disbelief slowly gave way to acceptance, even to excitement at what her new life might offer.

Oh, he could guess what she was thinking. She imagined centuries, eons, *forever,* by Darius's side. But even if Darius had loved her now, and Grayson knew he did not, eternal love was a mortal concept. When life was so finite, *forever* was a word of hope.

But not for Immortals. *In the end there can be only one.*

Grayson knew he would not say these things to Callestina.

She would learn; they all did. For now, this ever so short *now,* let her keep her illusions.

"Rome has fallen," he said, standing abruptly and holding out a hand to help her rise. "Alaric and Darius are within the Imperial Palace. The looting will go on, perhaps for days, depending upon their mood. Come, we must get you back to camp."

"But why?" Callestina asked. "If I am truly in no danger, why should I not go join my brother?"

Grayson stared at her as she put her hand in his. It was smooth and white, with long tapering fingers and nails as delicate as tiny pink shells. She came to her feet with almost liquid grace. Grayson's eyes roved down her body, down the generous curves the man's clothing she wore did so little to hide. He wondered if her naïveté was feigned.

"There is still danger, Callestina," he said. "Rome is in revolt. The gates were *opened* to us—from *within,* by slaves who saw in our presence the means of their freedom. Do you think that they, who have killed their own masters and who run through the streets drunk on the heady nectar of revenge, will hesitate at rape?"

Callestina's eyes grew wide and then angry. "I am Alaric's sister," she began.

Grayson snorted, a single dismissive sound. "From your own men that might save you—if they took the time to recognize who you are. But from the others in this city, from the slaves roaming free, from young men who have escaped the sword, from soldiers who have defected from protecting Rome—do you think any of these *care* that you are Alaric's sister?"

Grayson shook his head. "No, Callestina," he said. "We must get you out of the city and back to the camp. Alaric and Darius are too busy to accord you any protection—and how long the madness in the streets will continue, I cannot say. Your brother is intent upon teaching the Romans a lesson in the might of Gothic fury, and the men are eager to comply."

Callestina nodded silently and Grayson was glad she gave no further argument. Once she was safely back in the hills, he would be done with his duty toward her and he could return to fighting at Darius's side.

The place where he belonged.

He bent and picked up the short, ornate sword he had found clutched in her hand when she fell. It was a pretty piece of work, but it would not keep her alive through the centuries. Soon she would have to find another and she would have to learn how to use it. But that was a problem for another day.

"Here," he said, holding the sword out to her and drawing his own. "Stay close."

Grayson had brought the horses inside the temple, unwilling to lose them to rioters. They waited patiently by the door, no doubt glad to be away from the chaos. Grayson's horse nickered softly as he approached, and before mounting Grayson took a moment to run a practiced hand down its legs, checking for strains and injuries he might have previously missed.

Callestina was already mounted by the time he was finished. He gave her a brief nod of approval as he opened the great temple doors and swung himself into the saddle.

"Stay close," he told her again. "Keep your sword drawn. If anyone comes close, use it."

Without further word, he led the way through the temple doors and out into the madness that was Rome.

Darius strode through the ornate corridors of the Imperial Palace. Although his sword was still in his hand, the fighting was nearly over. Most of the famed Praetorian Guards lay as mangled heaps of dead flesh, overrun by the force and number of Gothic swords. The few who remained were holed up in the inner council chamber with the Emperor and several of the Roman Senators.

Walking next to Darius, Alaric was smiling. His soot- and blood-streaked face turned the expression into a primal war mask; his eyes, red from smoke, looked painted in fire and his gapped, yellow teeth seemed the grin of a death's-head. But his spirits soared.

They had taken the palace; they had taken Rome.

"Do we go for Honorius, then?" Darius asked him, returning his grin and knowing that his own face made an equally gruesome vision.

Alaric shook his head. "Let him wait," he said. "Let them

all wait. Let them cower in their chamber while they listen to the screams and breathe in the smells of death from their city. Let them wait while hunger and fear take turns gnawing at their bellies. Honorius will not say no to me again, I promise you that."

Darius's smile broadened. He was as amused as ever by the mortals surrounding him. Their lives, their deaths, their victories and defeats, all fed his own plans—plans of which they had no inkling. Only Grayson knew of the world Darius envisioned.

It was a world Darius would rule and mortals would serve.

Oh, Darius knew that Grayson still held to his dream, despite all the times Darius had told him that such was foolishness. But just lately, the possibility had begun to whisper within Darius's mind as well.

An army of Immortals—vast, unstoppable.

A kingdom, an *Empire*, ruled by Immortals that stretched across the earth.

The thought, if he let himself think it, was intoxicating. Perhaps, just perhaps, it might work.

The time for that world might be nearing—but it was not yet. Darius had watched empires rise and fall while he studied their mortal inhabitants. He had fought by their sides while he watched for weaknesses that could be used. And he waited.

For over three centuries now he had waited, prepared, grown stronger with each Quickening, as the tide of human history ebbed and flowed. He knew that soon it would crest—and he would ride that crest to domination.

Once more, Darius thought of the dream Grayson had proposed so often in the decades they had been together. *Could it be?* he asked himself. They lived The Game, facing one another in battle. They did not bond together in a common cause. But with the right leader—perhaps . . .

And *he* was that leader. If he could win their loyalty, as he had won Grayson's, he would make them see that ruling the world was the greatness for which they were destined.

There would still be mortals enough for menial tasks, the front-line fodder, the servants and slaves; mortals had been

Darius's tools for centuries. But the Immortals who joined him would be generals, princes, Kings.

And *he* would be at their head.

He would kill those he must; he did not fool himself into thinking Immortal loyalty was easily given. Yet, some would join him; *enough* would join him. Against an army of Immortals, what could a mortal army hope to do?

And if in the end there could be only one . . . Darius intended to be the one that remained.

Darius laughed out loud. Yes, it was good to be alive—and to be Immortal.

"Come, my friend," he said to Alaric. "While we leave Honorius to do battle with his fears, let us find the kitchens and the wine cellars before they are cleaned out. No doubt the vintages served to the Emperor will be very pleasing indeed."

"We will drink to our first night in the Imperial Palace," Alaric agreed. "The first of many."

Darius clapped Alaric on the back. "The first of many," he repeated, laughing again at the unsuspecting irony of Alaric's words.

As they strode down the palace corridors, Darius wondered after Grayson. He did not fear for his friend's safety— Grayson's skill with a sword was almost, *almost,* as great as Darius's own—but he missed the man's company. Grayson, alone, would understand the true nature of his laughter, and that understanding was the greatest bond between them.

Hurry back, Grayson, he thought to his absent friend. *Our time to be patient is nearly ended, and we have new plans to make.*

Chapter Twenty-four

For three more days, the pillage of Rome continued. Alaric's only orders to his men were, as always, that the Christian churches be spared; Darius ordered that all holy places were to be left in peace. The lucky of the Roman citizens found surcease from the violence within those walls.

But there was carnage in plenty. Rome burned as it had not since the time of Nero. Not the conquest of Egypt or of Gaul, nor the madness of Caligula, had caused so many deaths.

Grayson divided his time between the hours with Darius and traveling back to Callestina's camp to make certain of her safety. Although nothing in her words or actions showed that her attitude toward him had changed, his own feelings had only heightened since seeing her lie so still and fragile in death and being with her at the moment of her awakening into Immortality. He felt compelled to go to her, driven by a bond between them that he knew she did not yet feel.

And she would run to him as soon as she saw him approaching—but never for his own sake. She came to him always with the same questions: What news of Darius? Is he safe? Why doesn't he send for her? The questions ate at Grayson's heart, yet he answered them and continued to keep his growing feelings for Callestina hidden.

Yes, Darius was safe. He had laughed when he learned of Callestina's fall. Beyond that, he did not spare her a thought. He was too busy amusing himself with the treasures and whores of Rome while he awaited Alaric's next gambit, which the Gothic leader assured him would be a true *coup de grâce*.

Grayson told none of this to Callestina. Instead, he told her of the chaos that still filled the Roman streets. Darius and

Alaric, he said, had been busy restoring order and preparing their demands for the Emperor. These were not petitions such as they had presented before, but the demands of conquerors that must be worded carefully if conciliation was to take place.

Callestina accepted everything Grayson told her. Sometimes, when he looked into the blue depths of her eyes, he felt a twist of guilt grip his heart. He hated lying to her. He wished Darius would come to Callestina himself and put an end to the girl's pitiful dreams of a future together.

And if he told her the truth about Darius? Grayson knew Callestina would never believe him. So he continued the charade—but for whose sake? he wondered. For Darius's? Surely not; Darius did not care. For Callestina's? Perhaps. She did not love him, but she was coming to trust him and eagerly awaited his visits each day.

There was the truth. He did not tell her the truth about the person Darius was for his own sake. He liked to see the eagerness on Callestina's face when he approached. He wanted the hours they spent so well together. The gentleness in her voice when she spoke to him was unlike their past conversations, which had been only what courtesy demanded. Now there were smiles that he alone saw and that he thought of often during the hours they were apart.

These would all disappear once she knew the truth of Darius's plans—and that she had no place in them.

Darius's plans—Grayson thought of them as he rode once more up the hill toward Callestina's camp. Not tomorrow or the next day, but very soon they would leave Alaric behind and begin gathering their new army of Immortals. *Finally.* Darius had said so just last night, and with each passing hour Grayson felt himself more eager for that day to arrive.

But what of Callestina? something deep in his heart whispered—and he knew the answer. If Callestina survived these next few years, her pace in Darius's kingdom would be small. She would be one of a hundred, or a thousand, women Darius used or cast off at a whim.

Grayson wanted to be sure she survived. Each day he drilled her with her small sword. In the few hours they had, he could not teach her enough to keep her alive throughout the centuries, but it was a beginning and Callestina was a good student. Grayson knew he taught her for a selfish reason—he taught her in the hope that someday she would turn to him for comfort, perhaps even for love.

She was waiting, sword in hand, when he approached. She smiled and dropped into the slight crouch that imitated the posture her brother used when circling an opponent. Grayson laughed as he drew his own sword and swung himself from his saddle.

"So, little Callestina, you are impatient today," he said, keeping his sword raised and slowly turning to match her movements.

"Bored, mostly," she answered. "I practice the things you've shown me, but there is so little to do here alone. When may I come into Rome?"

"Today," Grayson replied, smiling. "I will take you back with me today."

"Finally," Callestina cried—and she lunged.

Three hours later, Grayson and Callestina rode through the broken gates of Rome. Callestina had grown increasingly quiet as they neared the city, and now all words left her. She could only look away in horror as they passed the bloated and stinking bodies that lay where they had fallen, rotting in the hot Italian sun. Rats, their bellies distended with fresh meat, scurried everywhere and smoke still hung like a putrid haze among the buildings.

Why would anyone want Rome now? Callestina wondered as their horses picked their way through the ruinous streets.

When they reached the Imperial Palace, Alaric was waiting for them. Callestina hardly noticed her brother; by his side stood Darius. In Callestina's eyes, the trampled gardens, the bloodstained tiles and steps, all faded away. She saw only Darius. Standing in the sunlight, with the soft breeze lifting the hair from his shoulders and the Imperial Palace at his back, he looked regal, almost godlike, in her eyes. He smiled at her and for a moment Callestina's breath caught in her throat. He was so beautiful, so perfect.

Next to Darius, Alaric held out his arms to her, and with the movement, the moment was shattered.

"Callestina," Alaric shouted, hurrying down the palace steps. Gone was any sign of the anger her presence had caused him. He reached her horse and, as she started to slide from the saddle, caught her and twirled her around twice before letting her feet touch the ground.

"Well, my sister," he said, smiling broadly at her. "What do you say of your brother now?"

"The same as I have always said, Alaric," she replied, returning his smile. "That you can do anything you say you can do."

She was proud of him, of this man whom she had called brother all of her life. He had promised his people he would conquer and he had given them Rome. But she knew now that she had been a foundling and that she and Alaric bore no blood together. Alaric, twelve years her senior, had never said a word or treated her as anything but the sister of his body. Her eyes filled with sudden tears at his kindness.

Alaric saw them and frowned. "Tears, Callestina?" he said. "Not for Rome, surely."

"No, my brother, not for Rome. Tears are a woman's way in more than sadness. They are tears of pride, and of joy, that you have always kept your word."

"Hmmph." Alaric looked away, embarrassed as ever by such emotion. "Women's ways are unfathomable, hey, Darius?" he said over her head.

"One of the true mysteries of the universe," Darius agreed.

Alaric pulled Callestina briefly into one of his gruff bear hugs. When he released her, he smiled at her once more.

"Come, sister," he said. "I am not yet done humbling Rome, and I want you, as my only family, to share this last victory with me."

He put an arm around Callestina's shoulders and began to lead her back up the stairs and into the palace. She glanced over her shoulder to see if Darius was following, but he was deep in conversation with Grayson.

As she watched, Grayson nodded once, then swung himself back into the saddle. He and Darius exchanged a few more intent words. As Grayson turned his horse and began to ride away, Darius hurried after Callestina and Alaric, his long strides quickly covering the distance that separated them.

He smiled at Callestina, but said not a word as he began to walk beside her. His smile had been pleasant enough, but there was a warmth missing from his eyes. Callestina wanted to throw herself into his arms and kiss him until she saw the fire of desire burning brightly again. Yet, with Alaric's arm around her shoulder, she could do nothing more than struggle to keep up with the pace the two men set.

They walked down the many twists and turns of the corridors. Callestina saw that most of the palace had been left untouched by looters. Statues stood unbroken in their niches—busts of past Caesars and images of gods—plaques, some adorned with gold and precious stones, still hung upon the walls, as did finely woven tapestries. The beauty of the tiled floor over which they moved so swiftly was marred by stains of blood, but no bodies remained. For this, Callestina was grateful; she had seen enough of death.

They reached the inner chamber where the Emperor Honorius awaited them. He sat upon the great carved and gilded chair. Those who were left of the Senators and bodyguard, all worn and bedraggled, ranged around him like the tattered petals of a dying flower. Honorius, alone, drew himself up straight when Alaric entered, striving at least for a moment to look like something other than the defeated ruler of a conquered city.

But the pose lasted only a moment. Soon his shoulders slumped and he hung his head once more. Too weary to even meet Alaric's eye, Honorius rested his forehead on the heel of his hand.

"Name the terms it will take for you to leave us in peace," he said, every nuance of his voice announcing how much he wished this meeting over.

Alaric stepped forward. As he neared the Emperor's throne, the few members of the Imperial Bodyguard who remained moved to place themselves between Alaric and the Emperor. Honorius waved them away with a weary gesture.

"Speak, Alaric of the Goths," he said.

Alaric waited a moment more, waited to show that he, and not Honorius, controlled the day. Callestina was again proud of her brother, and she sensed, even if Honorius did not, that he would soon wish he had not been so eager for Alaric's words.

"Honorius of Rome," Alaric began, his great booming voice filling the room, "weeks ago I sent you terms. Had you accepted then, we would have dealt with you in honor and our nations would now be living together in peace. It was *you* who chose to deny my message and to kill my messenger. It was *you* who chose this war. On your head lies the death of your people and the destruction of your city. It is your family who must, therefore, bear the price of your people's redemption.

"The majority of my terms are unchanged. My people demand full Roman citizenship, with all the rights and privileges such status accords. In return, our arms shall be made ready in defense of the Empire and of Rome herself. We also demand land of our choosing on which to settle our kingdom—and so that we might settle in prosperity, you will pay us four thousand pounds of gold and two thousand of silver. This we demand from the Roman Empire as tribute to their conquerors.

"But it is from you, Honorius, and from your house, that our final term of peace must be paid. I demand the union of our families by the hand of your sister, Galla Placidia, in marriage. By this, the world will see the place of honor the Visigoths hold in the Roman Empire, and only by this will a contract of peace between us be sealed."

A collective gasp ran through the room. Callestina was as shocked as the rest of them by her brother's words. But then she smiled; it was a bold and daring stroke.

Honorius's eyes had grown wide and his face blanched. He came slowly to his feet as the chalk of his cheeks changed into the high flush of rage.

"Never," he cried. "I will not soil my family line with the blood of barbarians. I will never—"

"*I* accept," a voice shouted from the back of the room. A woman pushed herself through the tired collection of men behind the Emperor's throne. Callestina looked her over. Placidia's face was dirty and her clothes wrinkled from three days of wear, but her bearing was royal. It was easy to see that the blood of the Caesars ran more true in her than in her brother, despite who sat on the throne.

"For the sake of my people, *I* accept," she said again. She turned to Honorius. "Because of your weakness and your arrogance, our people lie dead in the streets. Children wander, crying for parents who can no longer answer, and our beautiful Rome smolders in ash and destruction. Fool that you are, you listened only to the counsel of fools who had no care for anything but their own pockets. I care for our people, and *I* care for *Rome.*"

She turned and crossed the few steps to Alaric. Though her head reached only his shoulder and his bearlike frame made her look delicate as a child's toy, it was clear she had a spirit strong enough to match his.

She held out her hand and he took it gently. "I accept," she said one more time. "Let us be wed in the morning."

Behind her, Honorius sank slowly back into his seat, well and truly defeated.

Callestina looked at her brother, smiling down at Placidia's face. *It's over,* she thought. *We've won. Now there will be time for peace—and time for love.*

She looked over at Darius, but he was not looking at the handfast couple or the room full of men. His gaze seemed to be seeking something far away, something only he could see.

Do you look to the future, Darius? Callestina wondered. *What do you see? Do you see a time to put down your sword, despite this Game of which Grayson spoke? I have dreamed of the future also—and I know that ours will be such a love as the gods themselves will envy.*

Callestina smiled. Tonight she would go to Darius, wherever he was. She was Alaric's sister in all but blood, and if her brother could be bold enough to face the Roman Empire and win what he desired, she could do the same with the man she loved.

Chapter Twenty-five

They washed themselves in Roman baths, attended by Imperial servants. They were given royal apartments filled with soft cushions and sheets of eastern silk. This was the life of which Alaric dreamed and for which he had fought. Soon, he would call the rest of his people south and he would Romanize the Gothic nation.

That was *not* what Darius wanted. He had lived among the Romans two centuries before—as he had lived among the Persians and the Chinese. He had, at different times during his Immortal life, traveled throughout the East and down into Africa, and he had seen warriors grow soft with too much luxury and warmth.

His travels always brought him back to the north, back to the lands of the Gothic kingdoms. His heart drew him home to where men shunned a life that would turn their muscles into jelly, to where what was prized was a strong arm and a sharp sword—back to the place where even the wind and the rain, the snow and the storm, were enemies to be conquered and friends to be embraced. In the north, men knew that the struggle to survive kept a man's mind sharp and his body hard.

It was back to the north Darius longed to go now.

He paced the confines of his room, of his ornate cage, waiting for Grayson to return from his errand. Darius had sent him to spread the word among their own men to meet them at the gates at dawn. Darius had fulfilled the call of friendship by fighting at Alaric's side and helping the mortal win his heart's desire. Now it was time to be gone; Darius wanted nothing more than to put all of the obligations and associations of the long winter past to rest.

Those of his men who wished to stay with Alaric could do so with Darius's blessing. Darius was heading toward the destiny he had been born to fulfill and he wanted no one with him who would be pining after warmer climes or deserted women.

He could feel the call of that destiny pulsing in his veins, calling him north again. He would soon establish a kingdom such as the world had never seen. It would be the kingdom from which he would conquer and rule.

Darius planned to leave Rome no later than dawn—earlier, if Grayson could have the men ready. Darius had no desire to see this farce of a royal wedding. He'd had enough of mortal concerns and mortal desires. If only Grayson would return . . .

Darius felt the approach of another Immortal. There was a knock on his door and he spun around eagerly.

"Enter," he called, expecting Grayson to walk in, and to see him wearing the smile he so rarely showed to the world.

The door opened slightly—and it was Callestina who slipped inside.

She stood still and quiet for the barest moment, then she ran to him and threw herself into his arms. It was instinct rather than desire that made him catch her. When her lips closed hungrily upon his own, it was his body that responded, not his mind—or his heart.

The kiss ended and he disengaged her arms from his neck. She stood smiling at him, and Darius could see that she was waiting for him to speak. What was it the girl wanted from him now?

"Why are you here, Callestina?" he asked, not bothering to keep the frown from his face or his voice.

"I've come to talk about the future," she answered. "*Our* future."

"What do you mean?" Darius's voice was sharp. He did not care, not anymore. He wanted to be gone from the place—and he wanted her gone from his life.

"It's all right, Darius." Callestina's voice was light and cheerful, oblivious to the look of distaste that was spreading across his features. "I'm like you now—Immortal. We can talk openly with each other. The fighting is done. We've won against Rome and now our people can live in peace. *We* can live in peace—together."

Darius saw the eagerness in Callestina's eyes. He could feel the shape and the force of the fantasy she had built in her mind. He threw back his head and laughed.

"Like me?" he said, his voice heavy with scorn. "You're nothing like me. You—with your petty little dreams. You dare to think you have ever been a match for me?"

He laughed again. It was a cruel and biting sound. "There is no *peace*, Callestina," he continued. "Not for our kind. We must live by the sword until at last only one of us remains. That will not change, no matter what mortal empires rise or fall."

"But there *is* peace now."

"Peace." Darius spat the word. "We are not creatures of peace. You will learn that—or you will die."

Callestina had never heard him speak in such a way, and Darius could see the traces of fear growing in her eyes, replacing the happiness that had been there just seconds before.

Darius was glad to see the change. It was time and past that she knew the truth. By the gods, why had she followed him? Why couldn't she have stayed where she belonged and saved him from this—annoyance?

"You say we may speak openly with each other," he said, not softening his tone. "Then let us do so. We have no *future* together, Callestina. None. You were only a diversion to fill the long winter. Nothing more—*never* anything more. Well, the winter is over now, and *you* are boring."

Callestina backed away from him. She looked as if he had struck her. Darius did not care. He was tired of being genial to fools.

"I . . . I don't believe you," Callestina stammered. Her voice was hardly more than a whisper. "I love you—and you love me. You said—"

"Never. I have never said a word of love or made a promise of anything more than the moment. If you thought otherwise, then you are as much a fool as that man you call brother."

Again there was a knock on the door, this time hesitant and deferential.

"Come," Darius snapped, and a young woman entered, carrying a tray of wine and food. Her downcast eyes and the slave collar around her throat proclaimed her status, and the belted, thin linen shift she wore did nothing to hide the ripe perfection of her body.

Darius looked at her with a satisfied, predatory smile. He would make Callestina understand the finality of his words. He waited until the slave had placed the tray on the table and turned to leave the room. Then he grabbed her around her narrow waist and pulled her to him, one of his hands coming up to fondle her breast.

Callestina shook her head slowly from side to side, as if the action could make what she was seeing untrue.

"No," she said. "Darius, don't. We're meant to be together. Everything I've done has been so we *could* be together."

"Everything you have done has been for your own sake. But don't worry, little Callestina. I'm sure you will have no trouble finding someone else who can satisfy your lust. There is no great secret to it—after all, you're just a woman. Go away, Callestina—I'm tired of you."

She took another step back from him. Then another. "I'll go to Alaric," she said. "I'll tell him how you used me. He'll make you marry me."

Once more, Darius threw back his head with laughter. "Do you think I have any fear of your brother—of any mortal? Go—and perhaps in a century or two, if you survive that long, we will meet again."

Tears gathered in Callestina's eyes. "I'll survive," she said, "if only to repay you back for this moment. Somehow, I'll find a way to make you suffer."

She turned and fled—and Darius's laughter followed her out the door.

Callestina ran from Darius's room, down the corridor—and straight into Grayson. He caught her before she could run from him, too.

"I warned you, Callestina," he said, not bothering to ask where she had been. Her tears told the tale eloquently.

She tried to pull away, but he would not let her go. "You won't stop him—and neither will Alaric," he continued, guessing at her destination and intent.

Damn him, Callestina thought, *how does he always know?*

She stopped struggling, and Grayson loosened his grip slightly. "Let it go, Callestina," he said. "It is over. You cannot force love from an unwilling heart. But you have so much ahead of you now—centuries of life and love. Learn to use your sword well, so that you can live all the possibilities that await."

Callestina looked into Grayson's eyes. The intensity of his gaze had darkened his pale blue-gray eyes to the color of smoke on a winter's night, and she wondered what more he was not saying.

And she knew he was right. She had to let Darius go—for now. But only until she was strong enough in her new life to follow him.

She nodded briefly and turned her face away. Grayson dropped his hands from her arms.

"Good-bye, little Callestina," he said softly.

There was such an odd tone in his voice that Callestina looked up quickly, but Grayson had already turned on his heel and was walking away. Callestina felt a shiver race through her. She knew that she would see both Grayson and Darius again.

Someday.

She had time . . .

Grayson walked into Darius's room without stopping to knock. He found the other Immortal staring broodingly into a goblet of wine.

"The men will be at the gate," Grayson said without preamble. "Many seemed nearly as eager as you are to depart."

"And you?" Darius asked, not bothering to look up.

Grayson shrugged. He crossed the room and poured himself some of the wine from the pitcher that stood near Darius's elbow.

"I go where you go," he said. "It makes no difference where that happens to be."

Darius finally looked up and smiled with his usual wry amusement. "You're a liar, Grayson," he said. "But your lies are welcome ones. I know you did not want to come here and you've wanted to leave since we arrived." Darius downed his wine and stood. "So let us depart this place and leave mortal affairs behind us. We have other, better things ahead."

Grayson downed his wine too. Then, side by side, they strode from the room.

Over the last days they had become familiar with the Imperial Palace and it did not take them long to go to the room where they had stabled the horses. As Grayson swung onto the back of his stallion, it seemed to him as if the animals were just as eager to be off. Darius must have sensed it too, for he laughed and reached down to pat his own horse's neck.

"To the gate, then," he said to Grayson, "and then north— to Gaul and, perhaps, Germanica. From there, we'll found a kingdom that will shake the very pillars of the earth."

"Then let us ride," Grayson answered.

The horses' hooves made a loud clatter on the tiled floor, but soon they were in the streets. It was the last time Grayson would ride through this city, and he was not sorry to leave it behind. He was sorry to leave only one thing.

Good-bye, Callestina, his heart whispered. Yes, he loved her, as Darius did not—but he loved Darius more, owed Darius more, and had already pledged his soul in that service.

When they reached the gate, many of the men had already assembled, mounted and waiting. They cheered when they saw the Immortals approach. Grayson drew his horse to one side and waited, letting Darius ride forward among his men. He saw how their expressions brightened when Darius spoke their names and called to them individually, making each man feel important. Darius was the perfect commander; Grayson knew that each man here would happily give his small, mortal life at Darius's whim.

"We will wait for one hour," Darius announced, "then we will ride. Those who are not with us can follow or stay, as they will. You, too, are free to stay if you desire. Alaric has won his dream of Roman citizenship and it is offered to all who remain with him, here in this land of sunshine.

"But I will not stay. I ride north, back to the lands where we belong. I have no wish to be part of another man's dream or another King's empire. I ride north to build a kingdom of my own. Of *our* own."

Again, a great shout arose from the men. Grayson looked

at the adulation on their faces and at Darius, sitting so tall upon his horse, the breeze ruffling his tawny hair.

In the end they will make him not just their King but their god, Grayson thought. *I wonder if he knows that. I wonder if that's what he really wants.*

And the cheer went on.

Chapter Twenty-six

They rode north, as Darius had commanded, but not along the route by which they had arrived. They had neither the need nor the desire to return to Cremona or to cross the Alps again into the Danube Valley. They rode along the western coast of Italy into southern Gaul, following the curve of the land until they reached the Seine. Then, with the river, they turned north again.

The miles passed swiftly beneath their hooves. It was a good time of year to ride. There were lush grasses to provide fodder for the horses, and game was abundant for the men. They rode at ease, following their leader, content to serve his purpose with their swords.

Paris was their destination. Darius had decided to make that great and ancient city his base and the capital from which his new kingdom would be founded. It had stood on the Seine since before recorded history; now that Rome had fallen, both in symbol and in fact, Paris would rise from its ashes as the new Eternal City—with Darius as its eternal King.

Although his men were in good spirits, Darius battled a black mood such as had not touched him for over a century. He kept up a pleasant face to his men, for such was the duty leadership laid upon him, but in truth he was tired of them all. *Mortals.*

They are tools, he had often told Grayson, and his was the skilled hand that wielded them. But now he was like an artisan who has wearied of using worn and awkward tools and longs for new, better ones.

Immortals, an army of them—a *kingdom* of them.

Now that he had granted life to the idea, its possibility

would not leave him alone. Centuries of frustration with the pettiness of mortal lives fed it until each day now, each moment, it loomed larger in his thoughts. He knew Grayson was right.

But the old tools must be used until they were broken. Death would do that for him—death from battle, death from age. Poor little mortals; they did not realize that from the moment of their birth they were already in the grip of death.

Darius laid no battle plans as they neared Paris. He wanted to occupy it, not destroy it. He left his men two miles from the city gates with orders to make a temporary camp. He and Grayson would ride through the city alone, to scout out its weaknesses and take note of its population and weaponry. In a few days, they would return.

Riding away from the army, with only Grayson by his side, Darius felt as if he was leaving a great weight behind.

"It will not be long now, my friend," he said. "Are you ready for what is to come?"

Grayson gave him a genuine smile, untouched by the bleak shadow that seemed to have haunted his eyes so often of late. "I have been ready for decades," he replied.

Darius laughed; it was the first true laughter that had come to his lips in these past weeks. *Decades,* he thought. *Such a little time.* He had been waiting, preparing, for centuries. Yes, he too was ready.

"On, then—to destiny," he said aloud.

Darius frowned. Even from a distance he could see that the gates of Paris were closed. *Why?* he wondered briefly. *Why are they closed on a summer day?* He reined in his horse and sat for a moment, staring at the high walls and the shut gates, his mind racing through possibilities.

Overhead, the raucous caw of a crow suddenly split the semisilence of the hot afternoon. At the sound, a shiver ran down Darius's spine. In more superstitious times, the times in which he had been born, the crow's presence would have been called an ill omen.

Darius gave his head a small shake. Such superstitions were part of his past, part of his early days of mortality; they owned no place in his soul now. He, alone, governed his destiny.

But the crow's presence had disturbed his concentration. He frowned as he urged his horse forward once again.

It was Grayson who first saw the man dressed in priest's robes, who stood unmoving as a statue before the barred gates. He quickly pointed him out to Darius and both sensed the presence of an Immortal. Despite the clothes of a holy man he wore, his hands rested on the pommel of a sword. Its tip was stuck in the ground at his feet, so that it looked like the symbol of his professed faith, like an oversized cross, clearing the way before him.

Darius dismounted and handed the reins of his horse to Grayson. "Wait here," he said as he drew his own long and deadly sword.

"He wears the robes of a Religious," Grayson said. "He may not fight."

Darius's smile was dark and humorless. "He's one of us," he replied. "He'll fight—or he'll die undefended. Either way, his Quickening is mine. And so is Paris."

Darius walked away. Soon the little dips and rises in the land so easily ignored on horseback created a barrier between himself and Grayson. Darius did not care; this was a battle for which he neither wanted nor needed an audience—and Grayson would be waiting when the Quickening was over. Darius would return to his friend even stronger and more unstoppable than before.

A few more feet and the wave of the stranger's Immortality hit him, confirming what Darius already knew. He pulled back his lips, baring his teeth in a grin that looked like a mad wolf's snarl.

He kept walking, closing the gap between himself and this man who thought to bar his way. Foolish, so foolish; nothing would keep him from his goal.

"Come no farther, Darius of the Goths," the man called when Darius was ten feet away.

"You know me?" Darius asked.

"Yes, I know you, as I have known others like you since before the time of mortal memory."

"Then you know why I have come."

The man did not flinch as Darius took a step closer. He did not raise his sword; not a muscle of his body moved. He might have been carved of wood or stone, but for his eyes. They burned with internal fire. As they met and held Darius's own, Darius knew that his four centuries were as a passing night to the time this Immortal had existed.

"I have cared for my people through ages without number," the holy man said, as if reading Darius's thoughts—and still he did not raise his sword. "It was I who painted the walls of the caves in which we lived, holy pictures to guide my people's hands in the hunt or their souls to the afterlife. I blessed them at their births and at their deaths and sought the guidance of the spirits for all their years in between.

"It was at the ritual of Seeing that I died to my mortal life. I mixed the herbs for the sacred draught myself, but they were too strong that time. They did not bring me the Sight; they brought me death—and in that death, there was life.

"I have never forsaken my shaman's vows. I protected my people then and I protect them now. If I let you pass these gates, Darius of the Goths, you will plunge this world into an eternity of darkness. This I cannot allow. Though my way has been a way of peace, I learned to use a sword long before you were born—and I will use it now to stop you."

"What do they call you?" Darius asked. "I like to know the names of the Immortals I kill."

The holy man smiled mirthlessly. "I have been known by many names, words long forgotten to the human tongue. Among our kind, I am most often known as Emrys."

Darius nodded. He had heard the name and the legend of this man's existence. *Emrys,* the oldest of the old; Emrys, whose very name meant Immortality.

And of this Immortal other things were whispered, words of sanctity and of a holiness that outdistanced time itself. Darius had sneered at such reports before, and he dismissed them now. Holy men did not wield swords—and they died so very, very easily.

Darius smiled. "Well, Emrys the Immortal," he said. "I don't care how long you have lived. Today you die."

Darius brought his sword *en garde.* He waited for the other Immortal to do the same. Still the man did not move. It was unnerving to see him without a muscle twitching anywhere. He stood with centuries, eons, of patience.

Darius gave a mental shrug. He brought his sword up, down—and Emrys's sword was there. His movement had been so swift and silent, Darius's eyes had barely registered it.

For a brief moment Darius was confused. He had no idea of the man's weaknesses, his style of movement, his balance. Darius had never seen him walk, did not know if he was right- or left-handed. Emrys's stillness had been a good defense, and a dangerous one if a man lacked skill or speed. Emrys, it appeared, lacked neither—and his stillness had allowed Emrys to take Darius's measure while giving nothing of himself away.

Darius gave his opponent a savage grin. "Well played, Emrys," he said as he backed away slightly.

Then, suddenly, he lunged again, his sword aimed at Emrys's heart. The sword was deflected, but not quite enough. It pierced an arm.

First blood.

But this was no duel of honor to be ended with a wound. This was a fight to the death and both men knew it. As Emrys grunted in pain, Darius attacked again, bringing his sword low to sweep the legs and cut the tendons above the knee.

Once more Emrys parried, but barely in time. He brought the hilt of his sword up, smashing it into Darius's face. Pain exploded behind his eyes as the blood spurted from his broken nose. He staggered backward, giving Emrys the space he needed to attack.

Both men ignored their wounds; Immortal flesh would heal and pain would subside. All that mattered now was survival.

The clash of their swords rang out, hushing the songs of the birds and the cries of the waterfowl on the river. The breeze died and the afternoon sun beat down on them like a third weapon. In the sudden stillness it felt as if time itself was holding its breath, waiting on the outcome of this battle.

Darius was taller, with greater reach, but Emrys had shoulders that were massive with the strength he had built throughout the ages, and a speed such as Darius had never before encountered. Every time he swung his sword, Emrys's weapon was already there, waiting for him. It was a good match, a more even match than Darius had ever before faced.

Time was measured not in seconds and heartbeats, but in lunges and parries, in upward cuts, diagonal slices, and spinning blocks. Strike upon strike, the moments built and vanished. Darius felt his arms growing weary. His body was bathed in sweat and in blood from a dozen small wounds. He was slowing—and he knew it.

But so was Emrys. That amazing speed could last for only so long.

There, the opening was a little wider this time. Darius almost smiled, but he would not waste even that much movement. He reached down into himself, down deep where that last vestige of blood lust and battle fever might reside; he called upon every reservoir of strength his Immortal body held and began to rain down blows. There was no style, no finesse or skill, just blow upon blow meant to drive an opponent into the ground.

Darius felt Emrys's knees buckle. He went down. Then, even as Darius raised his sword for what they both knew was the final cut, the ancient Immortal turned his face toward Darius—and he smiled.

Darius's sword came down.

The Quickening began even before the body hit the ground. Tendrils of power shot through Darius, gripped his soul and held it in unmerciful fingers, as all that Emrys had been came crashing in upon him. This was a Quickening such as Darius had never felt before, for here was Age incalculable; here were time and humanity held captive in a single soul.

Above all, here was holiness.

It came not as ivory-tower brightness, a thing unsullied by the ways of the world. Here was holiness that had walked each path of the human heart, in joys and sorrows that mingled in patterns of dark and light. They played through Darius's brain and burrowed themselves deep into his spirit. Even as his body continued to be buffeted by Immortal winds, his mind swirled in the experiences that were Emrys's, and humanity's, past.

In scenes that shifted more quickly than the flicker of an eagle's eye, Darius saw humankind change with the ages.

Through Emrys's eyes, he saw them huddled around fires in darkened caves, faces painted with ocher and soot. He felt their fear of the night, their fear of the seasons, their fear of life and of death—and in all things they looked to Emrys for their guidance.

Darius felt Emrys's fear, too, for these were the years of his mortality. But he was their shaman and it was his calling to walk the holy paths. He loved his people with a love that was greater than his fear; for their sakes, he sought the way through the darkness.

Carried on the fire of the Quickening, the life and power that had been Emrys continued—building, pouring into Darius until he felt his mind must surely burst. Lightning tore at his body; lightning-fast the scenes came of Emrys's first death and reawakening.

For years he did not know what his Immortality meant. But his body did not change and death did not claim him. He could be forever with his people now and his love for them grew without bounds.

The ages sped past. Emrys's tribe grew and joined with others. Spiritual expressions changed from animal totems to the Mother Goddess, to a pantheon of gods, and still Emrys was there, seeking to give the heart of the Divine to all those around him. Finally came the teachings of the Christian Church and these, too, Emrys embraced, finding in those words of brotherhood and forgiveness an expression of all the ages had created him to be.

From distant places, other Immortals found Emrys—teachers who brought him the rules of The Game, disciples who sought the path of love he walked, and a few who came to destroy. But against these Emrys prevailed so that he could continue to protect and to guide, to keep his timeless vows.

He lived through famines, plagues, and wars—and now Darius lived them too. In each breath he took, in each beating of his heart, Darius felt the pain every human death caused in Emrys's soul.

This pain, born of compassion and tenderness, suffused Darius. It was bright and hot, the fire of the sun burning away the darkness of his heart; it was new and soft, the miracle of birth, replacing apathy with gentleness and selfishness with joy; it was the laughter of an infant, the selfless sacrifice of a parent, the innocence of a child and the patient wisdom of the aged.

Above all, it was love. Unsullied. Undemanding. Immeasurable. It was love that did not seek return.

Love.

The Quickening loosed its grip on Darius. Like a stone plummeting to the earth, he fell to the ground, his face in the dirt, lacking the strength to move himself. The images and memories of Emrys's life were gone—but the love remained.

Darius dragged himself to his knees, shaking his head slowly from side to side. For a moment he did not know where he was—*who* he was. He felt like a delicate mosaic that had been shattered into pieces until no hint of the original pattern remained.

He hunted deep within himself for the feelings that had guided him for so long. They were not there. Gone were the confidence, the arrogance and amusement that had tinged each thought and every action. But who was he now? What was he to be?

Then, in a sudden flash, it crashed in upon his soul, filling him—and he knew. He was forever changed; never again would he walk the path of war.

Darius dragged himself to his knees and looked around. It was like seeing the world for the first time. He felt himself newly created and a part of everything around him.

Is this why you smiled, ancient one? Darius thought as his eyes touched Emrys's body in both grief and gratitude. *Did you know what your Quickening would do to me?*

Darius looked at the sword he had dropped. He would keep it, at least for a time, for to deny what he had been was to deny what he had become—and the sight of the weapon that had caused so many deaths would keep him humble.

But he would not use it. Never again. From this day forward he would work for peace; from holy ground, he would continue the ageless and unending struggle against the darkness. All that Emrys had been, Darius had become and all that Emrys had done, Darius would continue. The chain of love that now bound his heart to the world and people around him, mortal and Immortal alike, was eternally unbroken.

Darius stood. He bent slowly and picked up the sword. Then, after giving a final salute to Emrys's lifeless form, he turned toward where Grayson awaited him. Darius hoped he could make his friend understand. He wanted Grayson by his side in this new life, working with him for peace as he had always worked with him for war. Together.

Chapter Twenty-seven

Grayson was waiting anxiously. He had seen the lightning of the Quickening, and although he wanted to believe nothing could harm Darius, a sense of foreboding filled him. It whispered to him that this opponent was like none other his mentor had ever faced.

When at last the lightning ceased, Grayson wanted to run toward the city gates and see who was left standing. But his fears stayed his feet—his fears and his loyalty. Darius had told him to remain where he was and remain he would, until either Darius gave him further orders or he knew for certain Darius was dead.

If it was the latter, nothing but death would keep him from revenge.

Grayson saw a figure walking toward him with unsteady steps. Even as he watched, the steps grew more certain as strength returned to the body fatigued by a Quickening's force. He stood taller, straightening his shoulders—and with the movement, so familiar, Grayson knew that it was Darius.

Grayson's heart soared with a pride that bordered on worship. Darius lived—Darius the Undefeated. There was nothing, no one, that could stop them now; Grayson knew it as surely as he breathed.

He leaned against his horse and smiled.

He waited until Darius was only a few yards away before taking up the reins of the horses and walking out to meet him.

"Are the gates of the city open yet?" he called as he neared. "Do we enter Paris today, or make camp and ride through the city tomorrow?"

Grayson found it curious when Darius did not answer. He furrowed his brow and looked sharply at the older Immortal.

Something's different, Grayson thought, but there was nothing he could see, nothing he could name. It was a feeling that grew stronger with every step until, when at last he looked into Darius's eyes, Grayson knew the man before him was not the man who had left his side so short a time ago.

"Darius?" Grayson said, making that single word ask a hundred questions.

Darius smiled at him, and it was in that smile that Grayson knew the change had not been imagined. Gone was the wry amusement, the dark humor, the superior air that had been the greatest part of Darius's smile. This expression was gentle, even tender; it was a smile such as a *mortal* might wear.

"There will be no attack on Paris," Darius said.

Grayson felt himself go cold. "What do you mean?" he asked. His voice was clipped and hard, deadly as the sound of a knife slipping its sheath.

"I mean that part of my life is over," Darius replied. "There will be no more fighting—not for me. Oh, Grayson, my friend, how can I make you understand? I've seen and felt things that—"

"No!" Grayson cried. He did not want to hear what Darius was saying. They had been together so long, ridden and planned and fought side by side. And now they were so close to making all he had dreamed for so long come true—

But Darius was continuing, heedless of the knife-edge his words were plunging into Grayson's heart.

"I've been wrong, Grayson. Everything I've been and done for over three centuries has been wrong. Mortal and Immortal, we are not different, except in the span of our years. Our hearts are the same, our needs are the same."

Darius stepped closer. He put his hands on Grayson's shoulders and looked deeply into his eyes. Grayson knew again that this was no longer the man in whom he had trusted—in whom he had *believed*. This Darius was a stranger who wore a familiar face.

"*That* is the Immortal kingdom we will build together. It will be a kingdom of peace, a kingdom *love* will build. Only love lasts forever. I know that now.

"Come with me," this new Darius said in the voice that had ruled Grayson's life for so long. "Walk by my side on this new path. We will build a kingdom just as we planned, but it will be built in a new way, a better way. Help me to right the wrongs that I've done. Help me to heal the wounds of this world."

For an instant, part of Grayson wanted to believe again. But the instant passed almost as it began. He did not want a new path or a new future. He wanted Darius back again—*his* Darius —as he had been, as they had been together.

Suddenly, his sword was in his hand. He lunged at Darius, his sword swung in a wide arc aimed straight at his mentor's head. He would make Darius fight, make him cast off the spell this Quickening had somehow cast over his soul. With blood and anger, he would make Darius remember who he was and who he had been born to be.

Instinct moved Darius. The sword he carried, that he did not want to wield, came up in defense.

"Grayson, don't," he said. "Listen to me. There's another way, a better way, for us to live. I've seen it now—let me show it to you."

"No," Grayson said again. "I won't listen. Not anymore."

Grayson attacked savagely, using every trick the years had taught him. He fought with a desperation that lent strength to his blade. But Darius was better; Darius was always better and it took but a few swift moments before Darius's blade was at Grayson's throat.

"Do it," Grayson snarled. "Take my head. You've taken my hope—now take my Quickening. Let it change you back to who you were."

"No," Darius said. He stepped back, dropping his blade to his side. "I won't kill you. Can't you understand? I don't want to kill anymore. There's been too much blood on my hands. Perhaps, with enough time, I can wash the stain away.

"Come with me, Grayson," Darius invited, pleaded, again. "Work by my side for peace instead of war. Together we can do so much good in the world."

Grayson felt as if the sword in Darius's hand had pierced his heart. He backed away. One step. Two. He swung himself up onto his saddle.

"This isn't over," he said. "You taught me many things over the years. You taught me about order, discipline, and purpose. Well, I have a new purpose now, Darius. I'll be back—to destroy this *thing* you have become."

With that, Grayson dug his heels into his horse's flanks and galloped away.

"Wait, Grayson. Please," Darius called after him. "Listen to me . . ."

But Grayson did not turn around. After a moment, Darius hung his head in defeat, and in shame; if he could not even persuade the one person to whom he had been truly close for centuries, what help would he be able to give the world?

With a deep sigh, Darius took up the reins of his own horse and turned back toward Paris. He would find someone who would give the animal a home.

For himself, holy ground awaited, and the years of trying to undo all that he had done. He would teach peace now, where he had once taught war, and compassion instead of destruction. He did not think the years ahead would be easy, but he knew with certainty that this was the road he must walk.

Inside his soul, he thought he heard Emrys laugh.

Grayson went back to the army and told them of Darius's demise. It was not a lie; the Darius he knew, *they* knew, was dead.

The news of his death seemed to take the heart from them. Grayson understood; he felt the same, but unlike them he had his new purpose to give him strength. It might take centuries, but he had time.

Darius had taught him that, too.

He sent the army north with the promise to rejoin them before the winter snows fell. They were happy to go back to the forests and mountains that had been home to generations of parents and grandparents. Grayson turned south. There was one person he knew would join him in his quest to destroy Darius. Betrayal had hurt her as well.

Callestina.

He rode like a man possessed, stopping only when his horse stumbled with fatigue, and then he begrudged the hours of rest. His new purpose was a taskmaster that drove him without mercy.

He covered the distance back to Cremona in a third of the time it had taken Darius and the army to march north. Alaric's people were still there—and Alaric was with them. They had built no permanent homes. Instead, they were preparing to march south again, to lands given them by the Roman Senate.

Grayson did not care where they went. He was here only because he knew Callestina would still be with her brother.

She must have recognized him from a distance, for she came out to meet him before he reached the camp. Her greeting was cold, but Grayson had expected nothing better. Her expression changed only slightly when he told her what had happened.

"Come back with me, Callestina," he said at last. "Join me—and together we'll find the way to make him pay for all his deceptions."

Callestina turned her head away from him. Grayson knew she felt pain and anger, but he knew of her love as well. And that love, which would not go away, only made the pain worse. His heart felt the same.

"Come with me, Callestina," he said again. "You don't belong here, not anymore. You need someone to teach you the ways of our kind. I will do that—and I will never betray you."

Seacover, present day

And he never did, Callestina—now Cynthia VanDervane—thought as she lay upon her bed beside the still-sleeping Victor Paulus.

Knowing that Alaric would have stormed heaven itself to find her had she just run away, Grayson had gone to the Visigoth and asked for Callestina's hand in honorable marriage. Alaric had consented eagerly, glad to be rid of his stubborn and wayward sister and settle down to his new Roman life with his new Roman wife.

Callestina and Grayson rode north, back to join the army he had left behind. When, many months later, she learned that Alaric had died, she mourned him only in passing. Under

Grayson's careful tutelage she was learning to leave mortal concerns far behind.

They stayed together for the first two centuries of her Immorality. He led his band of marauders through Europe, but without Darius's strength and finesse, Grayson never rose to greatness. He never established a lasting *mortal* kingdom of his own much less an Immortal one; he remained but one of the countless petty warlords inhabiting a bloody era.

From Grayson, Callestina learned many things, including how to use a sword and how to turn her mind to a single, unalterable purpose. Both these skills had kept her alive for over fifteen centuries.

She and Grayson had drifted apart and back together many times, always drawn to reunite for their single shared goal—the destruction of Darius and all he held dear.

Callestina knew Grayson had loved her, at least for a time and in his own way. *Did I ever love him?* Cynthia wondered. She still was not certain, even after all these centuries, what she had felt toward the man who had been her teacher, her lover, her partner—the one man who had truly understood her passion and her need for revenge.

Now the great Goddesses of Destiny have brought his killer to me, she thought with a smile. *Duncan MacLeod. After I kill Paulus—and MacLeod—my revenge will finally be complete.*

And then? a voice within her whispered, but Cynthia had no answer. She had lived for this one purpose for so long, she did not know what her life would hold once it was gone.

It did not matter; all that mattered were the deaths that would come at the point of her sword.

All that mattered was her *Purpose.*

Chapter Twenty-eight

Joe Dawson glanced at the wall clock and sighed. He had been at this work for hours, and now it was time to take his shift at the bar. That was usually the highlight of his day, but today his thoughts were occupied elsewhere.

With Cynthia VanDervane.

He had found her in the Chronicles, all right—under a number of different names and occupations. But her place of residence remained uncharacteristically constant, for an Immortal . . . and so did her goal in that place.

Dawson knew he needed to call MacLeod. *"Observe and record, but never interfere,"* the words of his Watcher's oath filtered up from Joe's subconscious. They were words by which he had lived for most of his adult life—until he met Duncan MacLeod. Actually meeting and becoming friends with the man he had already Watched for fifteen years, whom he had studied and admired, had changed the dynamics of everything in Joe Dawson's life. He owed it to MacLeod to tell him what he had spent the day learning. Considering who else might be involved, he thought he just might owe it to the world, too.

With that in mind, Joe Dawson reached for the phone.

Joe was standing behind the bar, checking inventory and setting up for the evening rush that would soon hit, when MacLeod walked in. As always, the Watcher smiled at the sight of his favorite Immortal.

"Heya, Mac," he said as MacLeod come over and sat down. "I'm glad you could get here so soon. What can I get for you?"

"Just some coffee," MacLeod answered, "and whatever information you thought was so important."

Joe noticed how tired MacLeod looked. *I guess Immortals aren't immune to jet-lag*, he thought as he reached for a cup and the coffeepot. He filled the cup and set it in front of MacLeod, then motioned to the other bartender to come take his place.

He walked around the bar and over to a table where he and MacLeod could speak in private. MacLeod followed him, but once they were seated Joe was not sure how to begin.

"Did you see today's paper?" he said at last, trying to ease into the subject.

"You mean the story about Victor's engagement?" MacLeod asked, his brows coming together in a confused frown. "I saw it. It was a good picture—I think they'll be happy together."

Joe shook his head. "I don't know, Mac," he said. "I've found out a few things about her that might change that."

MacLeod sat up straighter in his chair. "You checked up on her? Why, Joe?"

"Because, as a Watcher, that's my job," he replied. "And I was right—there weren't any reports coming in on her. That means she doesn't have a Watcher. So I started checking back to find out who she really is."

"What did you find out?" MacLeod asked sharply.

"You're not going to like it."

Joe took a deep breath. "Listen, Mac, this isn't our best effort. There's no first-death information. In fact, there's nothing at all before the tenth century—and that came from Darius's Watcher."

MacLeod sat forward in his chair, his gaze suddenly intense. Dawson could see the uneasiness on his face as surely as if he had felt it himself, slowly turning into a rolling boil somewhere near the pit of his stomach.

"Yeah, Darius," he said. "She really had it in for him, going back centuries. She tried several times to discredit him, to get him defrocked as a priest and thrown out of his Order. She even denounced him as a male witch once and tried to have him burned at the stake. None of her efforts worked, though. Each time, his own parishioners flocked to his defense and the only one discredited was Cynthia—at that time she was going by the name Celeste. She'd leave Paris for a while and travel—Italy, Russia, England—but she'd always come back to Paris and try again. And fail again. Then, about two hundred years ago, shortly before the American Revolution, she came to the colonies and disappeared."

"What do you mean, she disappeared?"

"Look, Mac, we're not infallible, you know," Dawson answered. "The New World was pretty big in those days and there wasn't exactly instant communication. Her Watcher broke his leg and by the time it had mended enough for him to move about again, she was gone. She was never spotted again and it was assumed she'd been killed. Her file was taken off active and put into the history archives."

"You're sure we're talking about the same woman?" MacLeod asked when Joe was done.

Dawson nodded. "It was that picture in the paper that made me certain. She's beautiful enough to have attracted attention. Several of her Watchers have sketched her. It's the same woman."

The two men sat in silence for a moment, each of them contemplating the possible impact of Joe's discovery.

"So, what are you going to do, Mac?" Joe asked at last.

"I don't know," was the answer. He could almost see MacLeod's mind sorting through the possibilities, trying to find the one answer his instincts told him was right.

"You know, Mac, I could be wrong. This might not mean anything," Joe said, wanting to give his friend some hope. "I told you we lost track of her for about two hundred years— and two centuries can really change a person."

MacLeod gave Joe a worn smile that held more than just time or wisdom. It was an expression of all the changes, all the good and evil, MacLeod himself had seen and felt and been in the long centuries past.

"They certainly can," he said softly.

MacLeod finished his coffee and stood. "Thanks, Joe," he said.

"I wish it had been better news."

"Yeah—so do I," MacLeod said. "Do me a favor. Keep

looking—I need to know about those two hundred years. I owe it to Darius."

Joe nodded. He would have kept looking anyway; that was part of his job as a Watcher. But on any other case, he might have turned the job over to the research department and let them spend the hours at the computer or in the archives that this job might take. For MacLeod, he would do it himself.

"And, Joe," MacLeod said hesitantly. Dawson could tell these were words he did not want to say. "Check Grayson's file first."

Again, Joe nodded, understanding what those words meant. "I'll call as soon as I find anything."

MacLeod nodded his thanks and turned. As he walked toward the door, Dawson could see that his step was a little heavier than it had been when he arrived.

MacLeod drove his black Thunderbird down the busy Seacouver streets, only vaguely aware of the heavy traffic. The greater part of his mind was turning over the current situation and trying to look at it from every angle. He kept coming back to the same point: Paulus had to know about Cynthia's years as Darius's enemy.

MacLeod realized with a start that he had been automatically heading back toward the dojo. The foundation's house, in which Victor Paulus was staying, was on the other end of town. MacLeod turned the car around.

The house was a modest two-story building, mock-Tudor and brick. It looked so quiet when MacLeod pulled up and got out of his car, he wondered if Victor was still sleeping, fighting the same sense of jet lag MacLeod could feel whispering to his muscles and his mind.

Perhaps he should leave and come back later, he thought, sitting behind the steering wheel and looking up at the house. Then Victor Paulus opened the front door and waved a greeting.

Well, here goes, MacLeod thought as he got out of the car and started up the walk. He still did not know what he was going to say, exactly, but he had the truth on his side. And it was the truth he would tell—if not quite the whole of it.

"Duncan," Victor said, smiling as MacLeod drew near.

"Come in, come in. I was going to call you today and let you know we'd arrived."

"Well, I saw the news of your engagement in the paper," MacLeod began. He let the rest die unsaid, for now.

Paulus's smile broadened. "Yes, that was nice, wasn't it. But I'm afraid you've missed Cynthia. She's gone shopping."

"It wasn't Cynthia I came to see," MacLeod said softly as he entered the house.

Paulus led the way into the living room and gestured toward the couch and chairs. "Please, Duncan, have a seat," he said. "Can I get you something? Maybe some coffee?"

MacLeod shook his head. "No, thanks," he said. Quickly, he searched for the right words, for gentle words, with which to begin this conversation. But he realized there was nothing to do but plow ahead. He owed it to Darius for friendship past; he owed it to Victor for friendship present.

"Listen, Victor," he said, "I've come to talk to you about Cynthia. I think there's something you should know."

The smile instantly faded from Victor's face. "Cynthia's all right, isn't she? She only left here about an hour ago—"

"She's all right," MacLeod assured him quickly. "It's about her past—and about Darius."

MacLeod took a deep breath, but Paulus stopped him before he could go on. "She's already told me," he said.

"She has?" MacLeod was surprised, but then instantly cautious again. "What did she tell you?"

Victor motioned again toward the chairs. "Please, Duncan, sit down."

He waited until MacLeod took a seat on the couch, then he sat in a chair across from him and leaned forward.

"You don't know Cynthia very well, in spite of the time we all spent together. Let me tell you something about her," he began. "She is a very beautiful young woman. In fact, I can hardly believe she would choose to love someone like me— but they say love is blind, and who am I to argue with my good fortune?

"She is beautiful, she is accomplished and well-traveled, but there are things in her past that have caused her a great deal of pain. Her relationship with Darius is one of those things."

"I'm not sure I understand what you mean," Duncan said cautiously. From the time he had spent with them in Sudan, and from what little Paulus just had said, MacLeod was fairly certain that Cynthia still had not told him about her Immortality. MacLeod wanted to hear exactly what story she *had* told him.

"Cynthia grew up in Belgium," Paulus began, "in a small town near the border of Picardy. Her family was Catholic. Unfortunately, the priest in that town had many problems—he was a little too fond of his wine, for one. That was easily overlooked—he was the only priest for miles around. But his other problem was much more serious, and much more secret. He was a pedophile. He molested several of the children in the parish, including one of Cynthia's best friends. Cynthia was the only one who would believe her—and that friend later turned to drugs and alcohol, finally dying of an overdose when she was eighteen. Cynthia blames what that priest did for her friend's death."

Yes, MacLeod thought, *that's just the sort of story that would touch someone like Paulus. She's clever—I'll have to be careful not to underestimate her.*

"Cynthia came to Paris when she was twenty," Paulus continued. "She found an apartment not too far from Rue St. Julien le Pauvre and after a while she began attending Mass at Darius's parish. You know how the children loved Darius—and he loved them. Cynthia saw him playing in the churchyard with the children and it made her uneasy. Then one of the parishioners told her that it often seemed Father Darius spent more time with the children than with anyone else. It was an overstatement and no doubt well-intentioned, but to Cynthia it was as if her childhood was happening all over again. She was determined to keep what happened to her friend from happening to another child. She became obsessed with discrediting Darius."

"But surely, no one in the parish believed her," MacLeod prompted. Cynthia had tried to discredit Darius many times throughout the centuries, according to the Watcher reports. Which century's story was she telling? Duncan wondered.

"Of course no one believed her," Paulus answered. "But in some ways that only made it worse—no one had believed her friend, either. Every time Cynthia saw Darius with the children, innocent though it was, it just added fuel to the fire.

"She worked for a magazine at the time and she was sent away on an assignment. When she returned, Darius was dead. It shocked her so much, and the grief of his parish was so genuine, that she began to see past her memories to the person Darius really was. After that, she quit her job at the magazine and began to work for the causes Darius supported. Reparation, she calls it, for her misjudgment of him."

"And that's how you met," Duncan said, finishing the tale for him.

Paulus nodded. "Yes," he said. "That's how we met."

"Have you ever checked out her story?" Duncan asked.

"Of course not," Paulus answered before Duncan could continue. "Have you ever been in love—Duncan? Yes, I see by your face that you have. Then you know that love, if it is to last, must be based in trust. I love Cynthia—and I trust her. I will not go behind her back to check on anything she has told me. I spend much of my life trying to persuade and promote trust between nations. Can I do any less in my personal life?"

"But, surely, this is important enough to be cautious. You're a well-known and very public figure, an easy target for many things—blackmail, assassination—"

"From Cynthia?" Paulus was incredulous. "No, Duncan, you really don't know her. Cynthia is every bit as sweet and beautiful on the inside as she appears on the outside."

Duncan could see that he would get no further with Paulus. Here was a man in whom Darius's teachings had truly come to fruition, who would see nothing but the potential for good, even for godliness, in all people. And he was also a man in love. What hope did reason and experience have against that—even four hundred years of experience?

No, Duncan knew he would have to deal directly with Cynthia. She would find that he was no Victor Paulus; it would take more than a sad story to convince him of her sincerity. Much more.

He stood and held out his hand to Victor.

"I know your concern is well-meant," Paulus said, "and is

based in the love we both had for Darius, but you can rest assured."

Duncan nodded but said nothing.

"You are still planning to come to our wedding?" Paulus continued warmly. "I know Cynthia will want you there, too."

Again MacLeod nodded. "Send me an invitation and I'll be there," he said, knowing that if Dawson confirmed what he feared might be true, he would do everything he could to prevent the marriage from ever happening.

As he left Paulus on the doorstep, MacLeod hoped Dawson found that information soon. The world had already lost Darius—Duncan had every intention of making sure it did not lose Victor Paulus, too.

Chapter Twenty-nine

Two hours later, Cynthia entered the temporary home she and Paulus were sharing, her arms loaded with packages. Victor immediately put aside the paper he had been writing and hurried to relieve her.

"I see you had a good day," he said, his arms loaded now as he followed her into the bedroom.

"Oh, I did," she said. "There are wonderful stores here. I found a shop down in the sari district, full of the most beautiful silks. I even bought you something."

Paulus put the packages on the bed and Cynthia began to rummage through them. A moment later, she shook out a shirt and held it up against him. It was pale green, raw silk, with tiny dark green dots.

"There," she said. "I knew that would bring out the green flecks in your eyes. You can wear it tomorrow when you give your speech."

Cynthia looked up at him. Victor was smiling, but there was also a serious cast to his face.

"So, how was your day?" she asked, turning to place the shirt on the bed. "Anything interesting happen?"

"No, nothing much," he replied. He was not very good at lying and Cynthia could hear in his voice that he was holding something back. She turned and looked at him in silence, knowing that if she waited he would tell her what was on his mind. It did not take long.

"Duncan MacLeod came by today," Victor began slowly.

"Oh? That's nice," she replied softly. Inside, she felt a sudden stillness grip her. She knew the feeling well; it was at such moments that the Goddesses of Destiny stopped their fateful weaving of time while the threads of the future were chosen.

"So what did Duncan have to say?" she prompted, knowing Victor both wanted to tell her and was hesitant at the same time.

"Well, you must understand—Duncan was a very good friend of Darius," Victor spoke very slowly. "He found out about your past . . . connection—"

"And he thought you should know about it, too," Cynthia finished for him, keeping her voice light. She turned back around to face him. "Is that all?"

Cynthia stepped closer to Victor and slipped her arms around his waist, nestling her head into the hollow of his shoulder. "But you already know all about that."

"So I told him," Paulus replied. He put his arms around her and kissed the top of her head. Cynthia felt him relax.

Damn that MacLeod, her thoughts were racing. *I'll have to take care of him sooner than I'd planned, before he ruins everything.*

She held on to Paulus for a moment longer, making certain that her presence lowered any subconscious defenses MacLeod's words had raised. Then, after a lingering kiss, she released him and turned back to the packages piled on the bed.

"I'd better get these things hung up before any wrinkles set in," she said, giving herself an excuse to be busy. She wanted time to think. She had planned to face MacLeod *after* she had killed Paulus. She wanted MacLeod to know that Darius's teachings were dead *before* he died. Now he had changed things by coming here today. How had he found out who she was?

"And I need to go finish my paper," Paulus replied.

"Let me know when you're done and I'll make us some coffee," Cynthia said. "I bought some delicious cake we can have at the same time."

"You spoil me," Victor said, and with another quick kiss, he left the room.

Once he was gone, Cynthia smiled, but there was no tenderness in the expression. Victor was so easy to reassure so easy to manipulate, it almost took the fun out of this little game. He would remain her devoted and trusting fiancé— right up until the end.

Well, he didn't learn that from Darius, she thought. Others might speak of Darius's goodness, his sanctity, but to her he would always be Darius the Betrayer.

Damn that MacLeod, she thought again. She hated it when her plans, so carefully thought out—just as Grayson had so long ago taught her—had to be altered. But there was no help for it; she would have to challenge MacLeod soon, before he could convince Victor of his danger.

Joe Dawson did not have the chance to get back to his computer until after the bar closed. But once he did, he was prepared to work through the night, if necessary. It would not be the first time he had lost a night's sleep on Watcher business, and he knew it would not be the last. And this was more than just *Watcher* business; this was about the life of Duncan MacLeod.

For any other Immortal, Dawson would not have felt the importance of these answers so personally. But Duncan MacLeod was something special, and not just because he was Dawson's friend. There was an ingrained honor about the man that Joe knew he could trust. It was there in all of the records of MacLeod's life, and it was there in a thousand instances since they had known each other. Duncan MacLeod *cared* in a way few other Immortals did—hell, few *mortals*, for that matter. And because MacLeod cared, he *mattered*—not just to Joe Dawson, but to the future of humankind.

Dawson turned on his computer and punched in the access code for the Archives.

Duncan MacLeod was punching the black hanging bag when Joe Dawson entered the hallway of the dojo early the next morning. He stood for a moment, looking through the windows at the strong athleticism of the man. Joe felt a quick, passing twinge of envy at the way MacLeod bounced on the balls of his feet.

Oh well, he thought, *that's life. You play the hand you're dealt.*

The truth was, if he hadn't lost his legs in Vietnam his life would have been far different—and he liked his life. He was proud of his bar and his band and all that he had accomplished. Without that explosion and its consequences, he would never have learned about Immortals or become a Watcher—or met Duncan MacLeod. The passing envy he sometimes felt over the man's physical skills did not begin to compare with the compensations of such a friendship.

He stepped through the double doors. In one fluid motion MacLeod completed the punch he had just thrown and spun to face Dawson, hands still at the ready.

"Joe," he said. It was both a greeting and an acknowledgment to his conscious mind that here was friend, not foe. He dropped from his fighting stance, then walked over and grabbed the towel he had left on the bench. Draping it around his neck, he used the corner to wipe the sweat of his workout from his face. Dawson followed him as he headed for the privacy of the office.

"It's not good news, is it?" MacLeod asked, studying Joe's face. Dawson shook his head.

"She was in Grayson's file," Joe began, "just like you thought. I told you we lost track of her about two hundred years ago when she came to the New World. It was easy to do in those days—communication was tough, life was difficult, at least for us mortals trying to colonize a new country."

"Joe, I know my history."

Dawson gave a little, self-effacing grin. "Yeah, right," he said. "Anyway, we lost sight of several Immortals in those days, but we kept watching for them until they resurfaced. This one didn't—except once, when she hooked up with Grayson about one hundred seventy years ago, in Canada. She had changed her name to Sharon Talbot and she'd dyed her hair red—perhaps that's why no one recognized her right away, and she didn't stick around long enough for any connection to be made. She became Grayson's lover and his business partner."

"Grayson," MacLeod said. His voice was soft, but there was no mistaking the deadly edge to it.

"Yeah, Grayson. Do you think she's here to continue his work?"

"I don't know," MacLeod answered, his voice still tight and hard. "But I intend to find out."

"Listen, Mac," Joe began, "be careful, okay? I mean—"

MacLeod looked at him, but Dawson shrugged. "She's lived this long," he said. The rest of the statement remained unspoken; both men knew what it meant. To stay alive in The Game took skill—and it also took luck. No matter how great your training, one unlucky step and it could all be over.

The phone rang, shattering the stillness that had fallen in the office. MacLeod grabbed for it. The conversation was short, his answers terse, and Dawson had no doubt who was on the other end.

"When?" he asked as MacLeod hung up.

"Tonight—nine o'clock. She says she just wants to talk."

"You believe her?"

MacLeod gave Joe a "you've got to be kidding" look, then he shrugged.

"Is she coming here?" Dawson asked.

MacLeod shook his head. "It seems she's intent on retracing Grayson's footsteps. She wants to meet at the waterfront. In the park."

"Do you think she knows what she's doing?" Dawson asked.

"Maybe—and if she does, it answers several questions at once."

Dawson thought carefully about his next words. Cynthia VanDervane, whatever else she was, was a beautiful woman. Dawson hoped MacLeod's long-standing sense of chivalry would not get in the way.

"Listen," he began, still searching for the necessary words. "I don't want another assignment," he said at last. "So watch yourself, okay?"

MacLeod flashed him a slightly world-weary grin. "I always do," he said.

MacLeod watched Dawson leave. He knew what the Watcher had left unsaid, and he was grateful for both the silence and the concern.

It was true—Duncan MacLeod disliked fighting women. He knew that some of the Immortals he called friend thought this attitude a weakness—Methos certainly did. But MacLeod believed women were to be cherished. Perhaps it was the teachings of his childhood—teachings that were never completely gone, no matter how long you lived—or perhaps it was just part of who he was.

He found himself wishing he could believe something of what Paulus had told him about Cynthia. Not the tale of her childhood; that was the type of lie all Immortals told, a tale of an identity that never existed and experiences that were never lived. What he wanted to believe was that she had changed and that continuing Grayson's revenge upon Darius, through the death of his protégés, was not her goal.

Maybe, he told himself, it was a coincidence that she wanted to meet in the same place he and Grayson had first crossed swords—an easily found place in an unfamiliar city. Or, maybe she wanted to meet there to show him that she was putting all of Grayson's enmities to rest. But he was no fool, and every instinct he had told him to prepare himself for the possibility of battle with Cynthia.

As he sat in the silence of his office, he heard Darius's voice speaking words he had first said to Duncan a century ago.

"Some people choose the path of their own destruction," the memory said, *"and nothing we do can turn them from it."*

Chapter Thirty

Paris, 1842

Duncan MacLeod stood on the deck of the river barge, *La Penèlopé*, as it glided up the river into Paris. He marveled at how much the city had changed in the last twenty-six years, how much it had grown—and how much had remained the same. Most of all, this still was Paris, home of a thousand joyful memories.

Those memories had drawn him here now.

For the last two and a half decades, MacLeod had dwelt in the New World, watching the growing pains of a young nation with world-weary eyes. Not all of what he had seen was good.

The peace for which he sought, that Darius had wished him when they last parted, had continued to elude MacLeod. Neither had the wanderlust that had been his companion throughout the majority of his Immortal life been stilled by the new country. He had seen mountain ranges and mighty rivers, waterfalls and primordial forests, unsullied by the march of "civilization." But that was all changing.

As the exploration of the northern continent expanded westward, MacLeod's own travels had taken him south. He had passed through Mexico and Central America, and seen the destruction the Conquistadors had wrought upon the native cultures. He knew the same thing was happening to the north, in the land he had just left.

He had pushed on, into the wildness of South America, into the heart of Peru, searching for the elusive *something* that continued to whisper in half-remembered dreams and drew him ever onward. Perhaps it was peace; perhaps it was the *be-*

longing he had known before Immortality had set him apart from all that he had once known, believed, and loved.

And perhaps it was none of these things. But whatever it was, his search went on.

Darius had often told MacLeod that his answers could never be found by searching other places besides his own soul; it was only within that greatest of unexplored realms that true peace could ever be found.

When MacLeod had emerged, worn and weary, from the jungles of Peru, his first thought had been to see Darius again. From Lima, he was able to catch a ship traveling around the Horn and on to Europe. He had disembarked at Le Havre, taken a barge down the Seine, and here he was again in the City of Lights.

The barge pulled up to the dock in the shadow of Notre Dame, and MacLeod found himself excited to see his old friend again. How much would Darius have changed? he wondered. Twenty-six years was not much time in the life of an Immortal, despite the incalculable differences it could make in the mortal world.

The ramp was finally lowered onto the dock. MacLeod threw a quick wave at the captain and crew who had been his companions on the voyage, then picked up his duffel bag and disembarked.

He could not help but smile as he walked down the street, still feeling the roll and pitch of the deck beneath his legs. He knew from experience that it would be several days before the feeling left him completely. But that was not what made him smile. It was the familiarity of the docks.

Gone were the men in uniform, maimed and wounded remnants of a recent war. Other beggars had taken their place, all asking for a *sou* from the passing stranger. Prostitutes still plied their trade. They had faces different from those of the girls MacLeod had known, but the offers were still the same.

MacLeod headed for where the *La Poule Aux Oeufs d'Or* had once stood, curious to see if the tavern in which he had once had rooms remained. The hotel that he found in its stead bore the same name, but little resemblance to the humble building where he had spent so many nights. The proprietor, Monsieur Vernier had the same name as the innkeeper

MacLeod had known before. The grandson, MacLeod guessed as he shook the hand of the young man before him, who was greeting guests with a practiced, professional smile.

MacLeod paid for his room in advance, then went upstairs to unpack and clean up before heading to the Rue St. Julien le Pauvre and Darius.

The afternoon had become dusk and the gaslights lining the Paris streets had begun to twinkle when Duncan finally left the hotel. He stopped and bought a bottle of red wine and a long loaf of fresh bread to take to his reunion. He thought he would stop and perhaps buy some cheese as well. It would be good to share a meal with Darius again, even one so simple. Better yet would be the conversation and the time in the priest's peaceful presence.

MacLeod rounded a corner and stopped as the presence of another Immortal seared through him, unmistakable as the clash of thunder or the roar of cannon fire. MacLeod quickly put his packages aside and drew his sword. He did not want to fight, but neither was he willing to die.

Carefully, slowly, he walked forward, senses on the alert. Up ahead, he saw someone bending over the prone figure of a man. The scene brought a wave of *déjà vu.*

It can't be, he thought as the figure straightened into the outline of a woman. But when she turned, bloodstained sword in her hand, there was no mistaking the face that was revealed by the distant streetlights.

"Violane?" His shocked voice was barely more than a whisper. But she heard it and came toward him, swinging her sword nonchalantly.

"Duncan MacLeod," she said, her hips swaying in a street-walker's saunter. "Back in Paris, and going to see Father Darius, no doubt. Have you come to save me a second time?"

MacLeod lowered his sword. "What are you doing here—like this?" he asked her. "You're not the child you were before. You know there are other ways for you to live now."

"What do you know about my life? About the ways open to a woman?" she said sharply. Duncan was dismayed to hear the hardness in her voice, to see the bitterness and anger marking a face that otherwise looked so very young.

"Aye," Duncan said placatingly, "here in Paris the choices for you may be limited. But there is a whole world out there, Violane—you've time to see it."

Violane laughed. It was a harsh, mirthless sound. "And do what?" she asked. "Be a healer, like Father Darius taught me?"

"Aye—'tis a good profession."

"I tried that," Violane answered. Again, Duncan saw bitterness twist her face. "But who wants a healer with a face that looks barely out of the nursery? What woman wants a *child* to deliver her baby? But on the streets—oh, here a young face is an asset. It works well for me."

"You could go to the New World, to America—start a new life. If it's money you need—"

Again Violane laughed. "Go to America," she sneered. "Start a new life—as what, a farmer's wife? Be some man's property, you mean, his beast of burden. Let him beat me because I cannot bear him children. No, Duncan MacLeod—I don't want your money. I want your head."

She raised her sword and swung at him. Duncan knocked it away easily.

"Violane—stop," he said. "It doesn't have to be like this. You could have a good life in America. I'll help you."

"I don't want your help—just your Quickening," she answered. She swung her sword again. "You're right about one thing," she said. "I know who I am now; I know about how Immortals stay alive. Darius sent me to a good teacher."

Her lunge was sudden and well-aimed. It almost caught Duncan off guard. Almost. He quickly sidestepped and parried.

"Violane," he almost pleaded. "Stop—I don't want to fight you."

"Then die for me," she answered.

Her movements were quick and practiced, but her aim was only for primary targets. She did not try to weaken her opponent by striking at the easier targets of arms or legs. That might have granted her some advantage. But Violane was too eager, and she tried to kill. It was easy for Duncan, who had learned from masters, to counter her moves. He trapped her blade with his own, circled and flicked. Her sword went flying, then clattered to the ground. MacLeod stepped, brought his foot behind her ankles, and swept backward. Violane fell—helpless and now weaponless.

MacLeod stepped back. "Violane," he said, "I will be with Father Darius. If you change your mind, come there. I meant it when I said I'd help you."

He turned on his heel and walked away. As he stopped to pick up the bread and wine he had left near the alleyway, he heard her rise. There came the sound of running feet and the cry erupting from her throat.

Duncan's instincts, his training for survival, took over. Sword again in hand, he spun around. Violane was nearly on him. Her sword was raised to strike; her face was twisted in murderous rage.

No time for thought—MacLeod swung his *katana*. Its polished blade caught the light and flashed like an arching silver rainbow as it descended, connected, sliced through.

Violane's body fell forward, carried by her own momentum. Duncan wanted to scream with the pain this action had caused him, but her Quickening caught him. It seared and twisted through him, squeezed the breath from him in its passing, until he was left limp and wrung, on his knees in the Paris streets.

Duncan's only thought now was to reach Darius. His legs felt almost too weak to bear his weight but he forced himself to rise and start to walk, knowing that the weakness would soon pass. But the other feelings—the sorrow, the remorse, the guilt at Violane's death—these would stay with him.

Darius answered Duncan's knock, but the joy on the priest's face quickly faded. "What has happened?" he asked as he ushered MacLeod into his familiar parlor.

"I met Violane," MacLeod answered dully. "I killed her."

For a moment, Darius hung his head in sorrow. Then he looked into Duncan's face, and MacLeod saw the fathomless depths of compassion in his eyes. He felt a little of his own sorrow heal.

"Tell me," Darius said.

Duncan dropped heavily into a chair and began to speak. Darius did not move as he listened. He stood in utter stillness until Duncan had finished.

"What happened, Darius? Tell me that," Duncan said at last, hearing the sound of desperation in his own voice. It had felt so *right* to help Violane. In the last quarter century, MacLeod had often thought of her here with Darius, happy and well, or wondered into what life Darius's teachings had taken her. The memory of Violane's soft smile and the look of peace on her face when he had last seen her had stayed with MacLeod through many a dark and lonely hour.

Now he had killed her; MacLeod felt as if his soul was bleeding to death.

Darius heard the pain in Duncan's voice. He sighed deeply. "Do not blame yourself, my friend," he said, coming over to take the chair next to Duncan's. "Some people choose the path of their own destruction and nothing we do can turn them from it. Violane was such a one.

"But what happened after I left?" Duncan asked again. "She seemed so happy here."

Darius nodded. "For a time she was," he said, "a few months. Then she began to grow restless. But if she was going to leave holy ground, I knew she had to learn the ways of our kind. I arranged for her to go live with Marie Guilliard and her husband and to learn from them. Hubert is mortal, but he knows the truth about Marie and he is an ex-solider. They are good people, and I knew that they would train Violane in the skills she needed to stay alive. Marie and Hubert have a farm a few miles south of Paris. Marie often acts as healer and mid-wife to the others in the area. She said she would be happy to continue teaching Violane in those skills also.

"Violane stayed with them for two years. Marie came here often with news of how Violane was doing—everything seemed to be well. Then one night Violane disappeared. She stole what money Marie and Hubert had and went off with a young man who had been working on a neighboring farm since shortly after Napoleon's defeat. Marie and Hubert were heartbroken. They had come to look on Violane as a daughter. They searched the countryside for her, but without success. They even came here, to Paris, but there was still no sign of Violane. She did not want to be found by them, just as she did not want to be helped by you. It is a difficult thing to learn,

my friend," Darius concluded, "but you cannot save them all.
No one can."

"Not even you?" Duncan asked softly.

"Not even me," Darius answered with infinite sadness.
"But come, let us have some tea and put this business behind
us. Violane now has the peace she would not let herself find
in life."

Darius's words, like his presence, were soothing. Duncan
let them wash over him. He knew what Darius said was
true—people did choose the path of their own lives, mortal
and Immortal alike; victor or victim, you claimed your own
role by the choices you made along the way.

"Tomorrow I will say a Mass for Violane's soul," Darius
said as he set the pot of tea on the table. Duncan smelled the
well-remembered scent of flowers and herbs.

"Aye," he said, "I'd like to attend."

Darius smiled his gentle, understanding smile. "I thought
you would," he said as he sat down. "Now, tell me all you
have done since we last met. It has been how long?"

"Twenty-six years," Duncan replied.

"So long as that?" Darius said. "I'm afraid I no longer notice time as I once did. But from all I hear, much has happened to that small country since its beginnings. It is not so
small anymore, yes?

"Oh, do not look so surprised, Duncan MacLeod," Darius
said in answer to the look on MacLeod's face. "I am not so cut
off here as you might think. I have many visitors—most of
whom visit me far more often than you do."

Duncan smiled as he took a sip from his tea, conscious
again of the healing effect of Darius's presence. Yes, it was
good to be back here. He did not know how long he would
stay in Paris this time, but he knew here was one place he
could always call home, one man he could always call friend.

That was the choice he made for *his* life.

Chapter Thirty-one

Seacouver, present day

Duncan stood at the park watching the play of the city lights across the water. It should have been a restful scene, but Duncan MacLeod felt no peace, no silence in his soul. A part of him wanted to hold on to the hope that this day would end without bloodshed. Another part of him, the greater part of him still whispered a warning.

Where is your wisdom when I need it, Darius? His thoughts sent the question into the ether. *Would you know what to say to Cynthia when she arrives? Will I?*

Then there was no more time to wonder. The familiar sense of an approaching Immortal announced her presence several long seconds before the sound of her footsteps reached his ears.

She walked past him without a greeting, over to the hanging sculpture that adorned this part of the park. It was modern, shaped like a great circle, yet somehow reminiscent of the ancient mysteries of the East. Duncan had always found himself attracted to it, yet now he shivered as Cynthia ran a finger down its outer rim.

"You met him here once, didn't you?" she said, still not turning to face MacLeod. "You started to fight, but you were interrupted."

"Who?" Duncan asked, knowing the answer but wanting to hear Cynthia say it.

Cynthia turned around slowly. "Oh, don't be coy, MacLeod," she said. "It doesn't suit you. I know all about you—you're rather famous among our kind. Let's see, what are some of the words I've heard to describe you? Chivalrous, certainly, though that seems to mean different things to different people. I've also heard you called a bloody nuisance and someone who lets his heart get in the way of his judgment. Do you think those are fair assessments, MacLeod?"

"What do you want, Cynthia?"

"Just to come to an understanding. Is that too much to ask?"

It was a cat-and-mouse game; Duncan knew it, but right now he had to play along. He needed to know her real intentions.

"Go on," he said.

"It's very simple," she continued. "A deal—you leave me alone and I'll leave you alone. For now, anyway."

MacLeod could almost hear Grayson's voice in her words. *"I'm prepared to offer you a deal, Duncan MacLeod. . . . All you have to do is nothing. . . ."*

Grayson had been after Paulus—also?

"And if I don't?" MacLeod asked.

Cynthia sighed. "Then this," she said as with a swift motion she pulled her sword from beneath her coat. MacLeod recognized it at once. It was a Kris broadsword, the same type of sword Grayson had carried.

Cynthia saw the recognition on his face and she smiled. "Yes," she said, "he was my teacher. But then, you knew that, didn't you?"

MacLeod did not bother to answer. He drew his *katana* and faced her. Neither of them moved for a moment as Cynthia went on smiling. Her eyes raked him up and down, assessing him in a manner that had nothing to do with swordplay.

"You know, Grayson always said you had great potential. It seems such a shame to waste you. Why don't you accept my offer, Duncan MacLeod?"

Once more, Duncan had a flash of *déjà vu*; Grayson had used almost those same words. Did Cynthia know she was echoing him? Just what *did* Cynthia know?

As she spoke, Cynthia was inching around to his right. Her voice was low and melodic and oh, so feminine. Here was an enemy, immensely dangerous; a tigress poised to strike.

"Victor said you came to see him today," Cynthia continued, still slowly circling, "to warn him about me. That wasn't very chivalrous, was it, Duncan? And what a waste of effort. Of course, he didn't believe you. He's mine, body and soul, for as long as I want him—the poor bloody fool. But then, he is mortal. Don't you think these mortals are fools, MacLeod? Oh, wait—I forgot. You like these pitiful creatures, don't you?"

"Why are you here, Cynthia?" Duncan asked again. "What is it you want with Paulus?"

Cynthia chuckled low in her throat. "So impatient for an Immortal," she chided. "What's your hurry—is the world waiting for you to save it? Oh, all right, Duncan MacLeod. I'm here to finish something, work that was started centuries ago."

"Darius is dead, " MacLeod answered her. "You can't hurt him now. It's over."

"No," Cynthia snapped, but she reined in her anger as quickly as it had flashed. "It's not over. It won't be over until everything he loved is destroyed.

"That was quite a pretty story I told Victor, wasn't it?" she said more calmly. "Of course, none of it was true—but you know that. Do you want to know the truth, Duncan MacLeod? Can you stand to hear the *truth* about your precious Darius?"

Duncan said nothing. Into what shape had her hatred, her obsession, bent and twisted the past?

"Darius was a liar," she said. "He lied with his words and he lied with his body. Oh, I can see you don't believe me, but there is so much about him you never knew. But I knew him—before he put on that brown robe and began the greatest lie of all.

"I was Darius's lover," she said almost proudly. "He was the greatest of us. I know—over the centuries I've been with so many. But none of them was as great as Darius. Warrior, leader, lover—no one else *ever* equaled him. He took me to his bed and, after I had given him my heart, he tossed me away like a broken plaything that no longer amused him. He used me and then betrayed me, and not even death can absolve him of that."

"You said yourself, it was centuries ago—" MacLeod began.

"What do the centuries matter?" Cynthia snapped again. "He betrayed us all. He could have created the greatest kingdom the world had ever seen. He let us believe in him, in who he was and what he could do, and then he abandoned us. He left us with *nothing*."

"No," Duncan said softly. "What he gave, what he taught, was so much more."

Cynthia laughed. "Well, you believe that, Duncan MacLeod. I do not."

With that, Cynthia lunged. She darted in, slashed her sword quickly across his left biceps and darted out again. MacLeod had time to do no more than gasp before she was out of reach. She was quick and well-trained—deadly, if he was not very, very careful.

He knew her voice had lulled him. It was a weapon and she used it well. MacLeod steeled himself against it, against all of her charms. May Ling had taught him centuries ago that a woman could be as deadly as any man.

She saw the emotions on his face, the set of his chin that announced his resolve, and she laughed. "It is a good Game we play, is it not, Duncan MacLeod? Do you feel your heart pumping warrior's blood, feel the heat surging through your veins? Is it not almost as good as making love, to feel this alive? *This* is what Darius would have denied us all, as he denied it to himself."

Once more Cynthia darted, but this time MacLeod was ready for her. As she thrust her blade forward, he spun outside her guard and brought the pommel of his hilt down on her wrist, deadening the nerves. Her sword dropped uselessly away.

Cynthia dropped with it, rolled, and picked up the sword in her other hand. Then she laughed once more.

"Very good, Duncan," she said. "I'd heard you were impressive. Oh, why are we wasting time on this. Come with me and I'll show you delights such as no woman has ever shown you. I've had centuries to learn them, and we have *time* to enjoy them all."

"And Victor Paulus?" MacLeod asked.

"Oh, why should his little life matter? Mortal men die every day and the world goes on without them. *Ours* are the only great lives; ours is the only Game that matters. Come play it with me."

Cynthia attacked, this time with her left hand. MacLeod had met few left-handed swordsmen in his time, but he had met them and he had trained against them. As her sword narrowly missed plunging between his ribs, slicing instead through flesh and muscle, he silently thanked the many teachers who had graced his past. The cut Cynthia's blade had left was deep and it was painful, but it would heal—and he still had his head.

This time MacLeod spun inside her circle of defense. Again he used the pommel of his sword as a weapon. He drove it back into her solar plexus, knocking the wind from her body and sending her lungs and diaphragm into a spasm that denied her air.

She doubled over with the force of the blow, instinctively taking a step backward. But MacLeod was not done yet. He brought his elbow up into her face, knocking her head back and robbing her of balance. His leg whipped out and caught her ankle. Cynthia fell. By the time she hit the ground, MacLeod had turned and had his sword at her throat.

He could not miss the sudden fear in her eyes as she stared up at him. They were blue eyes, framed in dark lashes, and they looked as deep as any ocean MacLeod had ever sailed. For a moment, MacLeod glimpsed the girl she must have been, the woman she *might* have been once—gentle, trusting, full of laughter, wanting love.

All that was the chieftain's son in MacLeod rose up, filling him with the urge, the need, to protect the weak and the helpless. Wordlessly, Cynthia's eyes seemed to plead with him for mercy; just as silently, the MacLeod of four hundred years ago longed to reach out, raise her to her feet and into the safety of an encircling arm.

Duncan fought the urge; she was no weak and helpless victim. He kept his sword at her throat.

Suddenly he heard Darius's voice as clearly as if the priest had been standing next to him. "*Stop*," it shouted within the silence. "*Don't kill her. Let her go.*"

I can't, Duncan's soul replied as he inched the blade higher toward the final stroke.

"Let her go. Put your blade down, Duncan MacLeod. The killing must stop." He heard Darius's voice again, speaking words he had heard from the priest in a hundred different discussions. If he was here, he would repeat them now—especially now.

Slowly, MacLeod lowered his sword. "That's enough, Cynthia," he said. "It's over—all of it. No more revenge, no more death. You'll leave Paulus—or I'll take your head now."

The air was finally coming back to Cynthia's lungs. She breathed it in with great gulps and she nodded, as she continued to stare up at him with those luminous blue eyes.

"Tomorrow," she said between gasps. "He has a speech. I'll leave while he's gone."

MacLeod hesitated. Did he dare believe her? *One soul at a time,* he heard Darius's voice again. *One soul at a time . . .*

"Would you rather I left Victor tonight?" Cynthia asked. "Do you want me to explain that if I don't leave, you'll kill me?"

"All right," MacLeod said, backing up a step so she could rise. "But if you harm him, I swear to you that *nothing* will stop me until I have your head."

Cynthia stood, her face only inches from his own. Silently, she stood there, their eyes locked for long, measuring seconds. Then she nodded.

"Tomorrow," she said. "I'll leave Victor tomorrow—for good. You have my word."

Cynthia picked up her sword and slid it beneath her coat. "I still think it's a shame, Duncan MacLeod. We could have had such *fun* together."

With a laugh, she turned and started to walk away. "Cynthia," he called after her. "You're wrong about Darius. He became something far greater than he ever was before. If he'd had a little more time, I believe he really would have changed the world."

"You go on believing that, MacLeod, if it gives you comfort," she called back to him.

"He did love you," MacLeod continued. "He loved us all."

Cynthia stopped and turned. Even from a distance, MacLeod could see that the expression in those blue, blue eyes was haunted, filled with too many memories. And centuries of pain.

Silently, she turned again and walked away. This time MacLeod let her go without another word.

Duncan walked over to where he had stood before her arrival and looked out again at the city lights upon the water.

All right, Darius, he thought, *we'll do this your way. I just hope it's the right thing. I miss your wisdom, my old friend. I miss it every day.*

A breeze stirred in from across the water. It was rich with the scent of salt and sea, and it lightly touched MacLeod's cheeks like a whispered benediction. He almost smiled.

Yes, Darius would have been glad he had let Cynthia live. Duncan could only hope—in Darius's memory and for Victor Paulus's sake—he had made the right choice.

MacLeod drew his coat tighter around himself and turned toward where his black Thunderbird was parked. Tomorrow he would have his answer. He intended to be at Paulus's speech and to follow him home afterward. He would make certain Cynthia was well and truly gone.

And if she was not—then tomorrow would have a different ending than today.

Chapter Thirty-two

Cynthia laughed out loud as she drove through the Seacouver streets. There were variations to The Game and she had just played one—and played it very well. Duncan MacLeod thought he had won. But he had won nothing, not even a few extra hours of life for himself or Victor Paulus. Cynthia controlled this Game and all the pieces were playing at her command.

This feeling of power was something Grayson had taught her to savor centuries ago. Victory was all that mattered, playing The Game to win. People like Duncan MacLeod, who were handicapped by strictures like honor and trust, stood little chance against her.

She laughed again. *Poor Duncan MacLeod,* she thought. *Four hundred years and he's still mortal in so many ways. He'll never know how great he could have been.*

Or what ecstasy we could have had together, her thoughts continued as she pictured his trim, muscular body, his dark heavy-lidded eyes, and his full, sensual mouth. *Yes, it would have been fun, if only there had been time to free him from the burden of his morality.*

Oh, but what a Quickening his would be—considering that was almost as good as the thought of his body over hers. And much more likely. She had shown him nothing of her true prowess with a sword, yet he thought she had—blind fool—and she had learned more from their brief encounter than he realized.

A less code-defined and honor-bound man would have taken her head while she was down. But not Duncan MacLeod. She had counted on that, and he had lived up to his reputation in every respect. She was certain now that when the crucial moment came he would hesitate, even oh so briefly—and in that hesitation, his head would be hers. With MacLeod's death, and Victor Paulus's, her revenge against Darius would at last be complete.

Game, set, and match.

And then what? the little voice inside her whispered again. *What will you do when all that you've lived for is finished?*

She quickly quieted the voice. She would not listen; she would never listen. She had a *purpose* and toward that purpose she had lived for fifteen centuries. It was all that mattered. When it was completed, *then* she could think about another.

Cynthia turned the car into the driveway at Victor's house, ready to begin the next set in the game she was playing. This one, too, was almost complete and victory was certain. As she turned off the key, Victor opened the door. He stood smiling and waiting for her. She had never known anyone who welcomed death so freely.

She got out of the car and walked quickly over to him, lifting her face to accept his kiss. "You were napping when I left," she said.

"And you were gone when I awoke," he answered. There was no accusation in his tone, as other men might have shown; it was utter trust, utter peace.

"I went for a drive," she told him, leaving out her destination. "I thought I should get to know the city. It's really very beautiful."

"Yes, it is," Victor agreed as he slipped an arm around her waist and led her inside, closing the door against the night. "Maybe tomorrow, after I'm done with the meeting, I can show you some of my favorite places."

"Did you get your speech finished?" she asked, carefully not agreeing to his plans and not letting him realize how she diverted his attention from their future.

"Yes," he said, but with a little frown. "I'm not sure I'm happy with it."

Cynthia laughed gently. "You never are," she said. "You don't have nearly enough confidence in yourself, Victor. You are very good at what you do."

"But will it be good enough? Can I get them to understand the horrors and the cruelty we witnessed? Sudan is so very far away, it's easy to forget the people there are suffering *now*. They need our help *now*."

"Victor, stop worrying," Cynthia said before he could go on. "Tomorrow will take care of itself. Let's just think about tonight."

She pressed her body up against his, sliding her arms up his back. He tightened his embrace and laid his cheek on top of her head.

"Oh, you are good for me," he said softly.

They made love that night with an abandon that Cynthia knew slightly shocked and yet delighted Victor. It was Cynthia's final gift to him. He *must* die tomorrow—from that nothing would dissuade her—but he had also been good to her with his love and at least he could die with such a memory to, perhaps, ease the passage.

Afterward, when Victor had dozed off, Cynthia lay awake thinking. For the first time, she could not get the question of her future out of her head. Where would she go? What would she do? For the first time in all the long centuries, her future was not already planned.

Grayson had had a dream once, and Cynthia had ridden by his side in those first years of her Immortality while he tried to bring that dream to fruition. An Immortal nation, a kingdom to rule the world—was it too late for such a thing?

Or, perhaps, it was the right time. Grayson had always maintained that the means of destruction was all that had truly changed in the world. With an army of Immortals, against whom bullets and bombs and gases meant nothing, the mortal world would be helpless. And in the age of instant communication, their demands—and their domination—could be broadcast immediately.

Oh, eventually they would fight each other—*In the end there can be only one*—but with the right incentive, *her* incentive, she was sure she could gather enough of them together to make the plan work.

Yes, that was the one goal worthy of her efforts—and she would do so in Grayson's memory. It would be the purpose that would drive her through the centuries to come. Fifteen hundred years ago the world would not have been ready for a woman to rule it, not even an Immortal one. In this, too, time had worked in her favor. Now was the era of equality, and she intended to show history exactly what that meant.

Cynthia smiled into the soft darkness of the bedroom and thought about the file of other Immortals Grayson had stored in the bank vault in Geneva. It was a file he had been collecting for hundreds of years. He had gathered together all of the stories and all of the legends on every name he heard whispered among their kind. He wanted to know who were the warriors and who were the visionaries, what were their strengths and weaknesses, how he might use them—or what could be used against them.

Cynthia was the only other person to have access to that file—the only person now alive. And she knew what to do with it; she knew what *Grayson* wanted done with it. They had always understood each other.

Well, not always—not in the beginning, before her Immortality. But from the winter of the year 410, when she had left the Visigoths in Italy and all connection to her mortal life behind, they had understood each other very well. They had known when they needed to be together and when they needed to be apart. Whether days or centuries, it did not matter; the bond between them was something no mortal would ever understand.

He had been her lover, yes—a lover of great passion and imagination. But most of all, he had been her teacher, the one who gave her the skills to stay alive and the drive, the *purpose* to carry on through the centuries. No mortal, with their frail little lives and loves, could ever imagine what that meant.

Cynthia's one regret was that she had not made that final trip with him. But he had been sure he would be back within the week and his plans had been so carefully laid. There was only one factor he had not taken into account.

MacLeod.

Well, this time MacLeod's presence was accounted for, and she had carefully neutralized him. For long enough, anyway. Soon, she would take care of him for good. By this time tomorrow, she would have MacLeod's Quickening—and after that, she would begin. . . .

Duncan MacLeod was not sleeping any more than Cynthia. He, too, was thinking about Grayson and the last time they had met. It had been a difficult fight, one of the worst MacLeod had faced.

"Another century and you might have beaten me," Grayson had said at one point, gloating over the victory he felt sure to have. For a time, it had felt to MacLeod as if he was in the final battle and *would* lose his head. It was not a feeling he cared to repeat.

But in the end he had prevailed—with an element of luck as well as any skill he possessed. If he had fallen farther away from his sword and not had time to retrieve it as Grayson came up behind him . . .

MacLeod stopped himself. He had played that fight over in his thoughts, and in his dreams, a hundred times. He did not need to do so again. He knew every step, every nuance of balance and thrust—and every mistake he had made. He had learned from them.

What is it Methos always says? "Live, grow stronger, fight another day." Well, it had certainly proved correct that time.

And Cynthia is not Grayson, MacLeod reminded himself. Aside from the sword she carried, he had seen no similarities of movement during their brief exchange today. He did not fool himself into thinking she had shown him everything of her skill; she would not have survived so long without knowing what she was doing. Would she?

Perhaps, MacLeod answered himself, with a powerful enough protector—like Grayson. Yes, he could have kept her safe in The Game.

And Cynthia's beauty . . . that, too, was a weapon that could weaken almost any man. Had it weakened him today?

That was the real question, the one that would not let MacLeod rest, and within it, one final doubt whispered. *Should he have taken her head when he had the chance?*

Darius would have told him no. Darius would have wanted her to live—Darius would have wanted Grayson to live.

Given the choice, Darius would have seen all killing, both mortal and Immortal, cease.

But the world was not the place Darius saw in his vision, and in the end, his beliefs had not saved him.

Duncan threw back the covers and got out of bed, impatient with the slow passage of the night. Tying a robe around himself, he went to the kitchen and poured a glass of orange juice, then came back to sit on the couch while he drank it.

On the low table before him stood his chess set, pieces spread across the squares in a half-finished game. MacLeod could rarely look at them without thinking of the hundreds of games he and Darius had played. Even as a priest, he had been a great general. "To deny what I was is to deny what I am," Darius had once told him as they sat over a game. But he had laid down his arms so long ago—did he really remember what the fight was like, or had it all faded into an academic exercise?

The chess pieces gave MacLeod no answer. Tonight they seemed to accuse him—but of what, he was not certain.

Someone has to be willing to fight for what is right in this world, he told them silently, as he had often told Darius. *Not just with words and ideals, but with a sword when necessary. At least for now, until the words and ideals of people like Darius—and Victor Paulus—have the chance to work their way into every heart. If that day ever comes.*

Darius had believed it would; Duncan, though he hoped for it, did not truly think it could happen. There was too much that stood in its way. Greed, pride, envy, anger; human nature, mortal and Immortal, forbade it.

What were you, Darius? Duncan wondered with the weary angst of sleeplessness. *An Immortal saint—or, like the rest of us, just a man trying to muddle through?*

The silent room gave Duncan no more of an answer this night than it had through all the years before.

Chapter Thirty-three

Victor's speech was not until afternoon, so Cynthia let him sleep late into the morning. She felt no need to rush with what she had to do. Time was her tool of destruction, as much as any sword, and she could play with it as suited her.

She had a leisurely breakfast while Paulus slept and took extra care in choosing her clothes and putting on her makeup. When at last she awoke Victor to his final few hours of life, she knew she filled his eyes—and his heart—as the perfect vision of female beauty.

Her clothes were all she had to pack, and that would not take long. As soon as she was finished with Paulus—and with MacLeod—she would be off. By the time the police discovered Victor's body, she would be on her way to Switzerland and the identity she had waiting there. She would spend however long it took putting her next plan into action. Fifty years, one hundred—it did not matter. She was Immortal, and this world was both her battlefield and her plaything.

They brunched on hot croissants and coffee, smoked salmon, and fruit. Then, while Victor showered and dressed, Cynthia wandered the house making certain that all evidence of her occupation was removed. The picture that had appeared in the morning paper the day after their arrival she could do nothing about—but in a few hours Cynthia VanDervane would cease to exist anyway.

Victor was dressed now. Another cup of coffee together and he would be ready to leave for his meeting. While he collected the notes for his speech, Cynthia went into the bedroom to retrieve the one object she had kept since the beginning.

It was a small sword, only slightly longer than a dagger,

and highly ornamental. It had been her first sword, found amidst the mayhem and carnage of the sack of Ravenna, and it fitted into her hand with a well-remembered ease. It felt right somehow that she should kill Darius's last and greatest protégé with the sword she had carried at the time of his first betrayal—just as it felt right to face MacLeod carrying the mate of the sword that had been Grayson's.

She heard Victor call for her. It was time that he was leaving, he said. *Yes,* she thought, *it is time.*

Sword in hand, she headed for the living room.

Duncan MacLeod sat among the crowd that had collected in the largest meeting room of City Hall. Present were the mayor and the city council members, representatives from radio, television, and newspapers, religious leaders from various faiths and denominations, company executives and known philanthropists; they had all come to hear Victor Paulus speak. He was due any minute.

MacLeod was here for a different reason. He supported Paulus's efforts with more than his time. He had already made a sizable—and anonymous—contribution to the foundation, and he would, possibly, return to the work in Sudan in person.

But he was here because Cynthia said she would leave Paulus while he was giving his speech. Afterward, Victor would need a friend.

The people were beginning to get restless. MacLeod glanced at his watch; Paulus was ten minutes late. MacLeod felt his insides go cold as a little warning voice began to nag him. He quickly stood and headed for the door, berating himself with each step. He wanted, he needed, to believe there was some innocent reason for Paulus's tardiness, but that same little voice would not let him.

Duncan knew he could not afford to let himself become upset or hurried. He would get to Victor Paulus as quickly as he could, hoping—praying—that it would be soon enough. But he must arrive calm and in control. If what he feared was true, Cynthia could well be waiting for him with a sword.

"A warrior's heart must be cold in battle," Hideo Koto had told him two hundred years ago as they trained on the banks of a quiet stream. *"Passion is for the bedroom, not the battle-*

field. A warrior who fights with passion—anger, revenge, frustration, arrogance—is not balanced. He misses opportunities and gives his opponent openings. He loses."

Hideo had said he liked to train in that place where the trees and the water surrounded him with their beauty and their serenity. In battle, he pictured himself there—felt the silent strength of the trees, heard the flowing calm of the water; he united his inner self with them, and he prevailed.

As MacLeod drove through the city streets, he took deep, centering breaths: in through the nose, out through the mouth. He breathed slowly, deeply, picturing the air as a stream of light flowing down to his *tant'ien,* his center, the place of his *chi.*

In all of the disciplines he had studied, from Western boxing to Chinese Kung Fu, this concept of centering, especially before a battle, remained constant. With the exercise he felt his frustration over the traffic drain away. He would be ready for whatever he found.

The windows were dark when Duncan turned his Thunderbird into the driveway. The house looked silent, still. For a brief moment, MacLeod thought—hoped—all his fears had been for naught.

But that voice inside him still whispered, and after four hundred years MacLeod had learned to listen to what it said.

He turned off the ignition and slipped the keys into his pocket. Then, pausing long enough for one final centering breath, he opened the car door and stepped out.

All the way up the walk and onto the porch he waited for the sensation that would tell him that Cynthia was here. It did not come—yet the warning voice grew louder with each step.

Duncan rang the doorbell. Once. Twice. He waited briefly, then he put his hand to the knob. The door opened easily to his touch, almost as if the house was willing him to enter.

"Victor," he called as he pushed the door open farther and stepped into the short hall. "Victor, it's Duncan MacLeod."

Duncan thought he heard a noise and he called again. Yes—it was faint but unmistakable. MacLeod hurried toward the sound.

Down the hall and to the left, into the living room where

just yesterday he had tried to warn Victor Paulus of his possible danger; it was only a few steps, but it might as well have been miles for all the help his presence could give Victor now.

Duncan found him on the floor, lying in a pool of his own blood. The sword thrust that had left him there had not been a clean, swift kill. MacLeod had had such a wound and he knew how much the man had suffered as he lay there waiting for death to come.

And for Paulus there would be death, final and complete. Duncan could not stop that now. But he could make certain Paulus did not die alone and abandoned.

He knelt by Victor's side. The smell of blood, with its cloying metallic-sweetness, filled his nose and raked the back of his throat. So much blood from one man, one life.

"Victor," MacLeod said softly. He took Paulus's hand into his own. It was so cold now, and MacLeod wanted Paulus to feel the comfort of a warm human touch. From experience Duncan knew how important that comfort could be.

He said Victor's name again. Slowly, Paulus turned his head a fraction and his eyes fluttered open. Although he had little time or strength left, the expression in his eyes was lucid and full of recognition.

MacLeod did not have to ask who did this, and Paulus knew that he knew. There was no need to waste those words when the few he had were precious.

"Victor," MacLeod said. "I'm sorry. I wish I had—"

"No," Paulus stopped him. His voice was weak, straining with the effort of speech. "Couldn't have stopped . . . anything. Just sorry I won't finish . . . my work . . . still so much . . . to do."

"The work will go on, Victor. It's too important to stop. You've given it enough momentum that others can shoulder the burden now."

"Darius—" Victor began.

"His words, his teachings, will go on too," MacLeod finished for him. "Darius would be so proud of you and all you've done. He always was."

Paulus gave a weak smile. It made MacLeod's heart ache to see it.

Victor closed his eyes for a moment. Then he opened them

again and looked at Duncan. MacLeod saw there was no ran-
cor in those eyes, only peace and, somehow, a tender compassion. For a moment, it was like looking into Darius's eyes
too—so full of timeless wisdom and infinite love.

"Cynthia . . . " Paulus said. His voice was even weaker now.
"Loved her . . . so much . . . it was good . . . to love that much."

"She won't get away with this, Victor," MacLeod said. His
voice was hard and cold. "I promise you, she won't."

"No . . . vengeance . . . Duncan," Paulus said, struggling to
make his words heard though his life was ebbing away. "No
. . . vengeance . . . only feeds the hate . . . hate must stop . . .
if world . . . to survive."

MacLeod was not going to argue with Paulus. Not now—
and there was too much he did not know. But even with death
so very close, Victor Paulus was a perceptive man. He knew
MacLeod was not someone to stand aside. And he saw the
anger stirring in Duncan's eyes.

"Let police . . ." he said. "Not you . . . find peace, Duncan
. . . live forgiveness . . . live peace. My death . . . doesn't matter . . . only peace . . . matters . . . for you . . . for the world."

Again, the presence of Darius was strong in the room. It
was as if, in these final moments, the teacher and the student
had merged into one spirit.

Paulus's breath had begun to rattle softly in his chest. Duncan recognized the sound. There would be only a few breaths
more. MacLeod searched for something, anything, to say—
but the lump that had risen in his throat would not let any
sound come out.

Paulus's eyes were clouding over. His lips moved; Duncan
leaned close to hear him.

"Peace be with you, Duncan MacLeod," he whispered. It
was Paulus's voice; it was Darius's voice.

The rattling breath stopped.

"And with you, Victor," MacLeod said softly, knowing the
benediction was unnecessary. He was at peace now, in that
place where nothing else abides.

Duncan did not move. He let his grief well up, wash over
and through him—grief for the death of this good, good man,
grief for the world that was an emptier place without him.

The sound of the telephone jarred through the room like an

explosion. MacLeod knew who it would be as surely as he knew whose hand had ended Victor's life. Duncan answered it on the second ring.

"Ah, MacLeod," her voice purred in response to his tight hello. "Did you find the present I left you? Oh, of course you did. I hope you had time for a good-bye; I tried to make sure he couldn't die too soon. Were his last words poignant? Victor did have a gift for that."

MacLeod's anger boiled and he did not stop it. Not this time. It rolled, up and up, like a tidal wave on the ocean drawing strength from the depths. It crashed in on him, destroying any hope of peace.

"Where?" he said, tight-lipped with fury.

On the other end of the phone, Cynthia laughed. "You're an intelligent man, MacLeod. You'll know where. Come at sunset. I'll be waiting."

The sound of her laugher was the last thing MacLeod heard as she hung up on him. He turned and looked again at Paulus's body. The blood beneath him was congealing now that there was no life to give it warmth. Yet, in spite of his slashed body, the blood that stained his clothes and soaked the carpet beneath him, Victor Paulus looked serene. It was as if he had absorbed all of the hate that caused his death and somehow—*somehow*—transformed it. He answered it with love.

There were still miracles.

But not for Duncan MacLeod. "This isn't vengeance, Victor," he assured the spirit of the man on the floor. "This is justice. *Immortal justice.*"

Judge and executioner—it was a role MacLeod resisted when he could. But not today. With an utter surety of purpose, he turned on his heel and walked toward the door.

Chapter Thirty-four

The stark yellow of the sulfur piles stood in bright contrast to the deep purple-black of the mountain silhouettes that rose as a majestic backdrop toward the lighter dusk of the sky. It looked like a scene by Salvador Dalí, beautiful and surreal.

But this was no painting. The smell of the sulfur hung like a living thing, a dragon with yellow breath that stained the air with each exhalation. Cynthia had arrived long before MacLeod, when the work crews were just leaving for the day, and she wandered through the area trying to sense how Grayson had fought and where he had died.

Showers that had fallen intermittently throughout the afternoon had left puddles of yellow water. Cynthia walked through them heedlessly, not caring how they ruined her fine leather shoes. Her thoughts were here, and yet they were on a hundred different times and places where she and Grayson had been together through the centuries.

Somehow, being at the place of his death made his life with her seem more real, more intense, than it had ever felt while he lived. Memories cascaded over her—of his smile, of his laughter, of his touch. She knew the way his mind worked so well, she could almost picture him standing beside her, almost hear his voice telling her the history of sulfur and gunpowder.

She missed him. Over fifteen centuries of his presence in her life, and MacLeod had robbed her of that one constant. At four hundred years of age, he was still a child by her reckoning. How could he understand what an emptiness Grayson's death had caused in her?

Well, it did not matter that he understand, only that he died. Here. Today. By her hand.

She turned toward the sulfur, toward the mountains, and raised her hand to the sky. It was an act of reverence. She knew, and the three great goddesses that had always guided her knew, that in this simple act she embraced their gift.

Her destiny.

Was that the clicking of their needles she heard, as they wove the threads of time? Or was it the beating of her own heart?

Was there a difference?

Then she felt it, felt him. "MacLeod," she screamed into the gathering night. It was a war cry, the name of her enemy.

"Right behind you," came his answering voice.

Duncan, too, had thought about Grayson as he walked among the sulfur. Being here again was like entering, waking, into the nightmare he had dreamt so often. One way or the other, today's battle would end that dream. But would it only replace it with another?

Then Duncan thought about Victor Paulus lying in his own blood, struck down by the woman he had loved. It was worth any sleeping nightmare to end the waking one that was Cynthia VanDervane.

MacLeod accepted the burden of that death upon the strong shoulders of his spirit. He knew that if he had not let Cynthia walk away from that first encounter, Paulus would still be alive.

"They all stay with you," he had once told Richie. *"Every one you've ever loved and every one you've ever killed."* MacLeod accepted that, knew it to be true, and would not let it turn his hand from what he knew he now must do.

I tried it your way, Darius, he thought, *and Victor is dead. Now I do it my way.*

He raised his sword to his opponent.

Cynthia laughed at him and brought out her own. Once again, she carried the Kris broadsword that was the match of Grayson's.

"So eager to die, Duncan MacLeod?" she asked. "No time for a little conversation? No pleasantries before we start our Game?"

"I think we've said it all," MacLeod answered.

"Have we? I wonder."

She swung her sword easily, round and round. But for all the nonchalance of the movement, Duncan recognized it for what it was—an exercise to warm up her wrists; he had done it a million times himself.

Cynthia began to walk around him. Duncan saw the little stretches she could not quite conceal from his practiced eye. Achilles tendon, calf muscles, right shoulder, left; she had no doubt grown cold and a little stiff in the time she had awaited him. He let her have her movements, let her think she fooled him. His own muscles, loosened by his morning routine of *kata*, were warmed and eager for the fray, and the heat of his rage had long turned to icy calculation.

As she walked, she kept talking. "What—no questions, MacLeod? No lectures on the *immorality* of what I've done? You *are* different from Darius. *He* would have had plenty to say."

"And you would not have listened to any of it," MacLeod countered, watching the length of her stride, where she put the balance on her foot. It was heavier on her right heel; that was her power leg, then.

"I listened once. I gave him everything I had, everything I was—oh, but you know all this. Tell me, MacLeod, did it ever strike you as ironic that Darius was killed by a mortal—after centuries of caring for them? Grayson would have called it cosmic justice, and oh, how it would have delighted his sense of humor. Do you have a sense of humor, MacLeod?"

"Not about death," Duncan answered, still watching, still measuring. She was almost ready to make her play. He could see it in the way her steps had begun to shorten and how her balance had shifted forward.

"Death, life, love, hate—they're the only things worth laughing about. We're all just playthings for the gods."

Her attack was sudden. She turned on her left heel; her right leg lunged while her sword arced sideways toward MacLeod's head, carried by the force of her body's turn. It was a good move, strong and sure; if MacLeod's perceptions had been a fraction slower, he could have lost his head at the first blow.

But his *katana* was there to stop her. The clash of the two blades rang in the still evening air. Cynthia stepped back as quickly as she had darted in, spun, and attacked from the other side.

Once more, MacLeod's *katana* was there. Cynthia laughed as they met, steel upon steel. Was that the biting edge of madness he heard within her laughter, madness born in that place where hatred crossed the line into obsession? Could an obsession that had been carried for so long leave room for sanity?

A part of MacLeod wanted to feel compassion. At another time and another place, he might have let that pity grow. But not now—not if he chose life.

And he did; life for himself, life for the world that Darius—and Paulus—had loved. It was his world, too, and all the people, mortal and Immortal—especially the mortals, who knew nothing of The Game—were the clan he had been raised to protect. He was still the chieftain's son. He raised his sword again.

Cynthia's attacks were like a stinging insect, buzzing all around him, darting in and out, trying to get past his guard. She aimed for his extremities first: biceps, hamstring, knee, forearm—trying to wound and weaken him. MacLeod felt like a lumbering bear swatting at a hornet.

He went on the offensive and began to attack. Cynthia was no match for his strength and for the power in his sleek, well-trained muscles. But she was good, fifteen centuries good, and more than once she spun away just under his blow. Nor did Cynthia forget the other weapons her body possessed. Hands, feet, knees, elbows—they were all part of her human arsenal.

She aimed a stomp-kick at MacLeod's right knee; he dropped and turned slightly, taking the blow on his thigh. The blow was a good one, full of power, that would have shattered his kneecap had it connected. As it was, it stunned his quadricep, making his leg feel numb and lame.

But these were tactics MacLeod knew well—and Immortal muscles heal quickly. Within seconds, he countered her attack with one of his own. Her sword came in with a thrust angled to slide between his ribs and up into his heart. He parried her blade to one side and drove the elbow of his other arm into her face. MacLeod felt bones and cartilage smash.

Cynthia wheeled back and to the right, shaking off the worst of the blood and the pain. She, too, would heal—if she lived.

Despite the blood pouring down her face, despite the split lip and flattened nose, she smiled at him again. Then she raised her blade in the briefest salute.

"Well done, MacLeod," she said. Her tone had a mocking edge, as if she played at being the teacher to an awkward student. "But is that the best you can do? I've had worse—and survived the battle. After all, what's a little pain . . . between friends?"

"I'm not your *friend*," MacLeod countered, "and there's much, much more."

The blood had stopped flowing from Cynthia's mouth and nose. MacLeod could almost see the bones knitting back into place, flesh pulled closed and new. Immortality at work.

Cynthia laughed as she drew the back of her forearm across her face to wipe the remaining blood away. "Oh, MacLeod," she said, "so fierce in your righteousness. You are *fun*. Too bad you have to die."

With that, she attacked again. The waves of her blade whistled through the evening air as it arced toward MacLeod's stomach.

MacLeod stepped just in time to parry. He turned; his *katana* sliced—at empty air. Cynthia had dropped, rolled, and now came to her feet behind him.

The battle continued, breath upon breath, heartbeat upon heartbeat long, as slashes and nicks began to appear on both their bodies where the tip of a blade or the final inch of a slice connected. MacLeod could not remember who had drawn first blood. It did not matter; only the last blow mattered.

Then MacLeod saw it—Cynthia was beginning to tire. The constant quick dashes, the slicing spins, the ducks and turns and sidesteps were taking their toll. She was not used to fighting an opponent who could counter her quickness for long. Silently, MacLeod thanked the spirit of May Ling Shen for her training in the White Crane system of Kung Fu. Without that training, and the others that had followed, MacLeod knew he might well have been dead by now.

Cynthia's spins were getting slower, her thrusts less sure.

The smile on her face had faded into a grimace. It was MacLeod's turn to smile. Internally: *don't let your opponent know what you know*.

There: the waver in her hand as she lunged toward his midsection. The tip of her sword wanted to drop. MacLeod moved, showing her the full extent of his own speed—speed he had kept partly hidden until now.

He parried and turned, spinning past her guard. As tired as she was, she could not pull back fast enough to stop him. His *katana* came down on her hand, slicing through nerves and tendons, biting into bone. She screamed as the sword dropped from her bloody fingers.

Then MacLeod's *katana* was at her throat. She looked up with eyes as blue as cornflowers in the summer sun, deep as the fields of time itself. He steeled his heart; nothing would stop him this time.

And she knew it. A small, sardonic smile tugged at the corners of her full red lips.

"Send me to them," she said. "We've been apart too long."

Duncan did not have to ask whom she meant. His sword moved.

Cynthia's Quickening swirled like a mist of charged ions around his feet. It rose, encircling his legs, shooting tiny shafts of power deep into his muscles. They contracted and jerked as the mist thickened. The power gathered and grew. It became lightning that flashed from him to the cloud-decked sky and back again. His *katana* stabbed the air overhead. His other arm flew out to his side, counterweight, to keep him on his feet and he opened his soul for what was to come.

Cynthia . . . Callestina . . . and a hundred other names she had used throughout the centuries; he knew them all, wore them all, felt all the people she had been. The *all* that was only one.

He felt the sunshine and laughter and the long twilight snows of her childhood years of mortality that had passed so quickly. He knew in his own soul the innocent she had once been.

The lovely child became a beautiful woman. All the young men wanted her and she laughed at the hunger in their eyes— and in their hearts. Her heart was already given.

To Darius.

MacLeod felt the burning passion and the need that had been Callestina's. Something in his own heart answered it. He, too, had known the fires of need and passion that could warm a chilled heart or sear an empty soul.

Her cry for Darius and his for Tessa—both loved, both gone—mingled. They merged into the wordless cry that was torn from his lips as Cynthia's Quickening continued to coil and strike—each strike an explosion of power that melded to his own. Building. Feeding.

And with each explosion came more of the feelings that were less than experience yet more than memories.

Devotion to the gods . . . a lover's arms . . . nights of ecstasy . . . dreams of a future . . . of love . . .

. . . that was not love. The bitter pain of rejection—Darius's rejection?—sliced through Duncan, sharp and deep as any sword thrust. He felt Callestina's heart, his heart, cut to ribbons.

Love twisted and blackened; his soul healed maimed and misshapen. Desire became obsession, fed with the fuel of Immortality. For all the centuries, he would feel her ire . . .

Still the Quickening came on, searing through sinew and muscle. It tore him apart with Immortal power and healed again with the same force.

Centuries built on centuries. Through them all, the long dark shadow of obsession stretched. Lovers came and went, meaning nothing; heads were taken to stay alive in The Game a little longer, until revenge could be complete.

Nothing mattered but vengeance . . .

Vengeance . . .

And Grayson . . .

He was the single thread that ran unbroken through her tapestry of time.

He was the love that could have been, should have been . . .

Love that had no room to abide in either heart . . . they were already too full . . .

With hope abandoned, denied, festering into the wound of despair . . .

With the shards of dreams never rebuilt . . .

With devotion, caged by the twisted wires . . .

Of laughter, stilled . . .
Of tears, unshed . . .
Withered souls that wanted, needed . . .
That could not receive . . .
Could not give . . .
Until, at last, all that was left was the long shadow and the silence of hearts that could only beat to the rhythm of revenge.

The Quickening was fading, taking the emotion but leaving the power. Duncan MacLeod had grown stronger, as he always grew stronger.

And he had been warned of the chasm that could await.

MacLeod fell to his knees and waited until the last of the Quickening winds dissipated. Then, slowly, he dragged himself to his feet and looked over at Cynthia's still body.

"Peace be with you, Cynthia," he said softly, repeating the words Darius had given to him when he left for the New World. He hoped her New World granted her more peace than he had ever found in his.

Epilogue

Duncan MacLeod stood by the graveside of Victor Paulus. The service was over, the mourners had gone home. Only Duncan MacLeod remained, bidding farewell to this man he had known too little and to whose aid he had come too late.

He did not wish peace to Paulus's departed spirit. Victor had always had peace; like Darius, he had carried it in his own heart. That was the lesson they had both tried to teach—and the lesson it was so hard to learn.

Who will take up the lesson now? he wondered. *Who would hold the shadows at bay?*

"You can't save them all, MacLeod," a familiar voice said behind him.

Duncan turned slightly and saw Joe Dawson standing there, his dark coat buttoned against the chill and his steel-gray hair darkened by the drizzle that had begun to fall. The grayness of the day matched the mood of Duncan's heart.

"I didn't save any of them, did I?" he replied. He was again—he was still—the chieftain's son, grieving over the deaths in his clan. Darius, Grayson, Cynthia, Paulus; lives so intertwined. They were shadows and sunlight, dancing the eternal dance, each a part of the others. Two he had killed, two he had failed to save; four lives, this time—but how much blood was really on his hands?

"Obsession and revenge—sides of the same dark coin." MacLeod spoke his thoughts out loud.

"What was that, MacLeod?" Joe asked.

"Something Darius said to me once—a long time ago. I wish Cynthia could have heard the truth in those words."

"Some people will only hear what they want to hear, and it doesn't matter about truth."

Dawson came and stood beside Duncan. In his presence was the silent offer of comfort and of burdens shared. Then Dawson put a hand on Duncan's shoulder.

"Come on, my friend," he said. "I'll buy you a drink and you can tell me some more about Darius. Darius, Grayson, Cynthia, even Paulus—we'll talk about them all. I'll get every word and every memory down in the Chronicles. And maybe someday we'll understand."

"Understand?" Duncan asked.

"Everything, man—why some love and others hate. When all is said and done, perhaps that's the best thing the Chronicles will tell us."

Darius was gone but his words and his spirit would live on, Duncan thought, the gray of his mood lifting just a little. That was the promise he had made to Paulus. Now, with Joe's help, he would keep it. In those words was an Immortality Darius and Paulus could share—the Immortality of remembrance.

As Duncan turned with Joe to leave the grave behind them, a few lines of a poem by Richard Cranshaw drifted through his thoughts. For the first time in two days, a soft smile touched Duncan's lips.

> *Let them sleep, let them sleep on,*
> *Till the stormy night be gone,*
> *And the eternal morrow dawn,*
> *Then the curtains will be drawn,*
> *And they will make into a light*
> *Whose day shall never die in night.*

Author's Notes

The conditions in Sudan, presented in the beginning of this book are, unfortunately, not products of this writer's imagination. The figures for deaths, the reality of torture and slavery, and other atrocities not mentioned in these pages, have all been verified with numerous sources. There are many organizations currently working to mount rescue and relief actions. Those of you interested in giving your aid to these efforts might try contacting the pastors or priests in your area or secular organizations such as Amnesty International.

Most of you reading this book will be familiar with the first season episode, "Band of Brothers," on which much of this book is based. You purists will have noticed the slight discrepancy in my presentation of the Battle of Waterloo.

The Battle of Waterloo took place on June 18, 1815, after a day and a half of torrential rains. However, while filming the episode the cast, crew, and scriptwriters had to contend with a sudden snowfall. They chose to incorporate it into the story; for the sake of history, I have taken it out.

I am most grateful to Mr. Erik Flint for all of his expert advice and patient explanations about the battles, uniforms, and weaponry of the Napoleonic era. Without his help, the Battle of Waterloo would have remained mere statistics on a page for me, and any mistakes in presenting this information are my errors, not his.

For those of you interested in learning more about the Napoleonic era, there are many fine books on the subject. The final book of Will and Ariel Durant's eleven-volume The Story of Civilization series is entitled *The Age of Napoleon* and is an invaluable source of information. For more fiction set in that era, the Sharpe's Rifles series by Bernard Cornwell is well worth the read.

The sack of Rome by the Visigoths in the year A.D. 410 is also grounded in fact. With the exception of the Immortal characters, it has been presented as accurately as possible, leaving out only the political intrigue of the previous years that had nothing to do with this story.

Alaric the Great, leader of the Visigoths, did indeed lead his army of 40,000 to the gates of Rome. As they began their siege of the Eternal City, the gates were opened to them by rebellious slaves from within the walls. The Visigoths entered and sacked the city that had stood for 1,000 years and survived everything from the greatness of Julius to the depravity and madness of Tiberius and Caligula. Peace with the Visigoths came at the price of total capitulation to their demands, which included Alaric's marriage into the Imperial family, in the person of the Emperor's sister. It was the end of Rome as the power she had once been. That power would be regained, though not in quite the same way, with the advent of the Holy Roman Empire and the spread of the pontifical authority of the Church. Had the Emperor Honorius been better advised in the years before 410, especially by his general Stilcho, who hated the Visigoths, the ensuing tale might have been far different. But that is a story for another book entirely.

Those of you interested in reading more about the Visigoths might try volume four of Will and Ariel Durant's series, *The Age of Faith*, and J.B. Bury's book, *The Invasion of Europe by the Barbarians*.

I am also indebted to the following people for all their help and support:

To Donna Lettow, Executive Script Consultant for Highlander, the series, and fellow novelist, for getting me the episode script and manuscript I needed to check my references, and to her and Gillian Horvath for a productive brainstorming session; and also to Donna for her wonderful work on *The Watcher Chronicles*, from which much of the background information for these characters was gleaned;

To David Abramowitz, who created the character of Darius, to Marie-Chantal Droney, who wrote the wonderful episode "Band of Brothers," that was the inspiration for this book, and to Bill Panzer and Peter Davis, who gave us the character of Duncan MacLeod, a truly heroic character who is fun to write;

To Betsy Mitchell, editor par excellence, encouraging, funny and kind, who is so good at handling a writer's occasional fits of angst;

To Jennifer Jackson, who reacquainted me with the good things about having an agent;

To Dianne, who kept the chuckles and cyber-hugs coming across the electronic waves;

To Debbie and Clay, from the local Videoland, who tracked down various obscure documentaries on the life of Napoleon and the Battle of Waterloo;

To my dear friend Donna, who has, as always, listened and read, encouraged and advised—in both career and in life;

And especially to my beloved Stephen, friend and husband, who is my sanity amid this world of words I inhabit;

My deepest gratitude to you all.

And watch for the new Highlander adventure
coming in July 1998 from Warner Aspect!

HIGHLANDER: THE CAPTIVE SOUL
by Josepha Sherman

AN ANCIENT EVIL

Over three thousand years ago, Methos helped the
Egyptian pharaohs in their battle against sadistic
Hyksos overlords. Then he fought Khyan, an
Immortal Hyksos prince, but failed to take his head.
Now a deadly madman stalks modern New York
City, hunting an ancient sword, killing all who stand
in his way. It can only be Khyan, seeking revenge. If
Methos does not destroy this darkness from his
past, he, Duncan MacLeod, and indeed all Immortals
will be doomed . . .